FIC   ANDER
Anderson, K.D.
The intrepid golfer : a
novel /
        R0043151858

MAR   2013

THE INTREPID GOLFER

A Novel

Donated By
Simi Valley
Friends Of The
Library

by

K.D. ANDERSON

Copyright © 2012 by Anderson Publishing Company.

The Intrepid Golfer is a work of fiction. The characters, names, incidents, dialogue, and plot are the products of the author's imagination. Any resemblance to actual persons or events is coincidental. An attempt has been made, however, to represent some locations and events accurately. Any errors are the author's alone.

Cover design by Zach Corbin.

All rights reserved.

ISBN 10: 1475010419

EAN 13: 9781475010411

Library of Congress Control Number: 2012915953
CreateSpace, North Charleston, SC

Acknowledgments

This book is dedicated to my life's partner, B.J. Anderson, who makes each day an adventure.

Writing a novel takes time and a lot of help and support. My thanks and gratitude to the following people:

B.J. Anderson, for adding so much to the tone of the book and for her expertise as an editor and source of common sense.

Early beta readers who gave me the encouragement I needed after a less than stellar first draft: Karl Braun, Bill Huber, Fritz Corbin, and my golf buddies, Sheri and Kevin Stroud.

Dr. Carrie Kubota, an early supporter of my efforts to write this book. She enlisted the aid of her mother, Marian Kubota, to read an early draft. Marian lived in Hilo, Hawaii, during World War II.

Dr. Lisa Oki, for her encouragement and valuable cultural feedback.

Dr. Gregg Hartman, for showing me how below the knee prosthetic work.

MAR   2013

Bill and Darlene Hughes, for local knowledge and for being great hosts during our visits to Kona.

Bob Wilson, executive director of the National Amputee Golf Association, for feedback and support.

Deb Davila, a fierce competitor and great golfer, for her knowledge of tournament golf.

Justin George of 141 Premiere Sports & Entertainment, for his firsthand knowledge of how the Sony Open works.

Jim Kefford, for local Honolulu knowledge and a newspaper editor's eye. Also thanks for the times we had together on most of the islands of Hawaii, which sparked my love for the area and the culture of Hawaii.

Alex Sokoloff, who as a speaker at the Ventura County Writers Club, assured me that the first draft is always crap and to just keep writing. Your blog has been a valuable reference.

Prologue

September 23, 1998

The fifty-year-old novice impatiently waited his turn to tee off at the tenth hole at the Makalei golf course. He took several deep breaths to ease his anxiety, grateful that the more seasoned golfers in his foursome tolerated with good humor his lackluster scores. Still, this didn't appease his desire for achieving excellence. A light breeze chilled his sweaty forehead as he stepped forward, the driver shaking slightly in his hands.

Even though Kenji Watanabe had the perfect build for a golfer—he was just shy of six feet tall, and his well-muscled torso gave him the upper body strength to hit a drive of more than 250 yards—he was frustrated that he hadn't yet reached this goal.

He felt the gentle breeze on his face and listened to the rustle of the fronds on the ever-present palm trees that dotted the landscape. It was ten thirty a.m., the temperature a balmy seventy-four degrees. It was another magical yet stressful day in this tropical paradise.

Suddenly a loud crack of thunder and a bright flash of lightning tore through the palms below. The golfers dashed to the shelter of their covered golf carts, heavy rain pounding on them sideways, to wait for a lull in the stormy weather.

Being soaked through to his skin from the pouring rain and feeling the notable drop in temperature prompted an impatient Kenji to swing too hard when he finally teed off at number ten. "Damn. That was ugly," he muttered under his breath. His ball ended up in the left rough near a five-foot fence with a steel pole gate that marked the golf course boundary. Kenji squished through the wet grass down to where his ball lay, knowing it was fortunate that his ball was sitting up in a spot clear of the tall grass. He pulled a four iron out of his bag, took his stance, and checked his back swing. He had plenty of room; he was clear of the fence gate by three feet. At the top of his back-swing, an explosive bolt of lighting struck the gate. Most of the one-million-volt charge traveled to the ground via the steel post, but part of the charge jumped to Kenji's four iron.

A jolt of pain tore through his body, and the force of the strike catapulted him ten feet through the air, out onto the fairway, where he landed with a thud. His shirt was torn half off; burns mottled the muscular tanned skin on his torso. Some of the charge went through the wet headband on his cap and singed his hair on the left side.

Kenji's body wasn't moving. He was dead.

CHAPTER 1

March 1998

He shut the front door of his shop and locked it, peering through the glass one last time before jauntily walking down the street where tourists thronged, in the balmy March evening. He attracted unwanted attention; several thirty-something females stopped to stare at the Japanese man, muscular and handsome in a casual, laidback sort of way, who passed them by with not so much as a glance. He was free. His days of catering to the whims of tourists were over. Kenji Watanabe, a month shy of his fiftieth birthday, was content with the decision to sell his chain of Hawaiian island T-shirt shops and retire.

The sale hadn't been without controversy. John Fletcher, his cantankerous landlord, had arrived at the shop one steamy morning—bulging in a tropical seersucker suit, his once-thick brown hair now a gray straggle—threatening a lawsuit over the lease arrangement. "You can't sell your stores on this island without my permission," he blustered. "I'll sue your ass if you try it!"

Kenji, unfazed, responded in a quiet, deadly voice, "It's a done deal. Nothing in my lease prevents the sale."

"We'll see about that!" thundered Fletcher as he stormed out the front door.

Later that week Kenji was served with papers announcing a lawsuit. Along with trying to prevent the sale, the cheeky old fart sought damages. Kenji immediately met with his attorney and countersued. Several weeks later, when the suit came before the court, justice prevailed and Kenji won. Fletcher was apoplectic, and Kenji overheard his comment in the hallway of the court: "That goddamn Nip will get his comeuppance soon enough."

Kenji shrugged off the remark. He had won. That was enough for him. The sale closed, and the new owners were capable and well capitalized.

* * *

Kenji liked running in the soft glow of early morning, the grass still wet with dew. Myriad birds chirped a welcoming chorus as he crossed the downtown street free of traffic. It seemed odd to leisurely run the daily route through his hilly neighborhood, then down the hill to the 7-Eleven to buy a newspaper and a cup of coffee before making the reverse trek. He was adapting easily to retirement, so far. Uncharacteristically, Kenji hadn't thought much about his future.

That afternoon he gazed moodily out the window of his home office. The hot sun was shining on a beautiful, calm spring day, yet he felt sad, alone. He had worked up a sweat taking care of the catch-up projects he'd been putting off — fixing the sprinklers, hacking back the lush tropical vegetation that threatened to envelop the lanai in the backyard. He was tired from the physical exertion and bored. He sat pensively in the executive leather chair in his newly refurbished home office. He hit the power switch on his personal computer, fired up the color printer, and sat admiring the elegant workstation furniture fashioned out of solid teak. Shocking, absolutely shocking, the amount of money he had spent recently. All should be right with the world, right? He flipped to the next page on his desk calendar. April 16, 1998. The significance hadn't crossed his mind until he saw the date. "Happy birthday to me. Happy birthday to me," he sang softly.

He sat quietly, reevaluating his early retirement. *What the hell am I going to do with the rest of my life?* he thought. He felt empty, passionless. Work no longer filled twelve hours of his day. He yearned to have a conversation with his wife, to hear the melodic sound of her voice whisper,

"Kenji-san, it's all right. Everything will be all right." But all he heard was deafening silence.

His love affair with golf began on a whim. That day, he was reading the newspaper and noticed an ad for the grand opening of a new driving range in Kona. Golf was something that appealed to him, though he didn't quite know why since he hadn't shown any particular talent for sports in the past. Some of the guys he knew played golf. He heard them bragging about a three-hundred-yard drive, a lucky putt from forty feet, or chipping the ball in the hole from a sand trap. He didn't know much about the game, even though an almost new set of clubs had languished in his garage gathering cobwebs ever since a frustrated customer had limped into the shop and thrust them into his hands. "Take the damn things or I'll throw them in the nearest water hazard!" the man had yelped.

Kenji was in good health, his powerful frame still trim and fit. His dark, thick hair, cut short, didn't have a hint of gray despite the profound losses he had experienced. He figured a little exercise on the golf course in addition to his daily run would keep him in peak physical shape. Retired people had hobbies, but he was much too young to wither away collecting coins or stamps. Why not master golf? After all, Misaki, a young girl that he and his wife had tutored, was doing exceptionally well with golf, winning tournament after tournament on the LPGA tour.

Over the next few weeks, Kenji tackled golf with a vengeance, as if he were on a crusade to conquer the world. He prepared and studied before even thinking about going to the driving range to hit golf balls or, God forbid, play an actual round. He read everything he could get his hands on about the game — books by Arnold Palmer and Jack Nicklaus — and devoured every sentence in *Golf* and *Golf Digest* magazines.

He meticulously cleaned his golf clubs before driving up to Makalei for his first lesson.

The golf pro, Mike Garza, had forged a reputation on the PGA tour as a short game guru. But age, injuries, and the rigors of constant travel had prompted his decision to retire and share his talents teaching others. His once lean, supple frame had succumbed to easy island living. He was curious about this new student who had signed up for three lessons a week. "Hi, Kenji! Welcome!" he said. "Let's go out to the driving range and get you started with the basics: the grip, balance, and the swing."

He watched Kenji hit balls and made minor adjustments as the lesson progressed. He was impressed with Kenji's burning desire to learn and wished all of his students had the same mindset.

"Kenji, to learn this game you must practice as much as possible to develop what we call muscle memory."

"No problem. I'll practice every day."

After the lesson, Kenji went home to work on his short game, using only the shorter irons. He had made a conscious decision to emulate the smooth swing of the two golfers he admired most, Freddie Couples and Ernie Els. He hit hundreds of wiffle balls in the backyard, startling the neighbor's yappy dog into howls of admonishment as they bounced off the fence into a scatter.

Kenji was a quick study, taking in the instructions, intense in his desire to master the game. After his third lesson, he drove directly to the driving range and parked his car. It was time for the next step. After retrieving his clubs from the trunk, he ambled nervously to the office and went in. Kenji handed the thirty-something, trim lady at the counter seven dollars; her nametag said she was Nita. He chuckled at the appropriateness of her name, which coincided with her appearance. She handed him a bucket that held a hundred balls. Kenji quickly headed to the driving-range tees, butterflies churning in his stomach.

He stood at the range entrance to get his bearings, breathing in the fragrance of newly cut grass while watching a teenage boy on an enclosed golf cart dragging a roller to pick up the balls strewn across the stretch of green grass. A line of palm trees helped soften the stark, tall chain-link fence that rimmed the range.

The air was deadly still, nary a whisper of a breeze, the only sound a "thunk" of a misguided shot and the occasional crack of a solidly hit ball. Kenji looked at the small greens in the distance, each with a flag proudly protruding from the earth. The flags were set at seventy-five, one hundred, 150, 220, and 250 yards away. He stood for a while surreptitiously watching others hit balls to glean as much information as possible. He walked past them to the farthest tee box, hoping no one would notice him.

He poured the balls into the tray as the others had done and leaned his golf bag on the rack provided for it. He paused to look around and relish the moment. He was excited but not cognizant of the potential importance this day would have on his lonely life. His competitive spirit kicked in, though he usually masked it with an easygoing way and the in-bred manners of his Japanese culture. Even before hitting his first ball, he was pleased with himself. This new pursuit gave him something constructive to focus on and help ward off the emptiness of his life. He enjoyed the planning, the reading, and the studying he had done so far. He was a good student and had listened intently to his teacher, always striving for his approval. Fantasy dreams of hitting a ball really, really well had filled his usually tempestuous sleep.

The joy of being outside on a beautiful Hawaiian day washed over him like a gentle wave as though he heard Mia's quiet voice murmuring, but it was just the sigh of a slight breeze high in the trees.

He removed the pitching wedge from his golf bag and held it aloft as he reached and stretched from side to side. He bent over to touch the club to the ground, keeping his legs straight to lengthen his muscles. After placing a ball on the mat, he stood to line up his body to the seventy-five-yard flag. He took a deep breath to slow his pounding heart and force himself to relax. He set his grip, holding the club loosely in his hands, took it back about halfway, and swung. The ball flew about halfway to the green, off to the right a bit, but not too bad for his first swing at the driving range.

Kenji's strategy was to learn something on every practice shot he made. Today's plan was to hit every club in his bag and note the results, good or bad, then review what he'd done with the golf pro during his next lesson.

The next few balls went about the same distance. Some were to the left of where he had aimed, some were to the right, and a few were almost on line. Then he started to take a full swing. Some of his shots missed by a lot, but a few actually hit the seventy-five-yard green, and one got to the hundred-yard green. It was a great feeling to see the ball fly straight and true and land on the green. No wonder so many people played this game.

Kenji hit a few balls with every club in his bag. He quickly discovered that it was more difficult to hit the ball straight when he used the longer clubs. This didn't concern him, however, as his goal was to get a feel for each club and gauge the distance he could achieve. Finally he took the driver out of his bag. *This is it!* he thought. *This is the big, bad boy.* He bent over to put the ball on the rubber tee then with deep concentration looked out at the green marked 220 yards. He visualized the ball flying through the air and bouncing once onto the green. He stood there for a moment to let the image burn itself into his mind. Then he forced himself to relax and hold the club lightly, as if he were gently holding a baby bird. He slowed his back swing then swung through the ball as though it wasn't even there. As the ball took flight, he stood watching, amazed. The ball was flying just as he had visualized it. Miraculously the ball landed and bounced once onto the green and rolled to within four feet of the pin. Joy leaped in his heart, and his eyes teared up. He quickly turned his face so the others wouldn't see his tears, then he looked again. His ball was the only one on the 220-yard green. He couldn't wait to tell the golf pro about this shot. He was hooked.

On that bright summer day, Kenji Watanabe became, in his fantasy, the intrepid golfer, and wonder of all wonders, he felt happy again.

CHAPTER 2

Kenji's life had started out well. He'd had caring parents and a solid home life amid comfortable surroundings. He remembered back to the night it all came crashing down.

Sergeant Bob Kualii hated this part of his job. There was never an easy way to break devastatingly bad news to someone, especially not to a kid. Sweat darkened the underarms of his uniform even though the air was cool, as he reluctantly rang the doorbell at the modest yet neat frame house, abundant flowers framing the doorway. Even though Kenji was seventeen years old, the picture in the police officer's mind was of him as a toddler in a playpen in his folks' T-shirt shop in downtown Kona.

Kenji was just finishing his homework, writing his name and the date, December 15, 1966, on the top of each page, when the doorbell rang. He looked up, a frown wrinkling his brow as he wondered, *Who can that be ringing the doorbell at this hour?* Perhaps his parents had forgotten their key; they were late coming home, he noticed as he glanced at the crystal mantel clock indicating 10:37 p.m. He quickly turned off the rock-and-roll music on the radio, knowing his parents disapproved. "Don't listen to that trash, Kenji-san," they would scold. Kenji opened the door and instantly recognized the policeman. "Sergeant Kualii," he said, "What's going on?"

"Kenji, may I come in? I need to talk to you," the cop said, prompting Kenji to motion him into the living room where they stood facing each other like opponents in a boxing match. The officer took a deep breath, his heart aching, and spoke quietly, "I don't know how to tell you this, son, but I have some really bad news. Your mom and dad were killed tonight in a head-on car accident on Highway 11. The driver of the other car died as well."

The teenager stood very still, the blood draining from his face, thinking maybe he hadn't heard correctly. "No, that can't be right! What do you mean, my folks are dead?"

"It appears a young driver was drunk or went to sleep and veered across the center divider and hit your parents' car head on. I'm really sorry, Kenji."

A buzzing sound seared through the boy's head, his vision suddenly blurred from involuntary tears. The sergeant reached out to grab Kenji under the armpits as he slumped to the floor. *Oh, my God. What am I going to do?* was Kenji's last thought before everything faded to black.

* * *

Kenji sat at the kitchen table staring off into nothingness, his arms clutching his stomach tightly. His insides ached as though a Howitzer had perforated the center of his body, leaving nothing but a dark jagged hole surrounded by wounded flesh. He couldn't believe the horror of the past three months. He went through the motions, making adult decisions about the funeral arrangements, the otherworldly choice of urns for his parents' ashes. He gratefully had accepted help from his next-door neighbors, Mr. and Mrs. Sato, when they offered to arrange for the food necessary to feed the people who came to mourn and pay their respects. He valiantly tried, yet sometimes failed, to be polite to the dozens of his parents' friends and neighbors who had brought flowers to the house. He inherently knew it was expected of him. He offered food and hospitality to them in the Japanese tradition. "Thank you for coming," he murmured over and over as he fought back the tears every time the doorbell rang, knowing he had to face more people.

The shrine he had set up to honor his parents gave him no comfort as he burned incense daily and dutifully spooned out a small portion of rice to leave on the table for the dead. "Mama, Papa, where are you?" he cried out in his sleep. "Why did you leave me?" He tried unsuccessfully to believe that his parents were watching over him, but he couldn't fight his way up and out of the dense stupor that enveloped him. The days passed in a blur. The ache inside his gut reminded him daily of the stark reality that he was totally alone, an orphan.

As he awoke every morning, inclined to be happy, reality slapped him in the face, as he knew he couldn't go to school that day. Instead he had to go to work in order to survive. He knew he had to take over the family business whether he wanted to or not.

Reluctantly he had gone to high school one final time on a Monday morning—to quit. The fuddy-duddy principal, reeking of too much aftershave, had motioned him to a chair in front of his tidy desk while murmuring his condolences.

"Thank you. I'm sorry, but I have to quit school and go to work." Kenji's shaky voice was just above a whisper. He was embarrassed because everyone in town knew about his circumstances.

"We're sorry to lose you as a student. You had so much potential," the principal had said, as if his future were now in jeopardy. He fled from the school in tears.

Kenji considered using his college fund but was reluctant to spend it because his parents had always stressed the importance of putting money aside for a rainy day. All thoughts of a college education were now a dream gone horribly awry. The palpable anger he felt surprised him. *I loved my parents. How could they abandon me like this?* he wondered, as the knot in his gut grew harder and harder.

Almost every evening, Mia Sato, the girl next door, stopped by the house to comfort him. They were the same age and had been good friends since early childhood. She wordlessly wrapped her thin arms around him and held him tightly as sobs wracked his body. "It's all right, Kenji-san. It's all going to be all right," she soothed. But he didn't believe her.

* * *

Kenji listlessly drove his mother's car to the T-shirt shop, her scent hovering like a ghost. Each day he reluctantly opened the door for business. He numbly went through the motions to serve customers — keep things tidy, lock up for the night, go home to an empty house, mindlessly fix something to eat — and then repeated the process day after day.

He knew the basics of running the shop. He had worked there since he was a kid, waiting on counter traffic, but mostly keeping the floor swept and the windows clean. His father, however, had never taught him the details of how to run a retail business. "Kenji-san, I work hard and save money so you can go to college and be an engineer," his dad had told him over and over.

Gus and Marion Olson owned the curio shop next door to Kenji's shop. Gus was only ten years older than Kenji, so he seemed more like a contemporary. With Kenji's folks gone, Gus immediately stepped in to teach him how to keep the books and order and manage stock. Kenji was quick to learn, even though he hated this crummy shop and resented having to run it.

One evening, Gus asked Kenji if he could hang around after closing the store. Curious about the request, Kenji agreed, hung up the Closed sign, turned off the lights, locked the door, and walked the few steps to Gus's shop. Gus closed up and motioned Kenji to join him at the table in the back room by the coffee machine.

He was surprised when Gus turned on him, eyes blazing. "What the hell do you think you're doing? It's been three months since your folks were killed, and you're moping around with a pitiful look on your face all day. You hardly talk to anyone except Marion and me." The next words cut to the quick. "Kenji, you dishonor the memory of your parents. This shop was their dream, and they built a good business and provided a nice home for you. They were living the American dream for their generation. What right do you have to treat all this as nothing but a pain in the ass?"

Kenji sat stunned, not uttering a word.

"I'll tell you something else," Gus said, "I believe in a higher power. I wake up each morning with my heart filled with gratitude for my family, for this simple little business I have. We live in one of the most beautiful places on Earth, and we get to experience it every day. It would be a fantasy for most people to have the opportunity to live in a place like Hawaii. I don't believe my higher power would want me to mope around with a sad look on my face and just put in the time day after day."

Tears streamed down Kenji's face, yet the barrage of words continued unabated.

"Kenji, if you continue your negative attitude, you'll look back thirty or forty years from now and see nothing but a wasted life. The way I look at it, we all have a special gift, and it's our responsibility to use the gifts we have to serve others."

Kenji's shoulders heaved with quiet sobs as he shielded his face with shaking hands.

"It was a terrible thing that happened to you at your age. Your parents were far too young to be killed. It was a tragedy. Now it's time for you to decide what you're going to do with your life. It's time for you to grow up. You can have a full life. You're incredibly intelligent, and you have good health. There's a saying that's attributed to Abraham Lincoln, 'People are about as happy as they decide to be.' It's time for you to decide."

Kenji sat there, his head hanging in his hands, the anger surging inside like a volcano about to erupt.

"I hope I haven't hurt your feelings, but you needed this talk, and since your father wasn't here to do it, I decided it needed to be me. See you tomorrow." With that, Gus walked Kenji out of his shop, locked up, and went home.

* * *

Two nights later Kenji sat dejected and alone on the dark beach just off Ali Drive, ignored by the other teenagers who laughed and talked as they passed around a joint while munching on Maui potato chips. Kenji listened intently to the roar of the waves crashing onto the lava rocks as if he were waiting for a message. While he pondered his fate, he heard the sweet chorus of birds in the nearby banyan tree as the cool air bathed his face, the gritty sand spilling through his fingers. He tried to make sense of the thoughts and emotions that had swirled through his brain since Gus's talk. Suddenly a bright light flashed through his head — an epiphany, a moment of clarity. His neighbor's harsh words had cut him deeply, but the more he thought about it, the more he came to understand that Gus was right.

His parents had left him a good business. It had made them enough money so they could live a comfortable life. Now it was all his. A kernel of satisfaction began to grow inside the hard knot of anger. Sure, some of the kids he had attended school with would be receiving a four-year college education, but when they got out of school, most of them would have to start from zero. *I'm seventeen years old and own a business,* Kenji thought. He couldn't think of any of his contemporaries who were in this situation. He smiled, suddenly pleased with himself.

At that moment he made what he would later come to think of as "the choice." *I will make a success of myself,* Kenji thought. *I will honor my parents and become a responsible businessman. I will try to help others. I will learn to live with the results of my daily choices. I will try to be happy. Tomorrow is a new day.*

Kenji left the beach feeling hopeful; the huge weight that had held him down had lifted. *Today I start the rest of my life,* he thought. *It's time to move on.* He saw his early memories in a new light. He felt loved, as if his mother

18

were reaching down from heaven to give him a wonderful gift.

As he walked from the beach, his mind flooded with his first distinct memory at the age of three. Kenji was in the shop with his parents, where he saw the T-shirts hanging all around, the intricate emblems that were printed on them a dazzling display of color. The shop was full of tourists. Some of the couples were dressed in brilliant Hawaiian shirts and matching fabric dresses — the "Sid and Gladys look," his father wryly commented. He saw his mom and dad respectfully waiting on customers at a tall counter with a glass display case. Kenji wandered around the display tables in the front of the shop. He remembered the big drawers that stored merchandise behind the counter. He occasionally tugged open a bottom drawer that held T-shirts — all folded, nice and colorful and soft. He remembered one time when he had woken up; apparently he had opened a drawer and crawled inside and gone to sleep. One of the customers pointed and laughed, and his mom came and got him. She was smiling and held him close as she kissed his chubby cheeks. She felt warm and soft, and he felt loved and safe.

Kenji's reverie continued, but now the demons took over and chilled him to the bone. It was the haunting memory of his first day of school when he was six years old. Several older boys, maybe nine or ten, were playing football, but one team was shy a player. Kenji stood on the sidelines watching. "Hey, kid," one of them said. "Come over here. Maybe you can run. We're going to make you a running back." All the boys laughed. They huddled together, talking about what they were going to do. When the huddle broke up, the leader of the group whispered to Kenji, "When I get the ball, I'm going to hand it to you, and you run like the dickens to the far end, okay?" Kenji, baffled by the situation, merely nodded. When the bigger boy got the ball, he handed it off to Kenji and said, "Now go! Run!" Kenji saw all the boys running at him, obviously intent on hurting him, so he turned around and ran in the other direction. This strategy made sense to his six-year-old brain; there wasn't anyone to stop him if he went that way. When he got to the goal line, the boys on the opposing team laughed like crazy. The big boy on his team said, "What the hell are you doing, you snot-nosed kid? Boy, are you stupid! Get out of here! I don't want you on my team anymore. We're better off playing short one person, because you're a total idiot!"

A feeling of humiliation washed over Kenji as he relived this incident eleven years later, making him angry all over again. It wasn't that big a deal, just kids interacting, he rationalized. But as an only child he hadn't been exposed to this kind of ridicule before, and the episode was seared deeply into his soul. His optimism about his future suddenly dimmed as uncertainty and doubt rose like bile in his throat.

CHAPTER 3

September 1967

Kenji, neatly dressed in chinos and a muted Hawaiian shirt, gingerly held a large box of chocolate-covered macadamia nuts, rang the doorbell, and waited patiently at the front door of Mia's house.

"Kenji-san, thank you for coming," said Mia's mother looking dowdy, though clothed in a colorful kimono, smiled as she opened the door wide to welcome him. "Come in. Come in and join the party. You're looking very handsome this evening. How are you doing? How's your business going? I'm so excited about Mia going to Stanford, but I'm going to miss her terribly," she rattled on and on.

He saw Mia's dark head across the room, her granny glasses perched on her straight nose, as she spoke in hushed tones with several girlfriends. He wondered at the courage it must take for her parents to send her thousands of miles away for college. *She's such a frail, little thing and looks so young,* he thought, *like a baby bird attempting to fly from the nest on its maiden flight.*

When Mia heard her mother welcome Kenji, she looked up and grinned. "Hey, Kenji. Come join us," she said, as the other girls' dainty hands covered their giggles.

Oh, God, what have I gotten myself into? Kenji wondered as he made his way across the room to the gaggle of girls. "Hi, Mia. This is for you." He handed her his gift. "Just to remind you of home."

"Thank you so much. I'll ration them out so they'll last a long time," Mia said with a smile. The other girls wandered off, sensing that these two preferred a private conversation.

"Are you packed and ready to go?" asked Kenji.

"Yes. I fly out tomorrow morning. I'm so excited but a little scared too," she admitted. "I've never been to the mainland before, and Stanford is such a huge school."

"Like you've told me in the past, Mia, it's going to be all right. Everything will be all right." Kenji reached out both hands to rest lightly on her shoulders.

Mia's eyes misted at the shared memory. "Thank you, Kenji-san. I'm going to miss you a lot."

"I'm going to miss you too. Just send me a postcard once in a while so I know you're doing okay. This is a terrific opportunity for you, and I know you'll be just fine. Will you be home for Christmas?"

"No, my parents are coming to California for the holidays. I'm their excuse to travel to the mainland. My plan is to take summer classes so I can graduate in three years. I may not see you for quite a while, but I promise to write, okay? Will you write to me too?" she asked eagerly.

"Of course." Kenji felt like an adult, if only momentarily.

He gave her a quick hug and said goodbye to Mrs. Sato as he made his way to the front door and left the party. Suddenly a feeling of abandonment washed over him, leaving him shivering, as bereft as an unwanted puppy.

* * *

June 1970

When the bell over the entrance to the shop tinkled, Kenji looked up to see a cute Japanese girl enter, her warm brown eyes smiling, her sleek black hair barely dusting her shoulders. "Excuse me. Do you have any Kona sweatshirts?" she asked knowingly.

Kenji grinned in happy surprise. "Mia, welcome home!" he exclaimed then rushed from behind the counter to give her a big hug.

She feels different — rounded out, soft, her fragrance of jasmine pleasantly wafting through the air, he mused. As he held her at arm's length, he noticed how her crisp blue jeans hugged her curvy body — size two, he figured. Mia was tiny compared to the tourist girls, who were tall, mostly blondes in short shorts over long tanned legs. They came to the shop in groups of two or three, flirtatious and too forward for Kenji's taste. He did enjoy the chitchat, intuitively knowing they had expectations of an island adventure with a handsome "local" they wouldn't be caught dead with on the mainland. Because it was good for business, Kenji flirted back, while tamping down his raging hormones against the barrage of firm breasts and too much skin. Yet when asked if he was available for a walk on the beach later in the evening and the implied promise of much more, he demurred.

"So how are you doing?" Mia asked, quietly pleased at his appraising glance.

"Just fine. Everything's cool. I haven't seen you in such a long time. You look so different, all grown up and beautiful. I can't believe you've been gone three whole years. When did you get home? Have you graduated from Stanford? You look amazing!" The questions and comments poured from Kenji.

"Thank you. That's very sweet. I arrived earlier today, and yes, I got my accounting degree by studying straight through. Now I'm looking for a job. I hope to find something here in Kona. As a last resort, I may have to go to Honolulu, though I would prefer not to."

Kenji marveled at the changes in Mia. She had become a stunning young woman, filled out in all the right places, with curvy hips and pert breasts he couldn't help notice.

He remembered her love of all things Minnie Mouse; the warm thoughts of her obsession with a cartoon character made him smile. He hadn't seen her since her going-away party but was grateful for the monthly postcards that had flown back and forth across the Pacific.

Mia smiled conspiratorially, as if they were still children. "You need to catch me up on everything that's happened around here," she said. "How about taking me out for a burger after you close the store tonight?"

"Sure, my pleasure. I can't wait to hear all about your adventures in California. You can regale me with stories about your many boyfriends on the mainland. You didn't have space to write many details on your postcards. I'll close a bit early and pick you up at eight, okay?"

"I'm not telling you anything about any boyfriends," Mia said with a wry grin. "See you later! I'm so happy to see you and to be home again. I've missed you." She gaily waved as she left the store.

Kenji couldn't help the wide grin that lifted his spirits. He was thrilled to see her again and astonished at how much she had grown up. "I've missed you too, Mia Mouse," he said under his breath.

* * *

That evening, Kenji went home early to quickly shower and shave before his date with Mia, excited at the prospect of resuming a relationship with his childhood chum. He hadn't been on any dates with girls, which was unusual for a young man of his age, but he'd had neither the time nor the inclination.

He stood at Mia's front door, a bouquet of fragrant flowers in hand, as he desperately tried to ease the fear that cramped his guts. *What if she's too good for me?* he worried. *What if she has a boyfriend on the mainland? What would she want with a simple shopkeeper like me?* He had a sinking feeling in the pit of his stomach as he summoned the courage to ring the doorbell.

Mia's mother opened the door, smiling in greeting. "Kenji-san, lovely to see you. I see you coming and going next door at all hours, but you work too hard, so we never have a chance to talk. Come in. Come in." She called to the back of the house, "Mia, Kenji-san is here!"

Mia gracefully glided into the room, wearing a colorful flowing skirt and a white sleeveless blouse, her slim waist cinched in with a wide belt. "Hi, Kenji," she said, smiling.

Suddenly shy, he thrust the bouquet into Mia's hand. "Welcome home!"

"Thank you," she told him. "That's so thoughtful and sweet, nothing like the frat-house guys at Stanford. Come on back to the kitchen and say hello to my dad while I find a vase and put these in some water."

Kenji followed Mia like a puppy trailing its mistress to face the stern countenance of Mr. Sato, who rarely smiled, self-conscious of his crooked teeth. He sat stiffly at the table reading a Japanese language newspaper. "Good evening, Mr. Sato," Kenji said.

"Hello, Kenji-san. So you're taking my daughter out to dinner. Don't keep her out too late," he cautioned.

"Yes, sir. I won't, sir." The image of Mr. Sato solemnly performing tai chi in the front yard popped into Kenji's mind.

Mia smiled, kissed her father on the cheek, took Kenji's hand, and led the way out the front door. Over time, the casual dinner that evening became a regular event, the two childhood pals rekindling old bonds of friendship that took on a new exciting form. Kenji was amazed at how easily and quickly they became a couple; all his fears had been for naught. Mia was as open and nurturing as she always had been, but she was different too — more worldly and polished. Maybe it was the contact lenses that had re-placed the granny glasses, revealing dark smoky eyes that highlighted her silky skin. They talked about her college experiences, including tidbits about the frat boys she had dated. Kenji shared funny stories about odd customers at the shop and his mentor, Gus, and all the mistakes he had made when he had first started running his business. They laughed about the forward white tourist girls and Kenji's refusal to fall into that trap.

The phone in the shop rang one day. "Kenji, hi. It's Mia. I got a job today at an accounting firm out in Kailua and guess what? As I was leaving, I overheard my new boss on the phone bragging to someone about 'the Stanford-educated girl' he had just hired. I thought you'd get a kick out of that." She laughed merrily.

His immediate reaction was fear and insecurity about his lack of an education. *Grow up, Kenji*, he told himself. He forced a smile. "Congratulations, Mia! This calls for a celebration. Want to go the Kona Inn for dinner tonight?"

"Sounds great! Thank you. See you about eight?"

"I'll pick you up then if you're willing to be seen in public with a humble shopkeeper."

"Stop that, Kenji," Mia admonished him. "You're as good as anyone. Get your head on straight!"

Kenji heard a click then a dial tone. *That was a stupid thing to say*, he chastised himself.

* * *

"I love this restaurant. There's so much history here," Mia commented as they walked across the polished wood floor and down the steps inside the Kona Inn to be seated at an outside table, the ocean waves lapping onto the shore. They sipped mai tais as they enjoyed the balmy summer evening. "It's hard to believe this used to be a hotel for ship captains and fishermen back in the 1920s," she said.

"This place is definitely a glimpse into the old Hawaii. I love the horseshoe-shaped koa-wood bar." The alcoholic drink emboldened Kenji to ask, "How about we pretend we're from another island, stopping by here for the night?"

"You're getting ahead of yourself, big boy," Mia replied, grinning at the thought of such intimacy and Kenji's boldness.

He raised his glass in a toast. "Here's to you, Mia Mouse. May all your working days be happy ones," he said.

* * *

Thinking back to the skinny kid he had been just three years ago, Kenji smiled as he glanced at one of the mirrors at the shop. He saw a well-muscled young man, hair neatly trimmed, with a tanned handsome face, if he were to believe the long-legged tourist girls. Since Mia had returned to the island, he opened the shop each day with new enthusiasm, knowing he would spend time with her in the evening hours. He liked the feeling of holding hands at the movies, the hugs of greeting, while gradually working up the nerve to kiss her goodnight at the door of her parents' home, noticing her mom slyly peeking through the lace curtains, smiling in approval. The months flew by as Kenji and Mia fell in love, their common heritage and long friendship a solid foundation for their future.

Mia's parents announced their daughter's engagement in the local newspaper soon after Kenji summoned the courage to ask her father for Mia's hand. Mr. Sato uncharacteristically grinned with delight. "Yes, Kenji-san, you have our blessing. We always hoped that you and Mia would get together." The lovebirds were soul mates, something that time and miles could not change, as if they were two doves destined to live together for life.

They were married in June in a small, quiet ceremony, with just Mia's parents and a few close friends in attendance as they vowed to love each other until death do they part. Kenji's heart brimmed with happiness as he watched Mia glide down the aisle on her father's arm. *I'm so lucky to have such a beautiful bride,* he thought, *dainty in a white-satin gown.* They were both only twenty-one years old.

* * *

The newlyweds quickly settled into the house Kenji had inherited from his parents. Their first fight began over something minor. Mia wanted to make a few decorating changes and replace some of the old-fashioned furniture. Her mother had counseled her to ask his permission, something that went against the grain of her personality, but she did it anyway.

"No!" Kenji exclaimed.

"What do you mean, no? This is the same couch I remember from my earliest childhood memories. It's old, faded, and falling apart," Mia argued, uncharacteristically stubborn. "And that old koa-wood table makes the house look dark and dreary."

"I don't feel right about it. What would my parents say? It was good enough for them, so it should be good enough for you."

"Well, it's not!" she shouted, slumping on the tattered couch, tears beginning to fall.

"Mia, let's not fight about this."

"Will you at least go shopping with me to see if we can find something we both like?" she asked, changing her tactic. "We can probably sell the old stuff. I don't want to fight either. Now let's kiss and make up." She went to him and hugged him tightly.

Kenji reluctantly agreed to the shopping foray.

"We're a two-income household, so paying for some new furniture isn't an issue," Mia told him. "Isn't it exciting, sweetheart? We're creating our own home, just like our parents did many years ago."

He began to see her point of view, and his doubts faded when they found two soft-green flowered couches and a pale ash dining table with matching high-backed cane chairs. He got into the spirit of things by choosing two modern lamps, while suggesting a new bedroom set and a white down-filled comforter. They left the furniture store after making arrangements to have their new treasures delivered, happy with their choices, the disagreement soon forgotten. The upgraded décor created an atmosphere that was both beautiful and serene, appealing to both of them.

For four years, Kenji had been running his business, and all was going well. He was pleased and a bit surprised at the knowledge and expertise Mia brought to their partnership. She continued with her career but spent evenings with him at the shop, pitching in to pay bills and do the accounting. They sat one evening, heads bent together, reviewing the year-to-date financials and decided that their cash flow warranted expansion to a second shop next year, then a third shop if business continued to flourish, partially because the cruise ships made weekly stops at the Kona port. Their youthful exuberance made it seem that anything was possible.

* * *

The lives of the Watanabes were blessed with their businesses growing and Mia's career in full flower. They enjoyed a comfortable, loving marriage, marred only by their inability to conceive a child. It certainly wasn't for lack of trying. They made love frequently, tuned into each other mentally and emotionally. The years passed in a state of near contentment, though Mia's internal clock struck louder and louder as she approached her thirty-fifth birthday. Her parents nagged her continually about the lack of a grandchild, blaming Mia for working too hard.

Finally Mia capitulated and resigned from her job at the accounting firm, telling Kenji, "I want to focus on starting a family, and I'll have more time to help you with the business."

"Why don't we both get checked out by a doctor?" Kenji suggested. "I want to make sure my little swimmers are potent," he sheepishly admitted. "Besides, with your good looks and brilliant mind, our kids will be perfect." They made appointments for the following week.

The news was devastating. "Mrs. Watanabe, I'm sorry to tell you that it will be difficult, if not impossible, for you to conceive. Your uterus is tilted," the doctor informed her matter-of-factly. "You and your husband may want to consider adoption."

Mia, usually optimistic and cheerful, fled from the doctor's office in tears, feeling stupid for having waited so long to get a diagnosis and dreading the conversation she'd have to have with Kenji. He would have been such a good father, and now she felt worthless.

Months passed as she grieved her loss of motherhood. She moped around the house, no longer showing interest in anything—not cooking, not cleaning, not the business, not Kenji.

Kenji became alarmed and then angry. "Mia, snap out of it!" he shouted at her. "You have so much to be thankful for, and you're burying yourself in self-pity. Frankly I'm getting tired of your whole routine!"

Mia looked up at him as if he were a monster. "Leave me alone," she told him, as the tears began to fall.

"I'll gladly do that!" he yelled as he stormed out of the house mad as hell. He ran and ran until he began to calm down enough to think things through. *I've been depressed before*, he thought. *I know how it feels.* Mia hadn't responded to anger or common sense. Though Kenji felt helpless, he decided to try a different strategy. Maybe women responded better to nurturing.

He opened the front door, went to his wife, knelt in front of her, and cradled her face in his loving hands. "Mia, my love, you are my soul. It doesn't matter to me that we can't have kids. I love you with all my heart. You're all I'll ever need. Please, just try to be happy."

Touched by Kenji's devotion and steadfastness, Mia vowed to snap out of her dark hole of depression. She started to walk miles every day in an attempt to enjoy the beauty that surrounded her. One day she happened by the Boys & Girls Club and heard the sound of children laughing. Something stirred inside her. Without further thought she walked into the club and asked whether they needed volunteers.

"You're a godsend," the director gushed. "We always need tutors. When can you start?"

The dark depression that had plagued Mia for months slowly lifted as she went to the club every day to tutor a select group of kids. She was enthusiastic one evening as she told Kenji, "You have to meet this little girl. Her name is Misaki. She's like a colt, skittish, uncertain, shy, somehow wounded in spirit. I feel compelled to try to help her."

"I'd be happy to meet her," replied Kenji, greatly relieved that Mia had found a spark of interest in something.

"She lives with her mother. Her father abandoned them when Misaki was seven. I'm tutoring her in math and science. Would you consider helping her with English? She needs a strong dose of confidence, and Lord knows you have plenty of that to go around."

Misaki, though shy at first, thrived under the attention of her mentors. Her grades improved at school, and by the time she was thirteen, she was getting straight As and exuded confidence.

One day she approached Kenji. "I hate to ask you," she said, "but could you help me go to this golf clinic? You and Mia already have done so much for me, but I hit some balls last week, and the coach said I have a natural swing and encouraged me to go to this clinic at the Makalei golf course."

"Sure, no problem," Kenji replied. That was the beginning of Misaki's adventure and quest in the golfing world.

Over time, the subject of adopting a child came up less and less. Kenji continually reassured Mia, "You're all I'll ever want and need."

"But aren't you sad that we can't have a family?"

"I'm not sad. I'm a realist. In a perfect world, having kids would be nice, but I learned a long time ago to accept what is and then move on."

Mia was mollified and finally came to accept their childless situation. She made a decision to fill her life with children even though she hadn't birthed them. Expanding her tutoring role at the Boys & Girls Club was the easiest path, and over time she had filled the void in her soul to overflowing. Her satisfaction grew with each new child she helped, bringing her joy and contentment.

Kenji and Mia continued to expand their business, opening shops on Oahu and Maui. Mia, still an active participant, suggested strategies for improving their marketing and put into place a program to guarantee a positive customer experience. Together she and Kenji devised sessions to train staff and managers while always keeping an eye on the bottom line. They traveled inter-island frequently to monitor each shop. Kenji and Mia were a loving

couple, equal partners, and very active in social and community activities in Kona. Life was good, and they were
happy.

At age forty-six the blessings seemed to run out. Mia
discovered a lump in one breast and immediately made
an appointment to see her doctor. After a nail-biting week
of fear and anticipation, a biopsy was performed, and the
results were pronounced. The tumor was cancerous — stage
four. There had been no symptoms, and Mia feared they
hadn't discovered the cancer in time. Kenji's world collapsed, though he remained steadfastly optimistic. Mia
was his heart and soul, and he was terrified of a future that
might not include her.

The next two years were a nightmare and a gift all
wrapped into one — doctors, surgeries, rest, chemotherapy,
and Mia's lustrous black hair coming out in tufts that piled
up on the floor. She was frustrated that she didn't have the
strength or will to tidy up the house. She struggled to fight
off the pain and nausea, quietly weeping in the middle of
the night so as not to wake her husband. He felt her pain,
cradling her gently to give them both some comfort. "Shh,
Mia Mouse. Everything will be all right," he whispered
into her lovely, pale, shell-shaped ear. "I'm here, right beside you."

Visits to the doctor became more frequent. The cancer
eventually spread to Mia's bones and brain. The doctor
strongly suggested she would be more comfortable in the
hospital, but she refused to go. The days took a dark turn;
the nights were worse. Kenji tended to Mia's every need
with selfless devotion. He lay holding her on the fateful

last night, as Mia took a long shuddering breath, then all was quiet, her still form wrapped in his loving arms. Mia died the same way she had lived, with quiet dignity and grace. Kenji, at age forty-eight, fought off his demons with a vengeance but involuntarily reverted to his teenage introvert self and was inconsolable, abandoned once again.

CHAPTER 4

June 1998

Kenji sat at the spinet piano, a remnant of his youth, nestled in a nook off the living room. His fingers caressed the keys as he mindlessly sang the lyrics of a song that ran through his head: "You don't have to say you love me, just be close at hand. You don't have to stay forever. I will understand. Believe me. Believe me." The gray, depressing day had put him in a somber mood, the rain beating against the windows, skies the color of dull pewter. Music usually lifted his spirits but not today. He switched tempos, pounding out a raucous rock song, but finally gave up in frustration. He wandered through the empty house, poured a cup of coffee, and brought it to his home office. He took a sip as he gazed longingly at Mia's photo in the seashell frame. To Kenji, the shells looked stupid and out of place in this masculine room, which was well ordered, neat as a new ship. It had been exactly two years since Mia had died. Nothing could fill the empty ache inside, not volunteering, not spending time with his friends, not making money, not even his burgeoning obsession with golf. The ringing telephone startled him out of his reverie.

"Hello."

"Hi, Kenji. It's Stu Garner." Kenji and Mia had met Stu and his vivacious redheaded wife, Gloria, at a charity event several years earlier, soon after Stu had launched his practice as an orthopedic surgeon in Kona. The four had hit it off right away. The Garners shared Mia and Kenji's passion for helping others.

"Hey. How are you doing?" Kenji responded listlessly.

"Great, Kenji. Listen, the reason for the call—I heard through the grapevine that you started taking golf lessons a while back. Is that true?"

"Yes, but I'm still learning. I've only played a few rounds and spend most of my time at the driving range."

"Good for you! Remember I told you about the foursome I'm in? We've been playing together for about three years. Well, one of our guys just moved back to the mainland, and we wondered if you might like to play with us next Wednesday."

"Oh, I don't think so. I've only been playing for a month. I'd be embarrassed to play with you guys."

"Not to worry, Kenji. It's fun, and I promise your game will improve, especially with all of us coaching you. Look at it this way — you'll be getting free lessons!"

"So who's in your merry little group?" asked Kenji, his mood beginning to lighten.

"Vince Whittaker is the athlete of the bunch. He has a low handicap, and our other guy is Ernie MacKenzie. We're a mixed bag when it comes to talent, so you'll fit right in. It's more about having fun and being outside, enjoying the beautiful weather, though today isn't a good example. So what do you say? Can we count on you for Wednesday?"

"All right. I guess I could try it."

"Awesome! We'll see you at Makalei at nine a.m. on Wednesday."

* * *

That Wednesday morning, a golden sun dawned, bright and clear in a cloudless sky, as Kenji prepared for his golf outing. He loaded his brand-new set of TaylorMade clubs into the trunk of his car. He had purchased them on a whim soon after he had begun to take lessons. *Perhaps not so frivolous after all*, he thought with a smile as he negotiated his car through the hills and curves that led to the Makalei golf course as he sang along with a rock song on the radio. He rolled down the car window, enjoying the

fragrance of pine trees and the fresh, crisp air as he pulled
into the parking lot of the club.

Stu was there to greet him. "Hi, Kenji! Glad you could
join us. Let me introduce you to the guys. This is Ernie
MacKenzie. He has a software company in Kona, and meet
Vince Whittaker, the real golfer of our group. He's a physical therapist."

"Good morning, gentlemen," Kenji said with a smile,
bowing in the Japanese tradition then shaking each hand
in greeting.

"Welcome to our little male-bonding session," said
Vince with a twinkle in his eye. "Why don't you ride with
me today, Kenji, and I'll give you a *real* golf lesson? You
can switch around golf carts and decide who you want to
ride with each week so you can benefit from all our bad
habits," he joked.

"Thank you very much. I'd appreciate that," replied Kenji, feeling a bit more comfortable than he had
anticipated.

The day progressed much better than his meager expectations. He hit enough good shots to entice him back
the following week, and he actually sunk a few putts. He
rationalized these small successes as beginner's luck. He
also was relieved that the guys seemed cordial enough,
though Ernie appeared somewhat preoccupied. Kenji had
heard rumors around town about "that genius MacKenzie
fellow" and some secret, classified government work but
hadn't paid much attention since he didn't know him
personally. Still, Kenji liked Ernie's easygoing style and
was awed by the power and length of his drives. The

eighteen-hole round of golf flashed by, the others holding true to their promise to give him advice along the way. He enjoyed the day, although it ended much too quickly.

"See you next week!" they told Kenji.

"Thanks for the golfing tips, guys!"

He drove down the hill, singing along with the radio, feeling as light as a feather floating on a breeze. He eagerly awaited the next golf outing, hoping to share a cart with Ernie and attempt to penetrate his mysterious persona while learning the secrets of his commanding drives—a challenge on both fronts.

CHAPTER 5

"Your golf game is coming along nicely," encouraged Stu, as he and Kenji stood talking before the Rotary Club meeting started.

"Thanks. Frankly I'm frustrated as hell. Golf is a lot more complicated than I thought it would be."

Stu laughed knowingly. "Hang in there and just have fun. That's why I play."

"That's not good enough for me. I want to win."

"Okay, just don't give up. Excuse me. I need to check in with this new guy I'm mentoring," Stu said as he went to greet a latecomer.

Kenji sat down at an empty table, wanting to be alone with his thoughts. The murmur of voices in the room suddenly grew louder. He looked up to see a stunning

Japanese woman, about thirty-five, he guessed, make her way into the room. She was almost too beautiful to be real. She had a perfect oval face, a straight nose, sculpted cheekbones, and ink-black hair that a cascaded like a waterfall down her back.

She was no more than a size four, Kenji figured, her medium height her only feature that wasn't extraordinary. Her red blouse shimmered in the morning light, attracting appreciative glances from men and women alike. He surreptitiously watched, curious about this stranger. She signed in at the guest table and paid for her breakfast in cash, her eyes searching the room for an empty chair. Her straight black skirt, flouncy at the hem, barely skimmed her shapely knees and long silky legs. She glided across the room in three-inch heels with the stature and bearing of an athlete or a dancer, her skirt seductively swaying with each step. *Oh, oh,* Kenji thought. *She's coming this way.*

"Good morning. I'm Lilly Yamada," she said, confident and self-assured, her hand outstretched.

Being a gentleman, Kenji stood up to greet her. "Hello, Lilly. I'm Kenji Watanabe. You must be new in town."

"It's a pleasure to meet you." She firmly shook his hand. "Yes, I'm a visiting Rotarian from the Los Angeles area."

"Welcome to Kona!"

The sergeant-at-arms rang the bell to announce breakfast. Somewhat relieved, Kenji guided Lilly to the buffet table, which was laden with fresh island fruit, scrambled eggs, ham and fried Spam, biscuits, and gravy. Other club members watched Kenji and Lilly as they made their way along the buffet, choosing various breakfast items. The guys, covetous of Kenji's good fortune, were astounded that he was being friendly to an unfamiliar woman. The women stared regretfully, feeling dowdy in Lilly's presence.

Kenji learned that she was an optometrist from Torrance, California; had just sold her practice and was thinking of moving to Kona. She had been here before on vacation, so this was a serious investigation trip to see whether she wanted to move here permanently. She was forthright and open in her comments, which was surprising, as Kenji was unaccustomed to talking with extremely self-confident women.

It was a frequent story; people often succumbed to the allure of the island while on vacation. The Big Island of Hawaii offered dramatic contrasts — the starkness of the lava fields north of Kona, or country living on the cattle ranches farther north. Hilo, on the opposite side of the island, was wet and tropical. Some visitors stayed, finding a new life, and became islanders. Others came and over time felt claustrophobic because it was a long way to anywhere else, requiring boat or airplane trips. The natives called it "island fever." The locals had a saying, "If you bring your mainland ways to the island, the island will send you home." The ones who adapted to the softer, slower way of life usually stayed and came to appreciate and love the islands.

"I'll be curious to find out if you adapt to the slower way of life here," said Kenji as he and Lilly returned to their table to eat breakfast. He doubted she would stay very long, as she struck him as a type-A personality, not well suited to island living.

"I've been here before and loved it," Lilly said with a broad smile. "We stayed at a condo in the Waikoloa area and played tennis most of the time."

He wondered who the "we" referred to but didn't ask. From what she had said, he assumed she was here alone on this trip.

"We didn't do much exploring on that trip, though. Are you available to show me the pleasures of the island one day this week?" she asked, openly flirting.

Lilly's request flabbergasted Kenji and instantly reminded him of the long-legged tourist girls in short shorts who came into his shop seeking adventure. *What kind of woman is so forward with a man she just met?* he thought. *What game is she playing? Is she looking for an island fling? Or is she serious about moving here?* This beautiful woman intrigued him. He enjoyed visiting with her, yet she scared the hell out of him. He decided to ignore her request as the club president fortuitously began the meeting. Afterward he surprised himself by asking her, "Would you like to have lunch tomorrow?"

"Thank you. That would be lovely."

"I'll show you where the locals eat so you can get a taste of the real Hawaii," he said and then gave her directions to a restaurant on Ali Drive.

"Terrific! See you there at noon."

A date. My God, this is my first real date in three years, Kenji thought. He was jubilant yet felt guilty about betraying Mia. Everyone noticed his jaunty step as he escorted Lilly from the building.

* * *

The next day, Kenji drove his car into a public parking lot off Ali Drive near the restaurant. He was nervous yet excited, wondering whether he would run into anyone he knew. *What will they think?* he wondered. *It's not a big deal. It's just lunch with a fellow Rotarian. Could it turn out to be more than that? Occasionally you meet someone for the first time, and you just click.* This woman had class; she definitely wasn't in the "bootie call" category, or was she?

He saw Lilly waiting at the bottom of the steps that led up to the restaurant. "Hi, Lilly. Seems we're both early," greeted Kenji, noting her stylish embroidered white pants and matching sleeveless knit top. Her high-heeled sandals made her muscular, shapely legs look even longer than he had remembered.

"Hi, Kenji. They say it's good to be fashionably late to appointments, but I tend to think it's rude. It's more important to let people know that I value their time." Her punctuality impressed him, as he also was conscientious about being on time.

They walked up the stairs to the restaurant, where the hostess seated them on the deck that bordered Ali Drive.

"There's a bit of traffic noise here, but I wanted you to see our little town from this perspective. The big days for the merchants are when the cruise ships dock just off to the right there," Kenji said as he pointed toward the disembark area. "Then, hopefully, hundred of tourists head for the shops around town to spend their money," he explained, vowing not to get caught up in the magic of this gorgeous creature. "So tell me about yourself. How long have you been in the Rotary Club?"

Lilly told him she had been a Rotarian for ten years in California and had been selected to serve as the club's first female president, much to the chagrin of some of the more senior male members. She had won them over, however, with a combination of guile and graciousness, she admitted, and was hoping to transfer her membership to the club in Kona.

"Guess I don't need to sell you on the virtues of Kona. You mentioned yesterday you were planning to move here?" Kenji asked.

Lilly sat comfortably, looking at this hunk of a man, considering whether he was viable as a future escort. He was plenty tall, so she could wear heels, always a plus. He and his quiet nature intrigued her. It hadn't occurred to her that she would meet such an attractive man so soon after her arrival. *Is he available?* she wondered.

"I'm ninety percent sure this is where I want to live, certainly for a year or so. I have a little time left on a consulting contract with the couple who bought my practice, but I've already signed a short-term lease on a condo to find out whether I like living in the islands. Hopefully I can get to know some people at Rotary, find a church family, and establish a social life. I may even open a practice here, but first I need to scope out the competition."

"You won't have any problems getting acquainted. Making friends is another story. People here are friendly but a bit wary of newcomers."

"Uh-oh, I may need some help in that area."

"Give it some time. Volunteer for something. That usually sends the signal that you're serious about living here."

Volunteer? While chairing Rotary Club projects at home, Lilly preferred to delegate the actual work. The notion of community service here hadn't occurred to her. What the hell had she gotten herself into?

"Actually," Kenji said, "we have similar circumstances. I just sold my businesses and am trying to figure out what to do with the rest of my life. I'm too young to *really* retire. Meanwhile I'm becoming addicted to golf."

Lilly pondered his last remark. *He must be set financially,* she thought. *Always a good sign.* "Have you always lived in Kona?"

"Yes. In fact I live in the same house I was raised in my entire life. I enjoy being a homebody."

Lilly wondered whether Kenji was married and had a family but decided the information wasn't important at this juncture. She was physically attracted to this comfortable-in-his-own-skin man. *He looks distinguished and casual at the same time,* she thought, *with those flashing, almost black eyes.* She fought the temptation to reach over to brush up a lock of hair that had fallen onto his forehead.

Sensing a need to fill in the silence, Kenji said, "I live alone now. I don't even have a cat. My wife died three years ago, and we never had kids. Her name was Mia. I miss her every day."

"I'm so sorry for your loss." *There's a red flag,* she thought. *He's still carrying a torch for his dead wife.* Lilly was disappointed. One quick comment had suddenly dashed her fantasies about possibly building a relationship with Kenji.

"What do you recommend for lunch?" she asked while perusing the menu, hoping the change in subject would lighten her dark mood.

"Everything here is good," Kenji said with a smile, "but the portions are large, so be forewarned. Perhaps you'd enjoy a salad. They use a lot of Hawaiian-grown fruit in some unusual combinations."

"Excellent. I'll try the mango-and-passion-fruit salad. That sounds exciting," she replied, flirting instinctively.

"Good choice. I rarely eat beef, but today is special, so I'm going to be a typical guy and order a burger and fries."

Lilly asked questions about Kona and the island while they sat comfortably, having lunch. He told her about the local coffee plantations, the flower and macadamia nut farms, and other typical tourist attractions before discussing the hazards of island living.

"The 1960 tsunami was caused by an eight-point-three earthquake in Chile. Waves thirty-five feet high struck Hilo, which resulted in sixty-one deaths and over twenty million dollars in damage. That side of the island was devastated. Not to scare you off, but the last eruption of the Kileuea Volcano began in 1983 and continues to this day. The lava spews into the ocean adding acres to the island every year. Kileuea is home to the fire goddess Pele, according to island lore."

"Scary stuff!"

"Yes, we have our share. Have you noticed that the more expensive homes in Kona-Kiluea tend to be at higher elevations? That's because those who can afford it prefer to live at least fifty feet above sea level, which is generally believed to be above the tsunami line."

"Guess I got lucky. My condo has a great view and it's up in the hills."

"Excellent. Bet you didn't know the largest cattle ranch in the US is right here on the big island."

"Really," she said doubtfully.

"It's called Parker Ranch. Here's a bit of history for you. In 1816, John Palmer Parker, a Western advisor to King Kamehameha, married royal granddaughter Kipikane and was awarded two acres of land for ten dollars. Over the next century, the ranch grew to a hundred and fifty thousand acres. Today the Parkers raise Angus and Charolais beef cattle."

"That's quite a history. You're right. I had no idea cattle were raised in Hawaii. Moo." Lilly giggled unexpectedly.

"They are indeed. The countryside in the upper elevations on that part of the island is spectacular. Do you ride horses?"

"I haven't in a long time, but I used to ride some in my wild, impetuous youth." Lilly laughed a bit slyly.

Surprising himself, Kenji said, "I'd like to take you riding up there one day."

"Sure, I'd love it!"

He felt more and more comfortable with this appealing woman, while fantasizing about how it would feel to touch her soft, glowing skin with his fingertips. He liked her laugh, which was merry and a bit raucous, so he told stories about island life that were funny, just to hear it ring out across the now mostly empty tables. They lingered over coffee and slices of mandatory macadamia nut pie.

As they headed down the stairs to leave, Kenji said, "I enjoyed having lunch with you. Will I see you next Thursday at Rotary?"

"Nah, I can't wait that long to see you again. How about that tour of the island tomorrow?"

Caught off guard by her eagerness, he was silent for a few moments, pondering what to do. He finally replied, "Sorry. I'm booked solid for the next few days with golf. But hopefully I'll see you at Rotary next week."

Lilly wasn't accustomed to being rebuffed. For a moment her lower lip jutted out in a charming pout, then she wisely changed tactics. "Have fun with that! Thanks for a lovely lunch, Kenji. It was fun. See you around." With an upraised arm, she waved over her shoulder as she walked away regally, like an Asian princess.

Kenji stood wondering why he had just blown off one of the most beautiful women he'd ever seen. So far it had been quite a day. He heard the birds singing more sweetly, felt the balmy air bathing his skin, saw the sun glowing brighter. This was new territory for him. He hadn't consciously felt single in three years, until today. The last time he had enjoyed the companionship of a woman was half a year ago in Honolulu. He had sat at the hotel bar after a long day of work, enjoying the solitude, when a thirty-something attractive brunette had sat down next to him. Her pickup line wasn't original, but it was effective. Her nonthreatening, bubbly personality was disarming. They chatted and ordered more drinks. Her playful, alluring way eventually led them to her hotel room. Emboldened by the alcohol, they tore off each other's clothes. The sweaty sex was passionate but brief. Afterward Kenji had performed the obligatory fifteen minutes of cuddling then quickly dressed and left with no promise of a rematch, sensing she didn't expect one. He felt twinges of guilt but rationalized it was just sex; it didn't mean anything. He already had forgotten her name.

CHAPTER 6

Several days passed. Lilly hadn't called Kenji, and he
hadn't called her, deciding after much thought to let fate
run its course. He was looking forward to playing golf
today. The Wednesday games and practice at the driving
range had shaken him out of his funk, lifting his spirits
while giving him something positive to think about; it
became one of the highlights of his week. He had come to
really enjoy spending time with Ernie, who reminded him
of the PGA pro golfer Ernie Els. He even looked a bit like
Els — a few inches over six feet tall, with a muscular chest
and in great physical shape at age thirty-seven despite his
lack of a regimented exercise program. His thick, straight,
blond hair and laidback demeanor also reminded him of
the pro golfer.

Ernie pulled up in his sports car, top down, in front of Kenji's house. He beeped the horn and waited. His new friend came bounding out of the house, lugging his clubs.

"Hey, Kenji. What's happening?"

He stowed his clubs in the trunk and lowered himself in the passenger seat before responding to Ernie's greeting. "Golf is happening. I have it in mind to kick your ass on the links today."

Ernie laughed. "I love your fantasy life, Kenji. It's so creative."

"Here's a serious question for you. How much do you understand about women?"

"Not much. My experiences in that regard have been disastrous. Why do you ask?"

"I had lunch last week with a gorgeous woman I met at Rotary. She came on to me a bit strong, and I think she may have some ulterior motive, but I haven't a clue what it is. It's not like I'm the catch of the year."

"Sorry. You're asking the wrong person. My track record with women would fill the shortest book on Earth, though it would be a thriller."

"Really? That sounds intriguing."

"Stick around," Ernie said. "I'll tell you all about the danger of liaisons with beautiful women some day."

As they drove out of town, heading for Makalei, Kenji was curious, but their discussion turned to more familiar and safer territory — golf.

Ernie MacKenzie enjoyed their weekly game of golf but didn't expend the time or effort to lower his scores. He played to relax and have fun away from the stresses and clandestine nature of his business. His drives typically flew more than 275 yards; that and his twenty handicap suited him just fine. Ernie was a genius, but few people knew this. Only his customers and a core group at the National Security Agency knew. Also, his watchers knew.

"So tell me Ernie," Kenji said. "What's your story? Did you grow up in a typical family?

Ernie's eyes crinkled as he laughed loudly. "Not really. My mom ran away with a sleazy used car salesman when I was ten. My dad was an alcoholic who took out his frustrations with the failures of his life on my mom and me with his fists. That's probably why she split. Pop drank, cussed, and drank some more, then would go out to get more liquor. One night he left and didn't come home. I never saw him again. I was twelve years old. There wasn't any money, so I ended up homeless, dodging the child-welfare people while trying to stay in school. I got by on two tacos and a cheeseburger a day while living under the bushes along the 405 freeway in Los Angeles and taking showers at the gym at school."

Kenji shook his head. "That's tragic. I'm so sorry you had to go through all that."

They drove in silence for a few miles, as Kenji tried to imagine how difficult Ernie's life had been. *God,* he thought, *Ernie's early years were a hell of a lot more tragic than mine.* He was curious to know how Ernie had become such a successful businessman after enduring such a rough-and-tumble past. "When did you start playing golf?" Kenji asked him.

"Not until a few years ago. I was a computer geek in school, focused on scraping together enough money to buy parts to build my own computer. I used to sneak into my Dad's wallet while he was sleeping off a drunk and lift a five or a ten. I mowed lawns, delivered newspapers, and did odd jobs so I could save up the two hundred dollars I needed to buy some computer parts from a catalog. I gave the money to a sympathetic teacher who put my parts order on his credit card."

"Really? Ambitious kid, eh?"

"You bet. The inner workings of a computer just made sense to me, so I wrote some code and started a consulting business when I was sixteen."

"That's beyond impressive."

Kenji learned that Ernie had finished high school at the top of his class and earned a full-ride scholarship to UCLA, where he had graduated summa cum laude with a computer science degree. The National Security Agency had recruited him right out of college in a rare instance of recognizing someone's genius.

Not for the first time, Kenji felt inadequate and inferior because he didn't have a college degree. He chastised himself, thinking he should have done better in life.

When they arrived at the golf course, they greeted Stu and Vince, checked in at the pro shop, then waited on the first tee. It was cool, the temperature only in the high sixties. In his mind, Kenji rehearsed the strategy he would use to beat Ernie. He knew he couldn't outdrive him, but he faithfully had been practicing his short game and putting.

His saving grace off the tees was the accuracy of his drives, typically right down the middle of the fairway. By the time they got to the tenth tee, Kenji, with his handicap, was tied on the scorecard with Ernie. Feeling more self-confident with every stroke, he decided to employ one more tactic — planting seeds of doubt in Ernie's mind.

"Hey, Ernie. Fifty bucks says you'll miss the fairway on this hole."

"Is that any way to talk to a friend? You're on!"

"I'm just saying…"

Competitive juices flowing, Ernie teed up his ball, swung harder than usual, and sure enough, it flew high and right, landing next to a pine tree in the rough. With a disgusted expression, he whipped out his wallet and handed a fifty-dollar bill to Kenji. "Happy now?" he asked.

"More than I thought, baby. More than I thought."

Kenji bent over to put his tee in the ground, took a couple of deep breaths, went through his pre-shot routine, and swung, smooth and balanced. He looked up to see his ball sail two hundred yards and land in the fairway, a bit left of center — perfect positioning for his next shot.

Ernie was quiet as they rode in the golf cart to where his ball lay. He didn't have a shot because the ball was inches behind the tree, so he took an unplayable lie and a one-shot penalty. He couldn't believe he had let Kenji's comment get inside his head.

While Kenji was fifty dollars richer, he already was regretting the bet with Ernie, as it wasn't in his basic nature to be unkind. Even so, he didn't regret it enough to give the money back; he was competitive to the core. The foursome finished out the round with Ernie remaining distant and uncommunicative.

The four of them usually would have lunch at the club's Peacock Grill after their round of golf. It was time to pay off the winner of the prize pot from the ten dollars each had contributed every week. The winner was based on who had the lowest score, with handicaps factored in. The group had assigned Kenji a high handicap, and today he was the winner through a combination of guile and luck.

"Thanks for the contribution, boys!" Kenji exclaimed. "I can't believe I got a birdie on that last par three. Beginner's luck, I guess!"

"You coached that putt in like it was the winning run at a Little League tournament," kidded Stu.

"Maybe more like shithouse luck," retorted Kenji, as he picked up the cash, a wide grin slicing his face.

The ride with Ernie back to Kona was quiet and uncomfortable, prompting Kenji to apologize and offer to return the bet money. Ernie accepted the apology but declined the offer. Kenji hoped he hadn't done permanent damage to a budding friendship.

* * *

The next week, as he took his stance in the tee box, Kenji struggled to fight off the demon thoughts that had taken up residence in his head. The voices nagged, *Don't shank it. Don't top the ball like you did yesterday at the driving range.* He backed away from the ball, bent over to get pinch of grass in his fingers, and tossed it in the air as if to check the wind on this windless day. *Damn! What's going on in my head today?*

"Stu, what do you do to get rid of negative swing thoughts?" Kenji asked.

"Read the book again!"

Kenji had read the book *Inner Golf* countless times, but today he couldn't mentally connect with the message.

"Stop thinking! Just swing and hit the damn ball!" yelled Stu, impatient for his turn.

At fifty, Kenji was the oldest golfer in the foursome, and his score was the usually the highest, not a recipe for self-confidence, especially now that Stu was getting cranky with him. He had been playing this game for several months, but despite his lessons with a pro and his dedication and practice, his game hadn't improved that much. He was embarrassed and humbled by his lack of skill on the course. He took one more practice swing as he nervously wiped the sweat off his brow with a white handkerchief. He checked the line from his ball to the flag 269 short yards away. The fairway was straight but perilously narrow, with sand traps lurking on each side.

"Are you going to surrender or hit the damn ball?" Stu groused.

"Straight and true, baby. Go for it!" encouraged Vince, the three-handicapper in the group.

Kenji's gaze honed in on a tuft of grass a few inches in front of his ball, and then he resumed his setup. He took one more look at the flag then peered intently at his chosen target and swung crisply through the ball. He watched, surprised and pleased, as the ball soared between the sand traps, landing about 180 yards out, dead center in the fairway.

"Well, that wasn't a great shot, but I'll take it!" Kenji told them.

He was happy not to look foolish to his teammates or lose face, a throwback to his Japanese upbringing. This was only his seventh round since he had been invited to join this usually jovial foursome.

"Nice shot!" the other three cheered almost in unison.

As the carts trundled down the pathway, Kenji was impatient to try his hand with a pitching wedge on the next shot. *If I can get it close to the pin, I could make a birdie,* the suddenly optimistic voice in his head raced on ahead of itself.

As the group arrived at Kenji's ball, Stu coached him, "Use about a three-quarter easy swing, put the ball back in your stance so you get some backspin, and hit down on the ball."

"Okay, thanks," replied Kenji as he lined up his shot. He was pumped, the adrenaline coursing through his veins. He swung, taking a large divot from the fairway, the ball flying past the pin about thirty feet.

"That buxom chick in the pro shop charges a dollar a pound for divots," Ernie chided, chuckling. "In fact the last time I saw one that big I was tossing a Frisbee to my dog."

"It's a good thing I've got a few bucks stashed away then, isn't it?" retorted Kenji, his moment of pride punctured by Ernie's comment. *He's getting back at me for last week's debacle,* he thought. *Okay, that's fair.*

His long putt against the grain of the grass came up short by five feet. Kenji squatted down to reassure himself that the putt was straight from his ball to the hole. There wasn't any break that he could see. His next putt lipped out, and he settled for a bogey five.

He was sharing a cart with Vince and getting to know him better with each outing. Vince was friendly and open, yet intensity throbbed just beneath the surface when it came to golf. Vince was a real student of the game. He had started playing as a teenager, qualified for his high school team, and won the state championship his junior and senior year — proud moments. His dad, a typical Midwesterner, had been hardworking and thrifty and had saved up money for Vince's college education. Together they had chosen Western Illinois University in Moline, Illinois, because it had an excellent golf program. By the time Vince was a junior in college, his coach began talking to him about pursuing a career as a professional golfer. In his senior year, Vince led his team to the championship, and everything was falling into place. His goal had been to qualify for the PGA tour immediately after graduation.

"How did that work out for you?" asked Kenji.

"Unfortunately it didn't. A few days before graduation, I was in a foolish pickup game of touch football out in front of my dorm with my buddies. God, I get nightmares just thinking about it. I was carrying the ball, going for a touchdown. I made a sharp right cut and felt a pop in my knee before I collapsed on the grass. My patella tendon tore where it attaches to the kneecap."

"That sucks," Kenji said. "You must have been devastated."

"You have no idea. Yeah, I whined about my misfortunes for a while after surgery, but my parents weren't having that kind of talk as I hobbled around on crutches. My dad said, 'You have a college education. Go get it figured out!' I toyed with the idea of becoming a golf coach, but I was less keen on the administrative tasks, so I tossed that idea. During rehab I developed a good relationship with the therapists who were helping me. They were young, bright, and enthusiastic every time I made even the littlest progress. It was then I decided to become a physical therapist."

A plan had started to emerge in Vince's mind, he explained, as he visualized a business in which his focus would be on finding and motivating good therapists and developing a business model that would allow him free time to play golf and indulge his other interest — flying. By the time he had completed rehab, he had outlined a clear path to reach his goals. The next challenge was to figure out how to pay for an additional three years of school, since the college money his parents had set aside was depleted. He scrambled, working several part-time jobs, waiting tables, bartending, and flying a crop duster to make enough money to plow ahead with school.

Kenji listened in awe. "Let me get this straight. You're an almost professional golfer *and* you're a pilot?"

"That's my other passion," Vince said. "A friend of my dad's taught me how to fly when I was a teenager. I kept up with it and finally got my license. I love it! Flying is such an emotional high. I'm jazzed because I recently joined a flying club here and bought a Cessna 172 with five other guys. I'll take you flying one day—that is, if you're up for an adventure."

"You're one surprising dude."

Vince chuckled. "Nah. I just work hard and play hard. Long story short, after I graduated, I came to Kona on vacation to check out the golf courses and the business climate here. After the third day, I knew I'd found the right place. Then I had to figure out how I could get a practice started."

With the arrogance and exuberance of youth, Vince had launched his practice in Kona with nary an idea about marketing. One of the first people he had met was Stu, who started to refer patients to him for physical therapy. Vince boldly schemed to attract the best and brightest therapists, spending his last nickel to place ads in the Boston, New York, and Philadelphia newspapers in January. Common sense told him that Hawaii would have a great deal of appeal to those living in cold weather areas—and it did. He quickly received a stack of resumes and hired the three top candidates. He sold them on his philosophy and enjoyed the time he spent training them. In the end, his patients received top-notch service, and the additional help allowed Vince some free time. "It doesn't get much better than that, does it?" he said.

"You're absolutely right! Very clever of you to put it all together," responded Kenji.

"Thanks."

Vince had finally come to grips with the notion that being on the PGA tour wasn't the best life for him. The brutal traveling and playing schedule would make it difficult for him to have a family life. He was content being a successful businessman, helping people, playing golf, and flying.

"One of these days, some lovely young thing may catch me — that is, if I ever take the time for a girlfriend," he said with a laugh. "More news on that coming soon. I have a yen for a gal in our medical building. What about you, Kenji? What are your thoughts about golf now that you've been playing for a while?"

"After the first good shot I hit at the driving range, my thought was, *I'm an intrepid golfer*," Kenji said. "Arrogant, eh? I'm learning that playing golf well is difficult. Yet there's no doubt about it. I've been bitten by the golf bug."

He had only recently accepted the reality about the difficulty of the game. Stubbornly he had mentally set a goal of scoring less than a hundred shots per round — a rather ambitious aspiration for such a novice, as the par rating for the Makalei Golf Club was seventy-two. Vince had explained to him that if a golfer averages par on his last five rounds, he can claim being a scratch golfer. Only five percent of golfers ever consistently break one hundred.

"Just keep your head down and swing through the ball," Vince said. "Your game will improve over time."

"Fine. But I'll be damned if I'm going to settle for mediocrity. What's the point of spending time and money to be in the ninety-five-percent loser category?"

His teammates smiled knowingly as Vince told him, "You'll get there soon enough, Kenji. You have the heart of a champion, but it takes patience and practice."

Kenji dismissed this comment as typical golf-buddy banter; they were just trying to psych him into being more competitive. Yet the seed of success had been planted in his mind, and it grew like a fire in a burning building, his imagination fanning the flames higher.

CHAPTER 7

Kenji had seen Lilly at the next Rotary Club meeting, but she ignored him, instead sitting with a group of fifty-something women at what the guys laughingly called "the menopause table." He had tried to catch her eye but got the feeling she was purposely avoiding him. His loss. He had turned down the opportunity to spend time with her, and now he was paying the price. He noticed the women laughing as Lilly obviously was regaling them with stories about God knows what; he hoped the conversation wasn't about him. He had been thinking about her a lot, especially in the evenings when the house was quiet. He longed to hear her voice on the other end of the phone.

Two weeks had passed since what he had come to think of as "the lunch." A few nights after the Rotary meeting, he sat playing raucous show tunes on the piano, the notes filling the otherwise silent house. He thought he heard the phone ring and abruptly stopped playing just in time to hear another ring. He rushed to the kitchen to answer it.

"Hey, Kenji, were you serious about taking me horseback riding?" purred the sweet voice of Lilly Yamada.

He instantly recognized her voice and felt relieved that she evidently was not *that* angry with him. Yet after getting the cold shoulder from her, he wasn't going to roll over like a mangy junkyard dog hoping for a tickle on its tummy.

"Hello. Who is calling, please?"

She laughed. "It's me, Holly Golightly, your friendly, flaky neighborhood Japanese chick, calling to see if you can come out to play."

"Oh, *that* chick. Well, yes, I can come out, but only on Saturdays, because my calendar is very full."

"Terrific. I'll bring my spurs."

They agreed that Kenji would pick Lilly up at eleven on Saturday morning at her condo, knowing it would be an hour's drive to the trailhead. The afternoon trail ride started at one o'clock, so he offered to pack a light lunch and bring a thermos of coffee. He suggested she wear jeans and bring a jacket because it could get chilly at the higher elevations above Waipio Valley. He got directions to her condo, which was located in an expensive part of town, and said goodbye. Heeding Ernie's caution about liaisons with beautiful women, he had made a stubborn decision not to call Lilly but felt a degree of satisfaction that she had reached out to him.

* * *

Kenji quietly watched the sun rise over the eastern horizon as he sat on his lanai sipping a cup of freshly brewed coffee. It was going to be another spectacular day on the big island, certain to be filled with adventures he couldn't imagine. Spending time with Lilly was interesting; she was unpredictable. He was excited at the prospect of seeing her, yet grounded in the safety of his daily mundane habits.

After finishing his coffee, he rose slowly to do some stretches before his three-mile run. He reminded himself to stop at the grocery deli to pick up sandwiches and fruit for their lunch.

When he returned from his run, grocery bag in hand and feeling invigorated from his daily workout, he quickly showered, carefully shaved, and purposely climbed into a pair of faded blue jeans that hugged his butt. He chose a sky-blue Western-style shirt with pearl-colored snap buttons. He rummaged in the back of his closet, searching for a comfortable old pair of cowboy boots made of snakeskin. He chuckled at the irony; there were no snakes in Hawaii. Fully dressed, he checked his email, reading a few golf jokes sent by his friends. He glanced at his watch again, noting it was still too early to leave. Kenji was getting nervous. He hadn't been on a horse in years and didn't want to look foolish in front of Lilly.

Noting a spacious lanai that ran along two sides of the building, he arrived at Lilly's very upscale condo right on time and rang the doorbell. The door flew open almost immediately, as if she'd been waiting for him. Lilly looked stunning in all black; her sleeveless sweater hugged her firm, ample breasts. Her skin-tight jeans were accented by tall black riding boots. *No spurs*, Kenji thought. *Damn.* She looked different, younger; her hair was casually drawn back into a long ponytail tied up with a narrow cord of leather, showing off the curve of her cheekbones, a dimple winking at him when she smiled. She had taken his advice and was carrying a fawn-colored suede jacket, the toasty sheepskin lining peeking out at the edges.

"Good morning." Lilly greeted him with a warm smile and a quick hug. "Nice ride," she commented, noticing the new silver metallic Honda parked at the curb.

"Thanks. I bought it a few months back — a retirement gift to myself. You look great. Ready for a ride?"

"You bet!"

He opened the passenger door, and Lilly seated herself comfortably. As they drove off, he decided to keep the conversation light, still a bit surprised, though not displeased, with her warm greeting. "We're going to go west, then north toward Waimea. Then we'll cut off and head up into the hills above the Waipio Valley. Have you ever been to this part of the island?"

"No, I don't think so, but riding sounds like fun."

"The group leaves at one o'clock for a two-and-a-half hour ride. Are you up for that?"

"Of course."

Lilly hadn't told him she had taken riding lessons as a child, or that she had competed in the hunter-jumper class with much success, beginning when she was only ten years old. Jack, her trusty chestnut jumper, had been ready for pasture at about the same time her interests had turned elsewhere, mostly boys. She smiled, remembering the joy she had felt as she and Jack had smoothly taken each jump. She couldn't wait to see the look on Kenji's face when she expertly galloped off across an open meadow. An accomplished woman always needed a few surprises in her arsenal.

"I haven't ridden in years," Kenji said. "Some of us guys used to go up to Waipio Valley once in a while for the fun of it. Are you a novice rider too?"

Lilly grinned. "I'll try not to fall off and embarrass you."

They arrived at the riding stables early, so they ambled to the picnic table just outside where the wranglers were saddling up the horses for the afternoon riding session. Kenji set out paper plates and plastic forks and unwrapped the deli sandwiches. He laid out slices of fresh pineapple and poured coffee from the thermos into mugs. Lilly watched him, impressed at the precision with which he handled these tasks. She wondered whether he had been trained well or was merely used to living alone.

The rolling hills, green and lush, provided a panoramic view as a backdrop for their picnic. As they finished eating, the head wrangler approached to tell them it was time to get their helmets on and gave them a preview of the trail ride. He asked them about their horse-riding experience. Kenji admitted he was a novice; Lilly confessed to being in the intermediate class. They decided to ride with the other novice riders. Once inside the stable, though, Lilly had a quick, private talk with the boss, John.

John and Lilly rejoined the group. "The wind is blowing in off the ocean, so put your jackets on," John told them. "It'll get colder as we go farther up into the hills." He presented an array of gloves and helmets to the group of twelve riders. "In Hawaii a cowboy is called a paniolo. One paniolo will lead each group of four riders, primarily to ensure your safety but also to share his knowledge about the area we'll be seeing today. Everybody ready? Let's mount up!"

Lilly and Kenji were assigned to John, along with a couple from the mainland. Once mounted, they rode across a large meadow, their horses walking until everyone got comfortable in the saddle. The meadows were tiered like a giant green wedding cake, so the pace quickened as they trotted up a slight rise to the next level. The other two groups of riders followed just behind them. All the riders trotted across the meadow, bouncing in the saddle, some holding on to their saddle horn, desperately trying to stay aloft. Up another rise and the paniolos stopped so the riders could take in the full experience of the spectacular view; from this elevation one could see the sparkling blue Pacific on two sides of the island. John rode up alongside Lilly and said in a low tone, "Ready for a run?"

"Let's do it!"

Kenji sat on his horse watching the pure joy on Lilly's face as she and John, mounted on powerful steeds, flew across the spacious meadow at a full gallop, Lilly's ponytail flying from beneath her helmet. The ring of her exhilarating laughter floated across the expanse of green. *What an extraordinary woman,* he thought. Somehow he wasn't surprised at her expertise and horsemanship. He suspected she had other secrets too and perhaps a few more tricks yet to be revealed.

After more than two hours in the saddle, Kenji and Lilly were tired, buttocks and legs sore, and happy to dismount. Lilly thanked him profusely for suggesting such a wonderful outing, all the while grinning like a schoolgirl who had just aced a finals test. Emboldened by the success of the day, Kenji suggested dinner the following evening, hoping the aches and pain in his body would magically vanish. Lilly quickly accepted his invitation. She was quirky, she was fun, and she was beautiful. He hadn't considered making an emotional commitment to her or anyone else, but he was more than ready to spice up his life in retirement with some fun. He couldn't deny that her firm yet voluptuous body stirred long dormant juices in him, but his shyness prevented the pursuit of a sexual encounter quite yet. He was content to settle for dinner and bide his time.

CHAPTER 8

Vince and Ernie didn't know much about Kenji before
he started to play golf with them. But between Kenji's
occasional comments and Stu's private conversations,
they were beginning to piece together who this quiet yet
interesting and enthusiastic guy with the bright spirit
really was.

Kenji wasn't inclined to talk about himself much—he
preferred to ask questions and draw other people out—but
he did admit that in high school he had been painfully
shy. Whether this was due to a personality defect or possibly the introverted nature of his Japanese heritage, they
didn't know. Kenji had accepted his quietness with more
grace than was typical of most teenagers. He confessed
that he hadn't been very popular in school and certainly

had lacked the courage and confidence to pursue any of the giggling girls in his classes. Mia, the Japanese girl next door, had been the only exception, and he hadn't pursued her either. They were tuned into each other and hung out together sometimes. There were no hugs, no kisses. They were friends. He hadn't played sports or learned the native dances. His focus had been on studying hard, achieving good grades, and being a good son to the parents who had encouraged him to further his education at college. "Kenji-san, I work hard and save money so you go to college and become an engineer," his father had told him time and again.

Kenji had been a dutiful son and obediently had agreed to his father's plan for his future, but fate had decided it wasn't to be. When circumstances had forced him to take over his parents' business, he'd had a rocky start and made mistakes—some large and some small. In the process of becoming a storeowner, he quickly had concluded that he had to overcome his boyhood shyness and by sheer will-power forged an outgoing persona that was necessary to interact with his customers. The uncertainty of his youth still lurked, however, fading only over time. By the time he was twenty-one and had gained some valuable, hard-won experience, Kenji discovered that he actually enjoyed the challenges of business and was fueled somewhat by the cash that freely flowed.

He was invited to donate his time and treasure to charity even though he was young compared to other business owners. "Kenji, would you be willing to serve on the board of directors of our non-profit?" "Kenji, I'd like to invite you to join our Rotary Club." Over time he had become one of the cadre of movers and shakers in the community.

As his solid reputation in Kona had grown, he became known as the go-to guy if someone wanted to get something accomplished. The only person in Kona besides Mia who had known Kenji was more than just a successful local businessman was his stockbroker.

"Kenji, I'm getting nervous about the high-tech investment you have," he had counseled him one day. "You're the only client I have whose portfolio is worth more than a million dollars, but most of your stock is in Sun Microsystems. You should be more diversified."

"Now that I'm a married man, I think you're right," Kenji had told him. I probably need to be more prudent. May I use your phone to call Mia? I'd like to hear what she thinks."

After a quick review of the situation with Mia, Kenji hung up the phone and said, "Mia agrees. So let's diversify. Sell it all and we'll take the hit on capital gains."

Kenji wisely had sold his shares before the dot-com bubble burst and was soon conservatively invested in a wide variety of assets — certificates of deposit, dividend-paying stocks, real estate, and Treasury bills. He had trusted Mia as wise counselor when it came to money, and she had helped with the financial planning for the business and the day-to-day operations.

They had met Stu Garner at a formal charity event. He and Mia had watched him from across the room, instantly captivated by his dynamic, gregarious personality. A mop of dark hair topped a deeply tanned face, with laughter crinkles setting off startling blue eyes, His Roman nose lent him an aristocratic air, a contradiction to his outgoing, friendly demeanor. His tuxedo fit perfectly on his trim, wiry frame; he was at least six feet tall. Stu's baritone voice exuded power as he and his beautifully gowned wife wended their way through the assembled guests, shaking hands with the gentlemen and giving the women a kiss on the cheek.

"God, it must be great to have such self-confidence," Kenji murmured to Mia as they heard his hearty laugh ring throughout the ballroom.

The handsome couple approached the table where Kenji and Mia quietly sat. "Hello. I'm Stu. This is my wife, Gloria," he said as he reached out to shake hands.

Kenji politely stood up. "Hi. I'm Kenji, and this is my wife, Mia."

The two couples chatted comfortably throughout dinner, and all were generous in the bids they placed for charity items, paddles raised, vying for a luxury trip to Las Vegas. Kenji allowed Stu to win the bid after running up the dollar amount to a healthy sum, knowing the money would go to charity.

During the course of the evening, Stu had described himself as a precocious, inquisitive kid who had been the beneficiary of good teachers—one in particular, Mr. Jonas, his science teacher in fifth grade. His life path had been set after he had sliced through a frog smelling of formaldehyde to marvel at the veins and muscles inside. In that instant he had decided to become a doctor. He hadn't played sports in high school; he'd been a nerdy, loud-mouthed kid, not coordinated enough to compete in basketball, football, or baseball. Fortunately, in the summer after Stu's junior year, his school offered a two-week golf program. The fluidity of the game appealed to him, and he enjoyed it, especially knowing that every self-respecting doctor played golf on Wednesdays.

Stu had graduated from high school with honors, receiving an academic scholarship to the University of Washington, as he had expected. Reluctantly he had agreed to live at home for the next four years, wishing instead that he could join a fraternity and reside on campus. The day he received his acceptance letter from the University of Southern California Medical School in Los Angeles was a momentous day in his life—freedom at last! He joyously bade farewell to his parents at Sea-Tac Airport, boldly promising he would become a great doctor while ignoring the tears that rolled down his mother's face.

Stu loved the weather in Southern California. He reveled in the sun and warmth, knowing he could play golf year round whenever he could steal a few hours away from his studies. He didn't find school a drudgery as some of his classmates did. Instead he eagerly spent time in the laboratory as he gained science skills. It became apparent that his two passions were science and golf, which led him to specialize in sports medicine then later to his specialty as an orthopedic surgeon.

That night at the charity event, Kenji sat enthralled by Stu's stories, prompting him to ask, "So how did you end up in Kona?"

Stu chuckled heartily. "Timing and opportunity! A friend told me about a Dr. Johnson who had a thriving practice here, but he was an older gentleman and wanted to retire. So I checked it out and made him an offer. I was surprised when he accepted. My other motivation for moving here was the beautiful golf courses and the fabulous weather." He went on to explain, "I spent my residency at Massachusetts General in Boston. It was a great experience but a mixed bag. I hated the cold winters, but I met Gloria and fell in love with this gorgeous creature." He tenderly brushed his fingers against his wife's face. "I fathered two children on those long, chilly nights, Emily and Peter, but vowed to move to a warmer climate when the opportunity presented itself. So here we are in the midst of a growth industry!"

Kenji, very impressed by Stu's life, the choices he had made, and his bigger-than-life personality, had felt a bit insecure about being in the company of such a powerhouse persona. "What do you mean by 'growth industry'?" he asked.

Stu explained, "Research shows that starting in the 1980s, the effects of working moms and the fast-food boom, combined with many hours of sitting in front of a TV — and later, computers and video games — have contributed to the majority of Americans being overweight or obese. The result of these trends is an increasing rate of worn-out hips and knees. The need for limb amputation also has increased, as more overweight people end up with diabetes. Orthopedic medicine has become a growth industry. My specialty also allows me to work with injured athletes and serve the growing population of seniors, many of them retirees from the mainland."

"Very interesting," Kenji told him. "I'm happy for your success."

"Thank you. It's such a pleasure to meet you and Mia. I've enjoyed this evening tremendously."

Over time, Kenji and Stu found themselves working on the same boards of directors and attending the same social events. As opposite as they were in personality and profession, they had forged an easy friendship, never suspecting how fortuitous the relationship would become in the future.

CHAPTER 9

Over the next two months, despite their vast personality differences, Kenji and Lilly established a routine, which puzzled even them, and became friends. He was pleased and proud to be seen with her and garnered stares wherever they went. He introduced her to everyone he knew to help her get connected around town. His friends and fellow Rotarians speculated endlessly about their relationship, but Kenji refused to offer any clues. "Are they dating? Are they sleeping together? They're such an unlikely couple, yet they aren't," the wags nattered and questioned.

The two spent more and more time together, going to lunch or dinner, seeing an occasional movie. Generous in her affection, sometimes spontaneously giving Kenji a hug or a light kiss on the lips and sensing he was reticent by nature, Lilly wasn't willing to temper her natural exuberance. Much to his surprise, Kenji began to trust her more and more, which prompted him to slowly reveal bits and pieces about himself and his family history.

The hostess at the Kona Inn greeted them warmly on a balmy evening, the air thick with the fragrance of gardenias, and escorted them to the bar to wait while a table was prepared. Ever adventuresome, Lilly ordered a Singapore Sling, with layer upon layer of rum and fruit juices; it was beautiful yet deadly.

"I'll have to carry you out of here if you drink all that," Kenji warned, certain of the outcome based on experience.

"Where's your sense of adventure?" Lilly teased.

"At home, worshipping a porcelain god!"

She slowly sipped her potent cocktail through a straw, defying him while smiling seductively. He had become accustomed to her unconventional behavior and actually enjoyed her quirky choices. He laughed merrily as he shared the story about his one and only encounter with this strong drink. He was unwilling to repeat the ugly aftermath that had left him hugging the toilet as he'd heaved his guts out.

"Watanabe, party of two," the hostess announced while motioning them to a table in the dining room as Lilly left her unfinished drink on the bar.

They ordered a salad, fresh-caught ahi tuna, and a bottle of crisp Chardonnay. Feeling more secure with Lilly now that they'd spent a great deal of time together, Kenji opened up and shared more insight into his background.

"Even though my dad only had a high school educa-tion," Kenji confided, "he was pretty smart. He acquired a wife to help him. I know that sounds sexist, but it really wasn't that way in our home. My mom and dad liked each other, and it seemed that they even learned to love each other as the years passed. It was a tranquil home, and for the most part, my childhood was pretty normal. He treated her as an equal, which wasn't the common model for Nisei marriages of that era."

"I know what you mean," Lilly said. "My parents were somewhat the same way, though my dad was definitely the head of our household."

She heard a catch in Kenji's voice when he told the next part of his story. "My wife, Mia, was a great help to me in running our shops. She was my partner in life and in busi-ness. She had an excellent financial sense and a Stanford education, which was a huge asset."

"Did you choose not to have children because of your business?" asked Lilly.

"No, Mia had a medical condition that prevented it. But we met a young girl through the Boys & Girls Club. Her name is Misaki. Mia and I tutored her after school at the club and came to love her very much. Misaki's mother worked long days as a maid in one of the big hotels just to keep a roof over their heads, so she was grateful for the time and attention we gave her daughter."

"What a wonderful thing you did, helping that little girl," Lilly chimed in, even more impressed by this man.

Kenji replied with pride in his voice, "She's not a little girl anymore. She plays golf on the LPGA tour and is making quite a name for herself."

"Is that how you became interested in golf?"

"Not really. Mia and I paid for a summer golf camp for her, and I drove her to the golf course for practice and lessons. Turns out she was a natural athlete, so our focus was on helping her realize her dreams and ensuring a good education. Golf wasn't even on my radar at the time."

Kenji revealed that he had enjoyed playing the stock market and had made some money but had enough sense to get out before the dot-com bubble had burst. Sill cautious, he didn't divulge the details or the large sums of money involved. Lilly continually fascinated him, but due to his inexperience with women he couldn't help wonder whether she might be a gold digger in disguise.

"It took a little more than a year to sell my business," Kenji told her. "My landlord, John Fletcher, tried to block the sale out of spite. He doesn't like Japanese people much. I finally got that settled in court. He owns a lot of real estate on the island, and he's on a power trip of huge proportions. He's an arrogant, vindictive SOB. I hate to admit it, but I felt some pleasure beating him in court."

Lilly looked at Kenji, thinking, *This guy is made of even sterner stuff than I'd imagined.* "Sounds like you had a real fight on your hands."

"Yes, it was a battle, but I won." Kenji smiled, remembering. "The new owners are nice people and are doing well. Now I'm trying to figure out what the next chapter

K.D. Anderson

holds. I'm having fun playing golf with my chums, so we'll see if I really get hooked or if it's just a hobby, just something to fill up my free time." He chuckled. "After all, we do have some of the best golf courses in the world on this island. Too bad you don't like golf."

"Yeah, and it's too bad you don't play tennis."

Kenji gazed fondly at the intelligent, nurturing woman sitting across the table, a real catch in most people's estimation. He confided, "I'm pretty shy about relationships because most of the people I've ever loved have died. The pain of their loss was so great that I'm not sure I want to go through that again. Of course, the trade-off is that I feel lonely sometimes."

"I get lonely sometimes too," Lilly said softly.

This comment surprised him. How could such a beauty ever feel lonely? Surely men would be lined up around the block just to spend time in her company, basking in her beauty, though he had heard no such rumors since she had arrived in Hawaii.

"Thank you for introducing me to so many people here," she said. "I really appreciate that. I'm getting along pretty well with the ladies at the Rotary Club, though I must confess that I prefer the company of men."

Some men might have taken that comment as a compliment, but it turned Kenji's heart to stone, creating doubt about Lilly's motives. *Am I just one of many?* he wondered. *Is she seeing other guys?* He had trusted her enough to open up to her about his family and his life, but he now questioned the wisdom of doing so. Golf, while difficult, was a much safer pursuit than women.

91

Lilly, unaware of Kenji's emotional withdrawal, reached out to touch his hand. She teased him with her fingers while smiling beguilingly.

"I have an early tee time in the morning," Kenji said abruptly. "Do you mind if we cut the evening short?"

Oops! What the hell have I done now? Lilly wondered as he quietly escorted her from the restaurant.

CHAPTER 10

September 23, 1998

The day it happened had started normally. Kenji tried to calm his nerves as he prepared to tee off. His nerves were jittery, his hands wet with perspiration, yet he couldn't figure out why he felt so tense. His love-hate relationship with golf bugged the hell out of him. He loved the game yet hated that he didn't play on a level equal to his partners. Most of the time, however, they tolerated his inconsistent performance with good humor.

Kenji pondered the major components in his life these days: golf, community service, tutoring kids at the Boys & Girls Club, and now this thing with Lilly. He liked Lilly a great deal and usually enjoyed her company, yet her madcap behavior sometimes embarrassed him. She was so aggressive. Weren't guys supposed to be the pursuers in a relationship? She was pursuing him— flattering, yes, but not the natural order of things in his experience. His guy friends teased him about it relentlessly, saying, "You're so lucky, Kenji. She's one hot chick." Instinctively, however, something troubled him; he was uncertain of her motives. He missed Mia, with her quiet, soothing ways. He'd had enough highs and lows in his life and didn't trust the bright flame that Lilly evoked in him. He felt he could easily get scorched.

A new year was about to dawn, and he'd been working on his goal plan for 1999 and reworking his five-year plan. He was convinced that one of the reasons he'd been successful in business was that he always had visualized and planned for the future. He chalked up his tidy sum of savings to hard work and luck. *Can one use goal planning for golf?* he wondered. There had to be some magical formula; he just hadn't figured it out yet.

Golf had become a growing obsession for him, he admitted somewhat sheepishly. *It's a stupid, difficult game. Who do I think I am, trying to master a game in which excellence is so elusive?* These thoughts raced through his head as he attempted to calm himself and hit his drive. Pride and bragging rights were up for grabs for the net-score winner of the weekly pot. Kenji's drive went left a little but was still on the fairway about two hundred yards away. *Wow!* He thought. The TaylorMade driver really felt good. Another morning of golf had started, and things in Kenji's life were looking up. Meanwhile, the clouds from the southwest were moving closer, though no one noticed.

"Golf is an uneasy mistress," Stu told Kenji, grinning mischievously. "It's a bit like sex. To become really good at it you have to be mentally tough, reasonably strong, but relaxed and flexible too."

Kenji questioned and pondered this wisdom as Stu continued his instruction. "You need to build muscle memory through practice so you can hit a good shot with every swing," he said. "There are no shortcuts in golf. At least that's what the experts say."

The lessons came at him from all sides. Vince advised, "Kenji, the grip you have on the club and the way you swing should be like the grip you have on your life, smooth and easy. Being disciplined and trying to stay in tight control isn't a recipe for success on the links." He continued, "Practice and technique are important, and you have the time and desire. Golf is one of the few sports that people of all sizes and physical capabilities can enjoy well into their eighties."

"Well, if that's the case, then I have a thirty-year career ahead of me," replied Kenji, smiling at the prospect.

He thoroughly enjoyed kidding around with the guys, collecting money for the betting pot, and forging these new friendships. He gazed at the stunning view from the tee box on the first hole at Makalei smiling at the competition—a half-dozen peacocks strutting their stuff, pecking for a bug here and there, impervious to the golfers.

Stu teed off first and hit a drive that sailed about 230 yards, a bit shorter than his usual 275-yard screamers. It was no wonder his patients liked him; he was open and friendly, his laughter booming across the hills, drowning out the screech of the ever present peacocks.

"Stu, were you holding back on that drive?" asked Vince.

"Nah," Stu said with a laugh. "I'm just giving you guys a chance to shine. Just like with my orthopedic patients—I hate to give them all the bad news upfront."

They all chuckled at that retort, happy to be in the moment on another beautiful day in paradise. It was misting a little as the foursome golfed through the first few holes. Rain at this elevation was common in Hawaii, but with luck it would blow over or only lightly dampen them for a bit and then stop.

Stu was two over par; Vince was one under; Ernie was four over; and Kenji was five over, having topped his fairway shot on number four, embarrassed to watch the ball skitter only fifty yards. He wished he could string together five or six good shots in a row, knowing consistency was the key to a lower score.

The fifth hole was a beauty—176 yards, a three par. Tall silver oaks lined the fairway like soldiers standing crisply at attention; a bevy of sand bunkers guarded the undersized green. The guys were grateful that the roofed golf carts offered some shelter while they waited for the group ahead of them to clear the green. Ernie appeared to be daydreaming. He had told Kenji once that he got some of his best ideas while letting his mind wander on the golf course. Their friendship had developed to the point where they felt comfortable with silence.

Stu and Vince's drives magically appeared on the green fairly close to the pin. Ernie was off to the right again, out about thirty yards, with a sand trap between his ball and the green. Kenji was also on the right; his ball had landed about fifty yards short of the green between two sand traps. Stu made his putt for a birdie, and Vince muffed a four-footer and settled for par. After an ugly encounter with the sand trap, Ernie got a bogey, and so did Kenji. "Not our finest hour," commented Kenji.

By the time they had reached the ninth hole, the highest point on the golf course at 2,860 feet above sea level, they heard the low rumble of thunder in the distance but paid it no mind. Suddenly there was a loud crack of thunder, and a bright flash of lightning tore through the palms below.

"It's here!" Kenji exclaimed, as a heavy rain began to fall.

The clouds opened up, and the rain came down in sheets, the freshening wind driving the rain on a slant. There was no way to escape the onslaught. The heavy rain took the fun out of this round of golf. Even though the temperature was seventy-six degrees, they felt cold.

"Let's wait it out. It rained like this the other day, and it stopped after five minutes," said Vince. But the rain continued, unabated, soaking them to the skin, their clothes clinging uncomfortably. They decided to quickly putt out and move on.

They were looking forward to the tenth hole, which was the beginning of the downhill leg of the golf course. "We should be out of any weather problems by the time we get to hole eleven or twelve," Kenji said, shivering.

Vince was first off with a 240-yard drive. Number ten was the longest hole at 580 yards. Just as Stu teed off, another loud clap of thunder crackled through the air. That should have been a warning to take cover. Instead they focused on the next shot and heading to a lower elevation.

Ernie hurried his shot, which landed about 130 yards out and left of center. Stu's drive, even in the heavy rain, was spectacular, almost three hundred yards, landing in the center of the fairway.

"Wow! That was awesome," Vince exclaimed. Did you have Wheaties for breakfast this morning, or what?"

"Yes, I did. Thank you very much," replied Stu, water dripping off his cap.

Perhaps being in the pouring rain, being totally soaked, and feeling the notable drop in temperature prompted Kenji to swing too hard when he teed off at number ten. The result wasn't good. "Damn. That was ugly," he muttered.

His ball ended up in the left rough near a five-foot fence with a steel-pole gate that marked the golf course boundary. A maintenance shack, rain bouncing off its roof, stood like a sentry on the other side of the fence.

As Kenji squished through the wet grass down to where his ball lay, he shouted to his teammates, "I got a lucky lie!"

Fortunately, the ball was sitting in a spot clear of the tall grass. He had 350 yards left to the green, so he pulled a four iron out of his bag, hoping to advance the ball 150 yards so he could reach the green with his third shot. Kenji took his stance and checked his back swing. He had plenty of room; he was clear of the fence gate by three feet.

He looked at the fairway where he wanted to land his shot and started his swing. At the top of his backswing, an explosive bolt of lighting struck the steel gate. Most of the one-million-volt charge traveled down the chain-link fence pole closest to Kenji to the ground, but part of the charge jumped to his four-iron.

It was like watching a silent movie, the force of the strike catapulting Kenji ten feet through the air, out onto the fairway, where he landed on his back with a loud thump a few feet from the golf cart; his body wasn't moving. One of his shoes lay forlorn in the middle of the fairway. His red polo shirt, torn half off in tatters, revealed ugly burns that scorched his shoulder and stomach. Some of the charge had gone through the wet headband on his cap and burned his hair on the left side, leaving only wayward tufts.

Ernie was flung to the ground on the far side of the cart. The flash temporarily had blinded Stu and Vince. When their vision cleared, they saw Kenji lying on the ground near the cart and Ernie in a heap on the other side of the cart with a dazed expression.

Instantly Stu jammed the accelerator to the floor and almost tipped the cart over as he headed toward Kenji. He jumped out of the cart and quickly straightened Kenji onto his back. He checked for a pulse and felt his neck, which didn't appear to be broken, and started CPR.

Vince, though dazed, was on his cell phone talking to the 911 emergency operator.

Stu yelled, "We need a defibrillator, Vince! Call the clubhouse. They may have one." He knew the oxygen supplied to Kenji's brain from CPR wouldn't be enough to prevent possible brain damage after ten minutes. He needed to get Kenji's heart working quickly.

Vince held the phone back. "The ambulance dispatcher estimates it'll take twenty minutes for them to get here."

Stu quickly checked the time. Kenji had been "dead" for no more than a minute; he was sure he had started CPR within thirty seconds of the lightning strike. Stu was panting from the adrenaline rush and the exertion of making compressions on Kenji's chest, desperate to keep blood flowing to his brain.

"Vince, take over the CPR while I check Kenji to see whether anything is broken."

Just then Kenji gasped, and his heart started to beat again. Stu stopped the compressions and lifted Kenji's eyelids, noting the pupils were dilated, a good sign. Stu took his pulse, which was strong and racing, not unusual at this stage of his trauma. He looked for external signs of damage. Kenji's hair, where his sweatband had been, was burnt. His hat, which was lying off to the side, had charred spots on the sweatband. He removed Kenji's remaining shoe and noticed the bottom of the sock on his right foot was slightly discolored. There were no signs of broken bones, and Kenji's pulse was slowing to normal.

Just then, Kenji's eyes fluttered open. He had a glazed, confused look on his face, and it seemed to Stu, maybe some sadness.

"Kenji, are you all right? Where does it hurt?"

Kenji gazed at him with a blank, dead look in his eyes. It occurred to Stu that his friend's eardrums might have burst due to the explosion of the lightning strike. *Perhaps he can't hear me*, he thought.

The minutes dragged by as the guys waited for help. The defibrillator wasn't necessary now, but Stu would feel better when it arrived, since Kenji's heart could go into fibrillation at any time, which wasn't uncommon in cases like this. He heard the hum of a golf cart racing toward them.

Ernie, though shaken and bruised, roused himself to an upright position. He was helpless, as a non-doctor, to be of any assistance to his friend and was worried sick about him.

Vince was on his cell phone talking to the paramedics in the ambulance that was racing to their location. Meanwhile two club employees arrived in a golf cart with a defibrillator.

Planning ahead, Stu asked the man who delivered the defibrillator, "Can the ambulance get here on the cart path?"

"Yes!" he responded. "And there's a golf cart waiting to guide the paramedics to this location."

Vince relayed this information to the medical technician in the ambulance. Now all they had to do was wait for the ambulance to arrive.

Just then Kenji's heart stopped beating again. He was dead.

CHAPTER 11

Kenji heard the faint beeps of monitors, opened his eyes, and looked around to see a white sterile room, not a picture on the walls, only a television set hung up high to rupture the room's starkness. *Where am I?* he wondered. His body hurt everywhere, especially his right foot. He felt very uncomfortable; tubes ran into his arm and nose, and he was so thirsty. He turned his head to see Vince and Ernie sitting in chairs alongside what looked like a hospital bed, confused because they both appeared concerned.

"Where am I? What's going on?" he mumbled.

"Hey, the man is finally awake!" Vince smiled, relieved that his friend, after being unconscious for four days, was finally awake and hopefully beginning to rally.

"You're in hospital in Honolulu, Kenji. Welcome back!" Vince said. He decided not to share the details of the lightning strike yet, fearing the information would only add to Kenji's confusion right now.

After a brief awakening at the golf course, Kenji had lapsed into unconsciousness again, and minutes later, as the paramedics loaded him into the ambulance, his body had gone into convulsions. They wondered why he was convulsing and whether they could get him to a hospital in time to save his life. Stu had been fearful that Kenji's brain had been damaged from the lack of oxygen, possibly leaving him in a vegetative state. He'd also been concerned that the electrical current from the lightning had caused permanent brain damage.

The paramedics decided to fly Kenji directly to Queens Medical Center in Honolulu 170 miles away. It was the closest place where Kenji could get intensive care and full diagnostic tests and procedures. They met the Medevac copter in the parking lot of the golf club. Stu accompanied the medics, holding Kenji's hand and talking to him in soothing tones as they loaded him in the helicopter for the flight to Honolulu. Vince and Ernie drove back to Kona, speeding through the curves heading to the Kona airport. Vince placed a call to the president of his flying club and found out the Cessna 172 was available.

Still baffled, Kenji looked at Vince and Ernie. Where was he? Why were his friends here? His brain clearly wasn't functioning properly. "What's going on?" he asked again.

They both started talking at once, then Vince took over and explained in broad terms what had happened, where he was and why he was in intensive care. Kenji was amazed that all this had happened to him.

"If I'm in Queens Hospital, how did I get here? How long have you all been here?" The questions spewed forth. Kenji felt foggy headed, like he had the worst hangover of his life.

"You've been here four days," Ernie told him. "You were unconscious, but it looks like you're on the road to recovery. Stu came over on the helicopter with you but had to go back to Kona to tend to his patients. He calls me about five times a day. We've all been worried sick, especially me since you're the only guy I can beat at golf. Oh, and by the way, you still owe me twenty bucks from the last bet we made."

Kenji managed a thin smile. "My body hurts everywhere, like I was hit by a truck."

This comment brought smiles to Ernie and Vince's faces. "That's good. You're complaining. That's an excellent sign," said Vince.

Their concern touched Kenji.

"You're lucky to be here," Ernie said. "Lucky you have a doctor for a golf partner. Some of the weather experts estimate the power of lighting is about a hundred million volts. It's amazing you didn't get totally fried. The doctors told us the reason you didn't is because the duration of the lightning pulse is very short, a few microseconds. Also, in your case most of the power of the lightning strike went down the metal fence pole that was next to you."

"I was struck by lightning?" Kenji couldn't quite assimilate the information. It felt like the words were flying over his head. "I have no memory beyond that ugly-ass drive I hit on the tenth hole."

"Yes, you were struck," Ernie told him. "I don't remember much either. When you were hit, there was a loud explosion and a rush of air that knocked me out of the cart. Vince said I looked like a sick cat about to spit up a fur ball when he and Stu got there."

"Yeah, Ernie was looking as confused as a virgin on her wedding night," Vince chimed in.

Kenji squirmed around in the bed, feeling uncomfortable and confined. "Ernie, can you find the controller and raise my bed a little? I need a drink of water. I'm so thirsty." He lay quietly, feeling helpless, legs twitching, the pain more intense than anything he'd ever felt and causing nausea. "I think I'm going to throw up," he said.

A buxom nurse came in just as Kenji felt his guts spasm. He dry-heaved into a pan held under his chin by Vince.

"So our friend has decided to rejoin us, eh?" the nurse said. "I'll get you some medication that will help settle that nausea." She checked all the readings on the machines Kenji was hooked up to and entered the numbers into a computer that protruded from the wall. "How would you describe your pain level, Mr. Watanabe?" She held out a plastic coated-card with different faces on it: a happy face, a face with a small smile, a face with no expression, one with a painful expression, and one with agony written all over it.

Kenji pointed to the face with the painful look.

"Let me get you something that will help with that." The nurse quickly left the room and returned a few minutes later with a needle that she inserted into the line of the saline bag that hung from its apparatus above Kenji's head. She explained how he could push a button on a controller when he needed to take the edge off his pain. He hit it instantly and felt an odd combination of peacefulness and euphoria almost instantly. "Ah, that feels good," he said, as a goofy smile spread across his face. His leg spasms stopped, the pain now magically washed away.

The nurse told the visitors that her patient would likely be out of it for the next few hours, and that rest was what he needed most. She suggested they come back later in the day and assured them that she and her colleagues would take good care of Kenji.

The visitors left the room and headed down the stark, overly bright hallway to the elevator, as they discussed their plans for the rest of the day. Ernie would phone Lilly, and Vince would call Stu to give them the good news about Kenji being awake. They knew both had been frantic with worry. The two chums decided on a nearby Italian restaurant for a celebratory dinner, relieved that their friend had survived and seemed to be doing well.

* * *

The next morning a tall, slender nurse making her rounds at seven was encouraged about the progress her "lightning strike patient" was making. After checking his vitals, she gave him a wide grin. "You're looking quite normal, Mr. Watanabe. How are you feeling?"

"Much better. Thank you."

"How is your pain level?" she inquired.

"Like a dull ache, but nothing I can't handle."

"Good. Looks like you're ready to stay awake for a while."

"Yes, ma'am."

Over the next couple of days, Kenji seemed to be recovering amazingly quickly, especially since he indulged in the pain medication only occasionally. The many tests the doctors ordered showed no internal damage, and his vital signs were above average for a man of fifty. The doctors voiced some concerns about the burn on the ball of his right foot, but they couldn't find any other negative after affects. The MRI showed no visible signs of brain damage, and Kenji's aches and pains were normal considering he'd been tossed through the air like a rag doll.

That night, Ernie and Vince delayed their visit until seven o'clock not wanting to get in the way of the nurses performing their daily tasks, while laughing and kidding with Kenji about the looks, talents, and sexual natures of the various nurses.

"I like the buxom blonde the best. She's got a rack on her that I could get lost in for a week," Ernie said dreamily.

"I'm a leg man myself. Did you check out the redhead with the legs that went up to here?" Vince said as he raised his hand shoulder-high.

"Yeah, you wish, in your wildest dreams, buddy," laughed Kenji. "Besides, I thought you were hot for that redhead in Kona."

"I'm working on it, man. I'm working on it."

After Ernie and Vince left, the blonde nurse got him up for a short walk around his room. "Just take it easy until you get used to being upright," she said. "Remember, you've been lying horizontal for several days now, so we've got to get the blood flowing to all your extremities."

Kenji felt unsteady on his feet but was able to walk as he leaned on the nurse for support, trying not to accidently touch her overly large breasts, while clutching his gown closed with one hand. He was embarrassed by the open back in the hospital gown but said nothing to the nurse. Later she brought in a cotton dressing gown to cover up his bare backside.

"Are you ready for a longer walk? Let's see if we can make it all the way down the hall and back so you can show off your new ensemble."

Moving about was the best medicine for Kenji, not to mention the attention he received from the attractive nurse, even though her abundant figure didn't suit his personal taste. After the first dozen steps, still relying on the nurse for support, he felt a new energy kick in and felt more confident with each step.

"I can make it on my own now," he told her, as they walked up and down the hallway side by side, making the trip several times. He set a goal of ten trips, which he completed to his satisfaction even though his right foot throbbed with pain after the seventh round. He limped back to his room, exhausted, gingerly climbed into bed, and hit the button to relieve the pain.

Just then the bedside phone rang. It was Lilly. "Hello, Kenji. How are you feeling?"

Still under the influence of the pain medication, inhibitions erased, he responded, "Lilly, you sweet thing, thanks for calling. Yes, I'm going to be fine. And how are you, my dear?"

Lilly lowered the phone, looking at it, wondering whether she had dialed the wrong number. *Is this Kenji?* she thought. *Shy, retiring Kenji?*

"I'm fine, but you sound different."

"I'm the same old Kenji, just a bit high from the stuff they give me for pain."

"Well, whatever they're giving you, I like it. I've been sick with worry about you. I was planning to come over to see you this evening, but when Ernie phoned, he said you'd probably be coming home sometime tomorrow. Is that right?"

He giggled. "Yes, in a private plane. What do you think about that? Pretty fancy, eh?"

"What are you talking about? You're not making any sense."

"So you were coming to see me? That's so sweet."

"Yes, I'm sweet. What plane are you talking about?"

"Vince's plane, my darling. He's buying new clothes for me so I won't have to be seen in public in my shorty nightgown." He giggled again, sounding crazy. "The doc won't release me until I get my own clothes."

Lilly couldn't make sense of anything Kenji was saying. Since when did Vince have an airplane? It was the first she'd heard that bit of news. *Why is he rambling on about clothes?* she wondered. *Maybe it's just the drugs talking.* And he thought *she* was nutsy.

"Do you want me to pick you guys up at the airport?" Lilly asked him.

"Sure. That would be great! I've been so confused I hadn't even thought about how to get from point A to point B. I am really anxious to see you!"

"Okay, I'll be there. Why don't you call me when you're boarding and I'll leave for the airport then," she suggested. "We should both arrive at about the same time."

As Kenji lay in his hospital bed for the last night, he couldn't help feel pleased that Lilly was coming to fetch him from the airport. The pain medication had worn off a bit, and his thoughts were clearer. Their friendship had evolved slowly over the past months, and they saw each other several times a week. Kenji enjoyed the time they spent together, especially the meals they shared. Eating alone was a forlorn pursuit.

He tried to figure out his feelings for her. Deep down he would like their relationship to go further, yet he had mixed feelings about Lilly. He had walled off his feelings for so many years that he was afraid to take the next step toward intimacy. He had loved his parents. They died. He had loved Mia. She died. If he loved Lilly, would she die too? Did he bring bad luck to those he loved? While lying in the hospital, he'd had time to really think about Lilly and their relationship. He had chided himself about his reluctance to take a risk. Perhaps it was time to jump into the deep water instead of just sticking his toe in the pond. Was it time to make a commitment?

Then Lilly's voice echoed in his head: *I don't want to get married any time soon* and also *I like men*. Plural. *What if I'm not the only man she's seeing?* he thought. Fear of the unknown prompted his decision. He decided not to decide.

Doctor Jacobs came in to see Kenji early the next morning before releasing him to go home. "How are you feeling today, Kenji?" he asked.

"I feel fine, although I overdid it on the walking yesterday. The bottom of my right foot hurt like hell until I took a hit of the pain medication."

"That's to be expected," the doctor replied. "There may have been some capillary damage from the lightning strike. We'll have to keep an eye on that. Meanwhile I'll write a prescription for codeine so you have a fallback position if the pain continues to bother you. Other than that, your tests results all look good. You're one lucky fellow. I want to see you in three months, okay?"

"Thanks, doc. You saved my life."

"No, your friends did that," the doctor said as he wrote out the prescription and release paperwork. "I'll send a nurse in with a wheelchair so you can leave. Sorry, hospital regulations."

Just then Vince burst through the door, shopping bags in hand. "You're going to love these cargo pants—it has pockets galore—and this pale blue aloha shirt. And I couldn't resist these tasseled loafers—size eleven, right?" He proudly displayed his purchases. "It's a coordinated ensemble, except for the underwear. I bought plain jockey shorts, but I almost got a red Speedo for you," he teased. "It's about time you stepped up your game, now that you're dating the fabulous Lilly."

* * *

Lilly inquired at the airport to find out where passengers disembarked from private planes. She was directed to one side of the main terminal after going through security. She saw Vince and Ernie climb out of a small airplane then watched anxiously as they assisted Kenji to disembark. She ran across the tarmac to drape a fragrant flower lei around Kenji's neck before giving him a big hug. She clung to him for an extra moment, despite the curious looks from Vince and Ernie. Kenji wrapped his arms around her, enjoying the feel of her body melded close into his. He wondered at the tears that wet her tawny face as she looked up at him.

Lilly noted the burn marks on his forehead and gently took his face in both of her hands, looked deeply into his eyes, and kissed him tenderly on the mouth.

Drawing back a bit she murmured, "Damn you, Kenji. I care about you, so you'd better stick around for a while." She had waited patiently for months for some overt sign of affection or approval or acceptance from Kenji, but he had continued to withhold himself from her.

Lilly was more than familiar with the kind of men who wanted a showpiece on their arm. She accepted the blessings of her God-given beauty, but she wanted to be more than an exquisite acquisition. Even though she had told Kenji that she didn't want to get married, she was beginning to have second thoughts. She could picture settling down in a warm, loving relationship with this man, but was Kenji ready?

"I will. I will," he promised.

This beautiful, affectionate woman cared about him. *Lucky me, lucky me,* he thought. He held her for another moment before they headed to the parking lot. They walked arm in arm out of the terminal, Vince and Ernie trailing behind. Though Kenji was grateful to have Lilly in his life, and amazed that such a beautiful creature actually cared about him, his prevailing thought was, *How soon can I play golf again?*

* * *

Three days later, as Kenji sat uncomfortably over lunch with Stu, he said quietly, "There's something I need to share with you, Stu, and I don't quite know how to say it."

"Why don't you just start talking?" Stu suggested, wondering about the mysterious tone of Kenji's voice.

"Well, when I was unconscious I remember floating up through space. I saw you working on my body and the guys frantically trying to help. I saw it all. Then I remember seeing a bright light in the distance. I had a feeling of total peace and serenity and security and warmth. My heart was filled with love. It was amazing. I don't know for sure if I was walking or floating, but the light kept coming closer and closer to me. I remember stretching out my arms and trying to reach out. Off in the distance stood three people. I could swear it was Mia and my parents. They were reaching out to me like they were urging me to come to them. Suddenly I was pulled away, and I kept fighting to get back to where I wanted to go—toward the light—but I was like a salmon swimming upstream. Suddenly the light faded then it was gone. Stu, was I dead, or am I just plain crazy?"

"No, you aren't crazy. When I got to you on the golf course, you didn't have a heartbeat. However, you didn't suffer from oxygen deprivation to your brain, according to all the tests they ran. It sounds like you had what's called a near-death experience, not an uncommon event. There've been similar reports from people who were close to death or even clinically dead. Around eight million Americans have experienced this, according to one article I read."

Kenji breathed a sigh of relief. "That would seem to rule out the 'crazy' part, I guess. The other thing, Stu, is that for the past few days since I've been home, I seem to carry with me a certainty about what lies ahead. As you know, I was raised in a Buddhist home, and then when my mom got killed I drifted away from its teachings. My friend Gus told me about the AA spiritual program. I went to a couple meetings with him when he got a cake for a certain number of years of sobriety. I adapted some of the ideas from him and merged some of the AA prayers into my daily meditation. The bottom line is that my concept of a higher power is stronger than ever. I know this is where that bright light was leading me. I have no fear of death, and I feel a profound gratitude for getting to see the light. I also feel I've been spared for a mission to do something significant in the world before I leave it. Does this all sound weird to you?"

"Wow, that's pretty profound. Kenji, helping others always has seemed to be a part of you, at least that's what I saw when you came on to the board at the Boys & Girls Club. You seem to have a commitment to service above and beyond most people I know. That may be one of the reasons you're so popular around town. Maybe your close encounter with death has amplified the traits that have always have been a part of you. The really big questions are 'What are you going to do with this newfound sense of assuredness?' and 'When will you be ready to start playing golf again?'"

Kenji hesitated. "I don't have a clue about the first question. About golf—I guess when you guys say it's okay. I'm not nervous about going out on the course again. It's like it's predetermined."

"You seem fine aside from hobbling around on the sore foot," Stu said. "There shouldn't be any physical reason you can't play. It's like getting back on the horse after you've been bucked off. You won't know how it works out until you try it."

That night, lying in bed, Kenji reflected on his conversation with Stu. His life was so full of promise. What he hadn't shared with Stu was the almost real and vivid replay of the events of his life to date that he'd experienced while he was unconscious or dead; it had been like watching a television special called *This Is Your Life, Kenji*.

It's time to begin the second half, he thought as sleep came.

CHAPTER 12

At the driving range, Kenji had become a minor celebrity because all the Honolulu TV stations had covered the news of his lightning strike. Kailua-Kona was a typical small town, and most residents gossiped about each other, which resulted in unwanted notoriety for Kenji. The other golfers speculated endlessly. *He's amazing, playing golf so soon. Is he limping today? I wonder what's going on with that? Did the lightning go through his foot?*

He felt more than a little self-conscious when he set up to hit his first ball out of a bucket of one hundred. He figured he'd loosen up his muscles and see whether he could get his swing back — not that it was ever that great. He stretched for a few minutes then took a pitching wedge and made a three-quarter swing, aiming at the seventy-five-yard green. The ball landed and bounced once to within four feet of the pin. *Boy, that felt good*, he thought, but he chalked it up to luck.

Kenji was startled when the people on the surrounding tees clapped and cheered. Hoping they'd pay him no mind, he gave them a friendly wave. Now he really felt self-conscious, so he concentrated on staying relaxed while working on his alignment for the second shot. The next ball also landed very close to the pin. He was relieved that no one cheered this time. *Thank God*, he thought. *Everyone has gone back to their practice routines.*

For his next shot, Kenji aimed for the one-hundred-yard green. It almost hit the pin, and since the greens were wet, it stopped about eighteen inches past the pin. Kenji hit a half-dozen shots with each club in his bag. By the time he had worked up to his five iron, he realized he hadn't hit a bad shot yet today. This was very strange, since usually only about one shot out of ten landed on the green.

What the hell was going on? His golf swing was the same as it was before the lightning incident. Why were the results so different? After Kenji had hit about seventy-five balls, he felt strong and had an inner sense of complete control. He noticed that as he concentrated on the spot on the ball he wanted to hit with each club, he actually could sense the spot on the ball that the club head would hit. How could this be? What had changed? Had something in his brain been affected?

Then it dawned on him. Now when he visualized the shot he saw a red pathway that showed the ball's flight all the way to the landing spot. It was like a bizarre movie in his head. The ball invariably would follow that path in the sky. By the time Kenji had finished the bucket of balls, he was in a state of euphoria. *This is great!* he thought. *Will this phenomenon continue on a regular golf course? Or is this just temporary? Maybe it's the drugs.* His foot had been hurting this morning, so he had washed down one codeine capsule with a glass of orange juice to dull the pain.

He reached for his cell phone and dialed the number for Vince, his unofficial coach. "Do you have time for lunch or a coffee?" he said. "Something weird is happening."

Curious about the "weird" remark, Vince quickly agreed. "Sure. I was just having a burger attack anyway. Meet me at Splashers. I'll be there in about twenty minutes."

Kenji quickly departed the driving range amid cheers and "Go get 'em, Kenji" comments and drove downtown. He arrived first and, wanting privacy, secured a table in the far corner of the upstairs deck.

Heads turned as Vince bounded up the stairs two at a time. He wore chinos and a dark-green polo shirt, his corporate logo tastefully displayed chest high. His handsome, even features — no doubt the result of his Swedish heritage — attracted the attention of women wherever he went. He paid no mind to the stares, comfortable with the attention, as he made his way to his friend's table.

"Hi, Kenji! It's sure good to see you out and about, walking upright, I presume. When are you going to start playing golf with us again?"

"Hi," Kenji said. "I need to give my foot a couple of weeks to heal. By then I'll be ready. In fact, golf is what I want to talk to you about."

After he shared his experience at the driving range, they both sat pondering how Kenji could have achieved that kind of perfection for a whole bucket of balls.

"Even the pros have miss-hits out of a hundred shots," Vince told him. "Do you think it could be the after effects of all the drugs they've given you these past weeks? Or consider this. Just maybe there's an excellent golfer deep down inside you, and like most golfers you can't stay relaxed during a swing. When this happens, the fantastic computer that is your brain is taken out of the equation and you start trying to guide the ball. Because of the residual effects of the drugs, maybe you're just very, very relaxed."

Kenji considered the different scenarios then finally spoke. "Well, I hope I stay this way. It felt awesome to hit the greens every time. Now I can see why you're so addicted to this silly game. I'm not going to count on this being a permanent thing. I'll just relish the day that I have had," he said, eyes twinkling. "Meanwhile, do you want to make a hundred-dollar side bet that I kick your ass the next time we play?"

"Tempting as taking your money is, my friend, I'm going to pass," Vince replied, laughing heartily, pleased that Kenji hadn't lost his quirky sense of humor after all he'd been through.

That night before he went to sleep, Kenji was edgy thinking about his game. Would he still be able to hit the good shots consistently? Would he be freaked out by the possibility of lightning striking twice at Makalei? He decided to give his foot another week to heal before he hit the links again. *Maybe I actually can be a contender,* he thought as he drifted off to sleep.

CHAPTER 13

Kenji was excited about his first golf outing since his release from the hospital. He felt calm and relaxed as he greeted his friends at the course.

"It's good to have you back, my friend," Ernie said, embarrassing Kenji with a bear hug.

"Thank you. It's great to be here. It's great to be anywhere."

Kenji was confident about his newly discovered gift, and his first drive confirmed it. The ball landed exactly where he had visualized it would, 270 yards straight over the center of the fairway, before bouncing onto the green and coming to rest about a foot from the cup.

"Geez, where did that come from?" Stu asked.

Kenji chose not to reply as he stood gazing at his ball, a goofy grin splitting his face. He was in great shape for his putt, and for the very first time, he'd be putting for an eagle. He glanced at Vince, who nodded slightly. Neither of them had shared Kenji's story with the others. When they were back in the cart, Kenji said, "I saw the ball trajectory trace again, Vince! It was there. I saw it again!" His heart was beating a mile a minute.

The number-one hole at Makalei was a short par four, one of the easiest holes on the course. The fairway was perfectly straight and only 269 yards to the pin from the white tees. A sand trap lurked just short of the green on the left and another at the left rear. The flag color was white, which meant the pin location today was approximately in the center of the green. Vince's ball was on the green, but a lengthy twenty-foot putt still remained. Ernie's ball ended up in the rear sand trap, and Stu's shot came up short, just in front of the green.

When they arrived at the green, Kenji couldn't help notice that his ball was closest to the pin, meaning that he would putt last. Stu and Vince got birdies, but Ernie duffed his shot out of the sand trap, ending up with a bogey. Kenji walked onto the green, putter in hand, nervous as a cat. He checked the line of his putt, set up, gingerly struck the ball, and jubilantly watched as it plopped into the hole for an eagle. The other three players stood in awe for a moment then rushed to envelop Kenji in a group hug, slapping him on the back, thrilled for his achievement. "Great hole, Kenji! What is with you today?" they asked, finally standing back and giving him a rousing round of applause.

"Lucky, I guess." He clasped his hands chest high to give them a traditional Japanese bow with a bit of attitude.

The second hole at Makalei was a par five, 550 yards. Kenji had honors at the tee box and was trying to slow his racing heart. He took a couple of practice swings to help calm himself down. He looked up and visualized the shot he wanted to make. Immediately, a red pathway came into view that duplicated the shot he envisioned. He blinked then took his position over the ball. He carefully set his alignment then focused his sight on the leaf he had picked out earlier. He aligned his club, thought about his swing strength, then relaxed his grip and swung. It was a picture-perfect shot. Kenji's form was that of a pro golfer. He held his follow-through to add a bit of drama and was amazed once again as he watched the flight of the ball duplicate his vision. It hit almost exactly where he had aimed then bounced twice before coming to a stop on the right side of the fairway. He had purposely aimed for that spot, knowing it would give him the best angle onto the green. The golf carts hummed down the cart path to where the balls lay. Ernie's ball was the farthest away, so he hit first, and then it was Kenji's turn.

Vince sidled up next to him, his voice low. "Okay, Kenji. You still have three hundred and thirty yards to the green. So a normal three-wood for you is about two hundred yards, right?

"Right. That'll leave about a hundred and thirty yards for my third shot."

"Let's see how your 'gift' will work for these next two shots."

The plan worked perfectly. The third shot rolled within eighteen inches of the pin, resulting in a birdie four, the best Kenji had ever scored on this hole.

Ernie watched his friend, curious to know why his golf game seemed vastly improved. "Did you have Wheaties with your noodles for breakfast this morning?"

"Nah, that's what I had for dinner last night."

"Oh, *that* explains it."

"Nice birdie, Kenji," said Vince.

"Thanks." He allowed himself to savor the moment.

As the round progressed, Kenji's teammates watched him with growing amazement. Their cheers turned to puzzled "Wows!" as he peeled off one great shot after another, no matter which club he selected. Now, instead of a typical weekend-golfer swing form, his form was as limber and smooth as that of Freddie Couples at the Ryder Cup.

In the end, Kenji had shot the best round of golf in his life—an eighty, only eight shots over par. This wasn't because of any bad shots, but because he had muffed a number of putts and on two occasions had gotten bad bounces on drives that were otherwise perfect.

Kenji noticed Stu was standing behind him on every swing, watching him intensely as if he wanted to take notes. Ernie was ebullient and actually played one of his better rounds. "You're setting a great example for me, Kenji," he said.

A couple of times Kenji turned and noted Vince looking off in the distance, as if he were thinking about something besides what was going on in front on him. It was clear to these three friends that something extraordinary was happening.

While the guys loaded their clubs into their car trunks in the parking lot, Kenji said, "There's something Vince and I need to talk about with both of you. It's about what happened today. How about we rally at the Big Island Grill for lunch? My treat. I feel a loco moco coming on." They all agreed to meet at the restaurant.

On the way back to town, Vince was totally excited about Kenji's game. The more excited he got, the faster he drove his late-model BMW. "Your game today was amazing," he told Kenji. "I've never seen a casual golfer shoot so well. Tell me what you see when you're putting. Does your new gift work then too?"

"No, and maybe you should slow down a bit before you get a speeding ticket," said Kenji.

"Okay, okay," Vince said impatiently, as he eased up a bit on the accelerator.

"My putting needs work. I'm still trying to figure out how to read the greens, where to aim, and how hard to hit the ball. My lack of putting skills does prevent arrogance, though," he continued half seriously.

"You're the least arrogant person I know. But the putting thing is strange, very strange," said Vince, as he slowed to the speed limit. "I wonder why your putts are different from your other shots."

"I haven't a clue. Not to be cliché, but I'm not looking a gift horse in the mouth. I'm thrilled to break a hundred, and today I scored an eighty. Can you believe it? An eighty! I'm so damned excited I could explode!"

"Not in my new car, please," Vince said with a chuckle, thrilled for his friend's success.

By the time they arrived at the restaurant, the lunch crowd had thinned out, and they were seated promptly. After ordering lunch, Kenji quietly shared his "red path in the sky" story with humility, fearing he would alienate his buddies if he came off sounding cocky, especially after the round he had just played. "I can't explain the how or why of it, and I don't know if this vision thing will last," he said. He also shared his near-death experience as the others sat in stunned silence. "Stu, could this possibly be the results of all the drugs they gave me in the hospital?" Kenji asked.

"Good question." Stu leaned forward as if to divulge a secret. "And strange that you should ask. I have a story to share with you. Last month I read an article in *Science* magazine about an orthopedic surgeon in upstate New York. The article was an excerpt from a book written by a prominent British neurosurgeon. It was a story about a doctor being struck by lightning and having a near-death experience just like yours, Kenji, and then becoming obsessed by piano music. In fact, in the following years, he became an accomplished pianist. The man also became much more spiritual and sometimes could see auras of light or energy around other people. The author gave the phenomenon the name, musicophilia. In fact that's the name of his book. Maybe you'll want to pick up a copy."

"Great idea," Kenji said with a grin. "I'll stop at the bookstore on my way home. Maybe I should talk to the author about how to write a book called *Golfophilia*."

They were silent while the waitress served their food, not wanting an outsider to hear any part of the secret held among them. Kenji continued to talk while they ate lunch. "You guys might think this is crazy or silly, but totally separate from this golf thing is my sense of oneness with the world. I don't want to freak you out, but it's like I have a direct connection to a higher power. I always thought I was okay with the 'Big Guy,' but now I'm sure of it. I just know everything is going to work out. I don't see the aura around people like that doctor did, but inside I sometimes feel this overall sense of love for the world and all things in it, you guys in particular. Is that strange?"

"That's not strange. We deserve it! Just don't get too lovey-dovey on us," kidded Stu.

"Not to worry. I prefer to get any affection I might desire from the female species." They all laughed, knowing Kenji was dating the fabulous Lilly.

For many years, Kenji had incorporated practicing gratitude and meditating into his daily routine and thinking, and most of the time it had governed the way he conducted himself. Since the lightning strike, however, he had an entirely new level of awareness about himself, Lilly, and his friends—as if he were operating on a higher plane. Although he'd been unable to articulate his feelings comfortably in the past, now it was easy. This ability to see things around him with total clarity—was it a blessing or a curse?

Vince said, "Maybe some of your energy is rubbing off on me. Ever since you told me about this, I've been completely stoked. I wake up early each morning, and I'm excited about the prospects for the day."

"I don't know if this golf thing is permanent or just a passing phase," Kenji said.

"I think you should register at the club so you can establish a handicap. That way we can measure your level of play. What do you think, Stu?"

"That's a great idea. The other thing, Kenji, is that I think we should keep this between the four of us for now. Otherwise all kinds of people will start bugging you for information. I noticed you at lunch the other day with Lilly. It looks like you two are getting serious." He put one hand behind his right ear grinning, "I think I hear the faint sound of wedding bells."

"Premature, my friend, premature," replied Kenji. "And yes, I agree with you. I don't plan to mention this to anyone, maybe not even Lilly. I haven't decided yet. I don't want to scare her off, and I sure as hell don't want to become a spectacle. It goes against my humble nature," Kenji said with a grin.

"No bells?" asked Vince, disappointed.

Kenji stared at Vince, hoping he would stop asking questions. "We're friends. I like spending time with her, and since we share the same culture, we have a lot in common. So why don't you tell us about your long-legged redhead?"

"Nope. It's too soon, my friend, too soon. But I'm working on it," Vince replied with a fake leer.

After lunch, Vince dropped Kenji at his car, which was parked at Walmart. Kenji had been unusually quiet in the car, as if he were pondering how to achieve world peace or some other huge task.

"Kenji, are you up to playing the Waikoloa Beach course tomorrow?" Vince asked him. "I know the starter there, and I'm sure he won't pair us up with anyone if I ask him."

"Sure. Sounds great. What about your work?"

"I'm all right there this week, and you know golf tends to be my first priority since I hired a good business manager to watch over things. I want to see if your newly found golf skills are exclusive to Makalei or if you can play that well anywhere."

As Kenji drove home, he turned on the radio in his car, listening to Celine Dion sing the year's number one song. "I'll be your cloud up in the sky / I'll be your shoulder when you cry / I'll hear your voices when you call me / I am *your angel.*" *Guess I do have a guardian angel, he thought. Thank you, Mia Mouse.*

CHAPTER 14

The next day, Vince managed to get a tee time. By nine a.m. they were driving up the Kohala Coast to the Waikoloa Beach course twenty miles north of Kona. Vince enthusiastically laid out his plan for the day. He wanted to watch Kenji's setup on each shot, especially the putts, to figure out the reason behind the wide disparity in results. It was to be a day of discovery. He also had a kernel of an idea about how Kenji could use his gift to benefit others.

Kenji agreed to the plan, deferring to his friend's wisdom and experience. As usual, Vince was driving fast but slowed to make the turn into the arched entrance to the Waikoloa complex. The Waikoloa Beach course was in Kenji's view the most spectacular golf course on the Big Island. The golf magazines had rated some of the other courses higher, but for Kenji's money, Waikoloa was a stunning place to play, with some holes skirting the ocean and others in the midst of treacherous lava fields. Most golfers pleaded with the lava gods after hitting an errant shot, praying their ball would spit back from the crusted landscape and land in a safe area, even though the ball was usually cut to shreds. Kenji had brought an extra dozen balls just in case.

His tee shot at the par four first tee was dead straight and landed right in the middle of the fairway, just at the turn of a slight dogleg to the left. Vince's shot was only thirty yards past Kenji's ball, also on the fairway.

"Did your shot land where you visualized it would?" asked Vince.

"You bet. I picked out a brown spot about two hundred and fifty yards out. That's about how far I usually hit the driver based on a lot of hours at the driving range, so I know pretty well how far I hit each club. The strange thing is I can tell by looking at the fairway where that distance is for the club I choose. The only thing I don't know is how it will bounce and how far the ball will roll."

Vince was amazed at the logic and thought Kenji brought to the game and impressed with his dedication and practice discipline. He was determined to help his friend put all the pieces together so he could excel at golf, but first he needed to get inside his head to understand Kenji's thought process with every shot.

Kenji selected his eight-iron for his next shot—138 yards to the green. "I'm just going to talk my way through this so you can know what's going on, okay?" Kenji said.

"First I stand behind the ball and look at the flag. Next I set my grip. Then I look again at the spot I've chosen, just so I have a clear aiming point. Then I move into position over the ball and square the face of my club to the spot in front of my ball. I look again at the landing spot and let my mind go blank and start my swing. Now here's the weird part. After I'm lined up, a red line of flight appears. It's like a roadway in the sky. At this point I feel totally at peace, and can't hear a sound. Then I swing. It's fun to watch the ball follow the red path and land exactly where I aimed." Kenji became deadly quiet and then swung. His form was perfect, and he held the follow-through until the ball landed, bounced once, then stopped six feet in front of the pin.

Vince was mesmerized. "Great shot! It was dead on line. Is that where you were aiming?"

"Yes, exactly what I had in mind."

Vince quickly drove the cart up the path to the green, anxious to see whether Kenji could sink a six-foot putt for a birdie. Competitive by nature, he couldn't help wonder whether his friend would kick his ass if he continued to land each shot.

Once on the green, Kenji checked the line from his ball to the hole, the ocean off to the right. Thinking the ball would naturally curve a bit to the right, he aimed his putt one-ball width to the left of the hole. He took a deep breath, stood over his ball, looked at the cup, then took his putter back about three inches and swung it smoothly toward his "spot." He looked up in surprise to see the ball stop a foot short of the cup on the left side.

"Damn. I thought it was going to break to the right."

"That's okay, Kenji. It was a good 'up.' We just need to work on your pacing. From now on I'll help you 'read' the greens until you get a feel for them, okay? The greens haven't dried out yet, so they're a little slower than later in the day."

Kenji tapped in his putt for a par.

The next hole was a long five par, 575 yards, with sand traps lurking on one side and the treacherous lava rocks on the other. They teed off, both landing in the fairway. Kenji's ball was out 250 yards; Vince hit a "screamer," out almost three hundred yards.

"Great shot!" Kenji exclaimed. "I've got to learn how to do that."

"Don't get ahead of yourself. You're doing just fine, especially with the accuracy of your drives."

They each hit their second shot perfectly, landing on the fairway thus avoiding the hazards.

"Now, Kenji, this next shot is one I think will be the key to a low score for you. Your three-wood shot was right at two hundred yards after the roll, so we're out about 125 yards to the center of the green. The flag is blue, so that means the hole is located toward the back of the green. There's no wind today, which is unusual for this course, but I bet the greens are starting to firm up, so you'll get a bounce and a good roll after it lands. Let's see... It's a hundred and twenty-five yards plus about thirty feet to the pin. I'd guess the roll to be about fifteen feet. Your job is to pick out a spot on the green about fifteen feet in front of the pin. It's more difficult to find a real target on the green, because the grass is all the same color, so you just have to make up a spot in your head. The rest is up to you. I don't know how hard you need to hit a pitching wedge to get there. Or would you prefer to hit a soft nine iron? The question is, 'Does that miracle computer in your head work for these kinds of shots?' "

Two things occurred to Kenji as he listened to Vince. One was that he had a lot to learn about golf, and the other was that Vince was a great coach. He was calm and logical and precise in his instructions. Kenji and Vince were tuned to the same mental channel.

Kenji pulled the nine iron out of his bag and did his normal pre-shot routine. He didn't worry about the distance, because he knew he'd have a pathway to follow. He tried to visualize the landing spot he sought and did the math in his head. The golf cart was about eight-feet long, so he needed to aim about two golf carts in front of the pin. He held this idea in his head. When he lined up over the ball and then looked for the imaginary spot on the green, the pathway appeared. Kenji felt a sense of well-being flood over him as he swung the club, kept his head down, then glanced up to see the ball track perfectly to his target. His semi-trance ended when the ball hit, bounced once, and rolled to within a foot of the pin.

"Yes!" Vince shouted. "Spectacular!" Vince was so excited he didn't even hit his own ball. He drove quickly to the green and watched from the cart as Kenji holed the putt. "Congratulations on a birdie, Kenji!"

"Wow. That felt awesome! This is better than sex, and I thought *that* was a spiritual experience."

Vince chuckled, continually amazed at the joy his star pupil displayed. He didn't play the rest of the round but instead focused on coaching Kenji. At each hole he shared his knowledge about the layout of the course and gave advice on the best angle from which to approach each hole and details about the undulations on the greens. The bond between teacher-coach and pupil grew with each hole Kenji played. The water, lava, and sand traps weren't obstacles for Kenji because he had his internal pathway to follow for each shot onto the fairway. The issue that did come up several times was holding the green with the second shot on the par fours. Club selection was the next lesson that Vince would teach him. Sometimes the club Kenji chose for distance would have too flat a trajectory, and the ball would roll across the green with no backspin.

He finished the round just four shots over par, amazing even himself. *So this is how it feels to play golf well*, he thought. He was euphoric!

On the drive back to Kona, Vince brought him slowly back to Earth. "You know, Kenji, on every shot you make perfect contact with the ball. The issue with distance is directly related to club head speed. This tends to be set by basic swing style and muscle strength, mostly in the legs. I wouldn't want in a thousand years to change your swing dynamics. Tell me, do you work out or anything to stay as trim as you are?" Vince inquired.

"I run every day. I guess the rest is good genetics."

Kenji, in most ways a typical Japanese man, preferred the kind of food his mother had cooked when he was a child. His meals were mostly comprised of fish, vegetables, and rice. He relished a tasty hamburger from Splashers and indulged in a rare steak on occasion, but he usually ate a low-fat diet. Mia's old treadmill gathered dust in the spare room at home; he preferred his morning three-mile run. He liked to be outside enjoying the views while checking up on the various activities around town. He wasn't inclined to gossip like the neighborhood ladies, but his keen sense of observation gleaned enough information so he could stay current on day-to-day affairs.

Vince switched to his most serious physical therapy voice. "Okay. Here's the reality of what happens to all of us as we age. Starting at about twenty-five years to around fifty years old, an average person loses about thirty-five percent of their strength. The way I think about it is that we lose about one percent of our strength each year, unless we have a resistance-training exercise program. One of the things I hear at my office all the time is, 'When I turned thirty, I started to get fat.' Most likely their body started to change its composition to more fat and less muscle earlier, but they just didn't notice it."

Kenji listened, a bit bored, wondering where this conversation was leading, hoping it would soon return to golf and, selfishly, his spectacular score.

Vince droned on and on. "When the body loses a pound of muscle it's replaced by a pound of fat, so your weight might stay the same. However, there are two important dynamics at work here. First, fat takes about twenty percent more space than muscle so you start to get bigger, especially around the middle. Second, a pound of muscle burns about eighteen calories a day, while a pound of fat burns two calories a day. The rate you burn calories is called metabolism. A good metaphor to think about is that muscle is like a fireplace that *consumes* fuel. Fat is like a gas tank in your car—it just *stores* fuel. If a person continues to eat the same amount of food each day, the ratio of body fat to muscle changes because his or her metabolism has slowed. So you need fewer calories to stay even or you'll gain weight. Add to this the effect of more inactive hours spent watching television, surfing the Web, or playing video games, and over time people start to get fatter and weaker."

"So what do you suggest I do with this heap of information?" Kenji asked, using a technique that he had learned during his years as a businessman.

"I'm so glad you asked. I think you should start a weight-lifting program. It doesn't have to be a big deal, and it'll help your golf game in terms of driving distance and stamina. Oh, and a side benefit is you'll thank me when you're in your seventies and eighties." Vince smiled, greatly enjoying his teacher role while noting the bored expression on his friend's face.

Kenji perked up and listened intently when the chatter finally returned to golf.

"I'm also thinking about a longer driver for you," Vince said. "Many people can't hit longer clubs because their swing dynamics aren't repeatable or as precise as yours seem to be. This means you may be able to increase your distance by simply using a longer driver. I have a forty-eight-inch driver in my garage. I'll get it for you to try on the driving range."

"Great. I'll try anything once."

"The other issue is the one-hundred-fifty- to one-hundred-seventy-five-yard shots. A lot of players are starting to use hybrid clubs. These clubs are a compromise between an iron and a fairway wood. Generally, for a given loft, a hybrid will cause your ball to go farther and fly higher. This means the ball will drop down on the green instead of skipping across it. Again, with your swing accuracy, you'd probably do well with a longer than normal shaft. Why don't we stop at the golf shop and see if they have a four hybrid club that'll suit you?"

"Sure, let's do it. Vince, thank you. I appreciate all you're doing for me. You're a natural coach, and I'm learning so much. And it is sure a lot more fun when I play well. No wonder so many people are involved in golf. It's like a whole new world has opened up for me."

* * *

The next day, Kenji, outfitted with Vince's longer driver and a new four hybrid with a long shaft, headed to the driving range and bought a bucket of balls. It was eleven o'clock on a workday morning, so the range was almost empty. Kenji went to the end tee, did some stretches, and hit a few pitching wedge shots. He took a few practice swings with the four hybrid then lined up with the 150-yard green. He did his normal pre-shot routine then took his shot. For the first time, the ball didn't follow the path he saw. It went about ten yards past his aiming point; it also flew higher than the path, with an abbreviated roll after landing. Kenji quieted his mind and considered this. He didn't worry or agonize. Rather it was like he was viewing a painting for the first time and seeing the nuances of beauty he hadn't seen previously.

He hit the 4H again. This time it tracked perfectly, like all his other shots. He stood in wonder, pondering that he evidently had some input into his mental computer for each club he used. Then it was as if he had stored the information in a vast databank, and he'd never need to think about it ever again. Amazing!

He tried choking down on the club to build a mental database of shorter shots. In each case, after the first shot, his pathway was accurate. He found by choking down he could vary the distance of the 4H by ten to thirty yards. With his newly found creation, he was as proud as a new daddy.

Next he tried the driver. The same thing happened on his first shot—the ball didn't follow the path. After Kenji meditated about the vision of the shot for a short time, the next shots were dead on. The good news was that he was consistently hitting the long-shafted driver 250 to 275 yards. Unbelievable! He couldn't wait to tell Vince, who would be as stoked as he was with the results.

Kenji had no doubt that these new clubs would change his game forever. His longer drives would get him to a point where he could use a more lofted club for the second or third shot. The hybrid would give him a lofted long shot that would hold the greens better so the ball would be closer to the pin.

As he drove home, he realized that although he had this gift, he still had a lot to learn about playing golf besides hitting the ball straight every time. *If I become a good amateur golfer,* he thought, *how can I turn this gift into something that's a force for good?* It would be interesting to hear what Vince had to say on this subject.

The minute he got home, he phoned his coach. "Hey, Vince. The new clubs are great! I'm nailing the driver two hundred and fifty to two hundred and seventy-five yards every time. And I love the hybrid. It has a different feel, and you're right, the ball does fly a lot higher. Your suggestion is going to work out fine. I was consistently hitting the four hybrid a hundred and sixty yards and occasionally a hundred and seventy. I guess the next thing is to figure out how this affects club selection on the golf course. What do you think?"

"I think a good test would be to play the Waikoloa Village course. It's hilly and occasionally windy, so you might find out how your gift works in the wind. Unfortunately I have to work tomorrow. One of our therapists is out sick. If I were you, I'd try to play alone. In the afternoon the course typically isn't too crowded, so get on as a single so you can really focus on each shot."

"Good idea," Kenji said. "I don't have anything on my schedule tomorrow. Oh, by the way, I joined the gym at the YMCA today. I'm starting a three-day-a-week weight-lifting program. The trainer I'm working with is a foxy blonde woman named Laura. She teaches yoga and kick boxing too. Not bad on the eyes either. She has a body that would rock your world!" Kenji added enthusiastically.

"Good for you! And for your information, I'm making progress with the redhead. We have a dinner date for tonight."

"Good luck with that, my friend."

After getting off the phone with Vince, Kenji noticed the red message light blinking on his answering machine and hit the "play" button. "Hi, Kenji, this is your taxi service from the airport calling. Do you need a ride today? Call me."

It occurred to him that he hadn't spoken with Lilly in several days. He'd been consumed with golf. He hadn't told her about his "gift" yet, not knowing how she would react and not willing to relinquish the euphoria he was feeling.

She sounded miffed, but he chose to ignore the call for the moment. He was excited about playing golf and didn't want or need any distractions right now. He'd return her call tomorrow.

Kenji thought about how golf was changing his life. He felt invigorated and challenged. He actually was having fun again. It was almost like being a child, a free and easy life. Not in his wildest imagination had he thought retirement would turn out this way. He lay in bed, relishing the feel of the crisp sheets on his skin, breathing in the fragrance of frangipani that wafted through the open window. *I'm so lucky to live in such a beautiful place*, he thought. *How could life get better than this?* On top of all that, it seemed God had given him the gift of the near perfect golf shot, at least for now. Was it all too good to be true? Unconsciously he rolled over to his side so the sheets wouldn't touch his tender right foot.

* * *

The Waikoloa Village golf course is located inland northwest of Kona. The west side of the Big Island is one of extreme contrasts. Most of the twenty-six mile drive is through the lava fields. Lava rocks jut out of the brown rye grass, dotted here and there by blood-red bougainvillea and white rocks arranged by tourists or teenagers to spell out the names of their sweethearts. Lore has it that if visitors take pieces of lava rocks as souvenirs they'll have bad luck, so the black lava rocks mostly remain in place. Millions of years ago, Mauna Kea erupted, and the lava flowed to the Pacific, thirty miles to the west and seventeen miles to the east. The contrast of the lava fields with the lush green near the ocean and at the higher altitudes is dramatic. It's been said that people who live around Kona believe they are closer to God than people in other locales.

On the drive out, Kenji pondered how he would play his game today. First he would try to get out as a single player so he could concentrate on his shots. Then he'd walk to see how his legs held up on a hilly course. He figured if he walked he'd have more time to think between shots.

He arrived at Waikoloa Village at eleven thirty a.m., noting the two-story condos that surrounded the golf course, holiday havens for mostly Midwesterners and Canadians of modest means. He felt the freshening breeze; the only sound was the rustling palm trees — the music of Hawaii. He gazed into the distance, the blue Pacific sparkling in the sunlight eight miles to the west. He should have brought a sweater, as it was cooler at the one-thousand-foot elevation than he had anticipated, especially with the breeze. Squinting his eyes, he looked up in wonder at the 13,700-foot snow-covered peak of the Mauna Kea juttin into the sky to the southeast; it was too far away for him to see any skiers.

The starter shack wasn't fancy compared to the amenities at the resort courses along the Kohala coast.

"Hi, Kenji," the starter greeted him. "Nice to see you out here in the hinterlands."

Kenji was still having trouble dealing with the fact that it seemed most people in the area thought they knew him. It all came from the TV and newspaper coverage of his accident.

"Good morning. Is there a possibility I can go out as a single?"

"Sure. It's a slow day now because the wind is beginning to gust. Most of our regulars are already on the back nine 'cause they typically tee off earlier in the morning knowing the wind picks up around noon. Go ahead and tee off. Have a good round."

"Thank you."

After a few warm-up swings, Kenji set up on the number-one tee, a 497-yard par five with a dogleg left and fairway bunkers about two hundred yards out. Kenji took out the long driver and visualized where he thought 240-yards out would be. Then he went through his standard pre-shot routine and set up over the ball. He let his mind go blank. The red path appeared, and he hit the ball. The ball tracked perfectly, hit the fairway, bounced, and rolled about fifteen yards, so the net length for this shot was 265 — great! He was way past the bunkers that would have spelled trouble for him before. *Wow!* he thought. *That was awesome!*

Kenji played the front nine with better than usual results. As he walked up the ninth fairway, his remembered the phone call he needed to make to Lilly when he got home. He knew it would be wise to pay some attention to her before she got bored with him and sought greener pastures. He shrugged off his slight guilty feeling about his lack of good manners and returned his focus to golf. Kenji pondered the ups and downs that fate had dealt him in his life, his mind flitting from one aspect of golf to another. *I must ask Vince how he shapes his shots,* he thought, *like a fade and a draw, bending the ball around in perfect harmony with the shape of the fairway.* The challenges loomed large.

Walking the course gave him plenty of time to think. There must be a reason for this gift at this time in his life. But what was it? Why did he receive it and not someone else? What did the future have in store for him? Meanwhile he had an overwhelming feeling of "all was right with the world." Kenji also knew that day-to-day life wasn't great for everyone. There must be a role ahead for him that had greater meaning than just a golf game.

Three and a half hours later Kenji suddenly felt bone tired as he trudged up the eighteenth fairway. It had been a good day. He was beginning to understand how to play in windy conditions. Vince had warned him that the Waikoloa Village course was hilly, and he now understood the warning; his legs ached with each step. *So this is why most middle-aged or older resident golfers elect to use a cart on this course,* he thought. Sharp pains emanated from his right foot, causing him to limp on the last four holes. The doctor had told him he might have some physical damage because some of the lightning's energy had gone through his foot. He remembered the slight burn on the sole of his foot and some discoloration on his toes. The doctor didn't think it was serious, but he had told Kenji to keep an eye on it. Kenji wasn't one to complain about his physical ailments and hadn't paid much attention to his foot, preferring to ignore it and hope for the best. He hadn't mentioned his foot issue to anyone, especially Stu. He pledged to himself that he would start to build up his leg strength and his stamina, heeding the advice of Laura, his trainer at the gym, who had told him the best way to build endurance for any sport is to play that sport.

On the drive back to Kona, Kenji took stock of his day. He had enjoyed having time alone with his thoughts on the golf course. It was a valuable learning experience. It occurred to him that there were three kinds of golf for him. One was to play in isolation. Another was to play with Vince. Yet another was the golf he played with his foursome. If he ever improved his game to the point he could play competitive golf, that would be a fourth type, and he was certain it would be different than the other three. Competitive golf? Where did that notion come from? Kenji's mind had gone off into fantasyland again.

When he got home, he again put off telephoning Lilly. Instead he called Vince to see whether he was free for dinner that night, wanting to recount his golf experience.

"Sure," Vince said. "After doing real work all day, I'm ready for a break." He was anxious to hear about his friend's day at the golf course.

As they chatted over juicy steaks at the Kona Inn, Kenji shared what he had learned that day. "The long driver is terrific. I can control it, and now I have a two-hundred-fifty-yard shot. And I'm in love with the four hybrid. I instantly felt confident with it, and I was quickly able to determine the distance."

Vince could tell Kenji was excited and enthusiastic about the things he had learned that day even though he hadn't scored particularly well.

"Now the wind is something else," Kenji continued. "I was amazed at how quickly I developed a sense of how to adjust each shot. I have a new understanding of how difficult it is to achieve a low handicap. I may be getting ahead of myself, but will you teach me how to hit a fade and a draw?"

"Yes, of course," Vince said, "but you need to walk before you can run. Let's focus on one thing at a time, okay? Since we last talked, I came up with some ideas for you to think about. You don't need to make a decision right now. This is just some food for thought. I was thinking you could join the men's club at Makalei. It would allow you the opportunity to play with different people in a competitive environment. Also in March they have the club championship tournament. By then I think you'll be ready to take on the world."

"I'm not sure about that," Kenji responded doubtfully.

Vince looked his friend in the eyes. "I have no doubt that you can become a competitive golfer. You just have to work on reading the golf course, and like you said, develop the ability to hit fades and draws and improve your putting. The physical-training program you started will keep you strong. That's the good news. The bad news could be that you'll get some amount of notoriety in this process, because I think you can win the Makalei tournament. Think about it—here you are, a fifty-year-old golfer who's come out of nowhere. You've played golf for less than a year, and you could become the club champion!"

"You really think so?"

"You bet. You're going to beat some really good golfers, many of whom are a lot younger than you. People will be curious and want to know how you're doing this or what you've done to become such a great golfer. You'll have to decide how you want to handle it all."

Kenji was skeptical. "I don't know, Vince. I've still got so much to learn."

"This is what I've really been thinking about," Vince said, "the reasons why you'll seriously want to consider my idea. The first one is the pure joy of playing competitive golf and winning. Second, the notoriety that comes along with this can be used for good purposes. For example, at the Boys & Girls Club auction, you could auction off a round of golf with Kenji Watanabe. There are other causes that you could put your name to that would be worthy, where you could benefit a cause or help a charity."

"Other than my sparkling personality, why on Earth would anyone pay good money to play golf with me?"

Vince grinned. "Notoriety. Everyone wants to play the tournament winner. It's all about the male ego. Thinking further into the future, you might want to enter some state amateur events. This will open up a whole new world with a whole new set of issues, like the expense of traveling to other islands. Also you'll compete with a lot of high school and college golfers who have dreams of gaining a professional tour card. Some of them are really top-notch golfers with egos to match. For now maybe you'd like to think about the path of an amateur as it relates to the Big Island. If you decide to go this way, hopefully you won't leave your foursome buddies behind."

In the back of his mind, Kenji kept thinking he had been given this gift for some purpose. Perhaps getting involved with the men's group at the club would be a good way to explore those possibilities—and he had no intention of telling anyone else about his gift.

"I haven't talked to Lilly about my new abilities. I haven't even seen her. I've been so consumed with golf."

Vince shot Kenji a puzzled look. "You're kidding, right? You're ignoring that stone fox so you can play golf? Lilly's a keeper. She seems like a really nice person, and she's a good match for you. I wonder about you sometimes, Kenji. No, actually, I *worry* about you, especially now that I know your priorities are so screwed up. What are you waiting for? The next thing you'll be telling me is that you're sleeping with your golf clubs."

Kenji winced, certain that he was *not* going to tell Vince that he hadn't slept with Lilly yet, fearing this revelation would diminish him in his friend's eyes. He knew Vince was right about one thing. His obsession with golf had taken over his life.

Vince sensed he had stumbled onto a sore subject and decided to back off. "Lilly aside, I have to tell you that sharing your golf experience and sharing my knowledge of the game with you has been really fun for me. If it's all right with you, I'd like to continue that."

After years of protecting his feelings, Kenji was beginning to understand what it was like to have friends. Because of his community activism, he had many acquaintances — some closer than others, but what was always missing in his life was crossing that invisible barrier to trust that another person truly cared about him. Later Kenji would remember this day as his friendship with Vince blossomed.

"Now, Coach, let's talk about a schedule going forward," he told Vince. "I'm retired, so it's easy for me to organize two or three or even four games a week. But you still have a business to look after, so what makes sense to you in terms of a training program?"

They agreed to continue the Wednesday foursome, playing just for fun. Kenji would join the men's club and test his game in that environment, then play at least one or two coaching games with Vince every week.

"Then I propose we put together a game plan just like a business plan for a company," Vince advised. "We'll mutually decide how to proceed so at the end of the program you'll be a well-rounded and complete golfer. You and I will play as a twosome when possible so we can focus on whatever part of your game that needs work. I predict that within six months you'll be an eight- handicap or better golfer. That would put you in the top five percent of everyone in the world who plays golf."

Kenji flashed Vince a wide grin. "I'm stoked just thinking about it."

"In addition, depending on how you handle the pressure of competition, you may even be our club champion and perhaps win some other competitions around the island. Of course the big unknown in every tournament is the young bucks you'll compete against. It seems that from age sixteen to twenty-one or so they're fearless and occasionally put together great games."

"Not to dampen your enthusiasm, but I have to admit that I've been having a little problem with my right foot," Kenji admitted. "I got an ugly blister on it today after walking eighteen holes at Waikoloa Village, and this isn't the first time it's happened. The doctors told me to watch for ulcers and or any other problems that might occur with my foot. Apparently it could be similar to the problems a diabetic has with circulation. I'm not worried about it, but I thought I should mention it because it could be an unknown factor going forward."

"Okay, Kenji. Thanks for telling me. It's a good thing that all of these amateur events let you ride in the cart. Just pay close attention to what happens to your foot. We see lots of diabetics that come in for therapy, and circulation in the extremities is a big issue for them. Have you talked to Stu about this?"

"Not yet. I'll see how it looks on Wednesday, and, if isn't showing signs of healing, I'll ask him about it."

"Check it every day, okay?"

"I will," he agreed, though he was totally in denial that his foot could possibly be an issue in his plans for his future.

On the drive home that night, Vince pondered what Kenji had told him about his foot. His concern was a lot greater than he'd let on at the restaurant. His friend's description of his sore foot sounded like a classic case of damaged capillaries. He shuddered knowing the options more than likely weren't good.

CHAPTER 15

Since Kenji had started to play golf, his life had completely changed. In fact it was difficult for him to remember a day when golf wasn't even on his radar. Now he was obsessed. His friendship with Vince was flourishing. Not only was Vince his coach, but he also had become Kenji's closest male friend. He was getting in seventy-two holes of golf every week. *Nothing obsessive about that,* he thought, while rationalizing that his profound interest in golf was all part of his master plan. The plan was working fine, except for the growing problem with his foot. He walked as little as possible, but the sore on his foot was becoming worse.

When Kenji finally got around to phoning Lilly, he apologized. "I'm sorry I haven't been quick to return your calls. I'll do better in the future, I promise," he said, turning on ample charm. "Are you free for dinner Saturday night? There's a new Hawaiian fusion restaurant out at the King's Shopping Center that we need to try."

Lilly, though her feelings had been hurt by Kenji's inattention these past weeks, agreed to the date. She was confused by his attitude toward her and hadn't seen him in quite a while. Of course she had spent several weeks in Los Angeles as part of her consulting contract, but still...

Kenji knocked on Lilly's door on Saturday evening promptly at seven o'clock. He hadn't played golf that day and instead had prepared for this evening by getting his car detailed, getting a haircut, and carefully selecting a large bouquet of fragrant flowers from his favorite flower shop. Even though most locals didn't dress up—even for dinner in the better restaurants—he decided to take the high road. His light tropical suit with a European cut showed off his lean, muscular build. Gold links in the French cuffs of his blue shirt lent an elegant air to his bearing. He was trying to impress Lilly and worm his way back into her good graces. *She deserves better than what I've been giving her lately*, he conceded.

Lilly answered the door and exclaimed, "Wow! You're one handsome fellow, all duded up in a suit! You're looking *fine*." She grinned mischievously. "Come on in."

"Aloha." Kenji leaned in, his hands behind his back. He gave Lilly a light kiss on the cheek, catching her completely by surprise. He made a sweeping gesture and thrust the bouquet into her hands.

"You're full of surprises, aren't you?" she said with a smile. Her sleek hair was held up and away from her face with combs made of ivory, a striking contrast to the inky blackness of her hair. Her simple strapless sheath—the color of fresh peaches—highlighted her figure and golden tan. She had chosen her ensemble carefully, not above using feminine wiles to reignite a spark of interest from this man.

"Come into the living room," she said, "while I put these beautiful flowers in a vase. I have a bottle of Cristal on ice."

Not one to spend his money frivolously, Kenji vaguely knew it was an expensive brand of Champagne, but he had never tasted it. He glanced around the room, noting the eclectic collection of wall décor from primitive masks to modern art—exotic just like Lilly.

She carried two crystal Champagne flutes, expertly popped the cork—not spilling a drop—and poured the glasses full. "Cheers!"

"*Salut!*"

They clinked glasses, the bubbles tickling Kenji's nose as he swallowed his first sip. "Ah, sweet nectar! This is delicious."

"Oh, is this your first time?" Lilly asked coyly.

"I hate to admit it, but yes. I'm a simple man, not accustomed to the finer things in life—that is, until I met you."

Somewhat mollified by his charm, Lilly relaxed, determined to fan the flames of interest, sexual or otherwise. She had played the waiting game long enough.

On the drive along the Kohala Coast, they chatted about Lilly's travels and her plans to open an optometry practice in Kona. "There's hardly any competition here, so it's a great opportunity," she told him enthusiastically. "The ones who can afford it fly to Honolulu to get their eyes checked, and the poorer people go to a clinic where they can get glasses at a discounted price. I figure there's an untapped market in the mid-range for my services." Kenji nodded while not saying much of anything, but she sensed something simmering just below the surface.

He had decided, somewhat motivated by guilt, to share the news about his newfound magic on the links with her but wanted to do so over dinner in more amenable surroundings. They arrived at the restaurant, the trees out front lit up with hundreds of twinkly lights. They walked hand in hand up the steps and into the restaurant to be greeted by a friendly, attractive Asian hostess. The place was obviously new, with sleek furniture, eclectic tableware, and candles aglow on each table to set the mood for a fine dining experience.

After they were seated, Kenji ordered a bottle of white wine and they perused the menu. The young waiter explained the specials in enthusiastic detail, after which they both decided on the three-course prix fixe menu that featured a choice of salads, giant sea scallops, and the restaurant's signature dessert, a melting chocolate mousse cake.

Lilly could no longer restrain her curiosity. "So, Kenji, what have you been doing to stay so busy?" She had called him before she had left for the mainland just to say goodbye. No answer, so she had left a message to return her call. She had phoned twice from California and still hadn't received a return call. She attempted to hide the hurt in her voice but didn't succeed a hundred percent.

"I have the most fantastic story to tell you!" Kenji said. "My life has changed beyond recognition, and I've been waiting for the right moment to tell you all about it."

Lilly sipped her wine, wondering what in the world had happened to this man. Kenji went on to tell her about his incredible experiences on the golf course. He shared everything that had happened lately—including the golf lessons from Vince and his near-death experience when he saw his parents and Mia—then went on to explain his physical regimen with the goal of winning the local men's club tournament and perhaps even playing in some tournaments around the islands.

The waiter served their salads and poured more wine. Kenji assumed Lilly would be supportive of his new passion for golf and all the plans he had made, together with his hopes for the future.

"That's quite a story," Lilly replied quietly. Her thoughts were totally different from the words she spoke out loud. *What am I, just a beautiful plaything, like a toy he plays with when he's bored?* she thought. *He didn't even mention my name in any of his plans. I thought I had competition before. Now in addition to a dead wife, I have to compete with a golf obsession?* She was livid with anger, frustration, and a feeling of abandonment.

"What's the matter? Are you upset?" Kenji asked.

"I'm furious with myself for wasting so much of my time on someone who obviously doesn't have a clue about how to be in a relationship. I thought we had something going on, but I'm obviously mistaken. I'm so far down on your list of priorities that any relationship we might have had will never see the light of day."

Kenji sat across the table, stunned by her reaction. "Lilly, let me explain. This is a gift, the ability to visualize the ball in flight. It's an amazing gift. I can't squander it. I can use this phenomenon to help others in some way." Dumbfounded, Lilly sat in silence. Kenji reached across the table and grazed his fingers across her hand. "It's going to be all right, I promise. I have more than enough time in my life for you. And you're absolutely right—you need to be a higher priority. Let me prove it to you, okay? I don't want to lose you."

The tenderness of Kenji's words and the gentle look on his face took the fight right out of Lilly. She took a deep breath to relax her body before speaking in a somewhat skeptical tone. "I'm not sure I believe you, so let's just see how things go." She had been falling in love with him almost from the day they had first met, but Lilly, with her independent streak, didn't want to admit it, either to herself or to Kenji.

"Okay, then." *She's so beautiful when she's angry*, Kenji thought, while acknowledging that he had been selfish in his pursuits and unfair to her. As they sat there on a balmy Hawaiian evening, publicly holding hands, he made another potential life-altering decision. *I will not let her go*, he thought. *I want her in my life.*

They finished their dinner and dessert, talking about other things, neither wanting to resurrect the anger or the hurt. After the drive into Kona, Kenji walked Lilly to her door, tenderly touched his lips to hers, and said, "Good night, my sweet. Sleep tight. I'll call you in the morning."

Lilly went into her condo and gently closed the door. All the pent-up feelings came crashing down on her like a giant avalanche. She listened for Kenji's car to drive off before finally giving in to the tears. She sobbed for a while, her shoulders heaving in spasms of self-pity, then chided herself. *Stop this, Lilly. You haven't lost him yet.* Still, the pain in her gut reminded her of her father's passing.

* * *

The cool shower felt good against Kenji's skin. It had been an eventful night. Lilly's reaction had totally surprised him, and he had felt confused and uncertain at the restaurant—but only for a few moments, then the confidence and peaceful tranquility clicked in so he could reassure her that everything would be okay. *I like her independent outlook*, he thought with a smile. *That's definitely part of the attraction.*

Kenji took stock of all the qualities he liked about Lilly. She had a good value system, and their philosophy of life was generally in sync. She had an active mind and an intellectual curiosity. She loved to read and kept up on current events, and he had discovered her acute political mind over lunch one day when they were discussing presidential politics. Of course he couldn't overlook the fact that she was gorgeous and had a traffic-stopping figure. He couldn't wait for the moment when he could leisurely undress her and touch that lovely golden skin from the top of her head to the tips of her elegant toes and all places in between. As Kenji drifted off to sleep, he pictured Lilly in a flowing white dress, her arms reaching out to him, and the fantasy dream continued into the night.

* * *

The next morning after his daily run, he phoned Lilly with a cheery "Good morning, sweet thing. What are your plans for the day?"

"I'm playing tennis with my new friend, Sandy, at ten, then we're going to lunch. After that we're checking out some real estate for my new office." She couldn't help think, *Hmmm, 'sweet thing.' Now that's an improvement.* "Did you know Sandy's dating Vince?" she asked coyly, already knowing he probably didn't.

"Really? Is she the redhead he's been blabbing on about?"

"Yes, she is."

"How did you meet her?"

"I was checking out offices in their medical building. We got to chatting about tennis, and she invited me to play."

"I told you Kona is a small town," Kenji said, knowing that sooner or later Lilly would meet everyone involved in the community.

"I think she's in *looooove*." She drew out the word, laughing, enjoying the gossip session with Kenji.

"Good for her," he responded diffidently, selfishly hoping Vince's involvement with a woman wouldn't interfere with his golfing plans with his coach.

"There's a luau at the King Kamehameha Hotel tonight. And I know how much you love poi," Kenji teased. "May I pick you up about eight?" he asked politely, subtly continuing to make amends.

"Sure, sounds like fun, and you can stick the poi up your you-know-what!" She laughed as she hung up the phone.

Kenji's life was good — at least for now — aside from his nagging worry about the increasing pain in his foot. He'd checked it out closely, and there was no sign of healing.

CHAPTER 16

March 1999

Kenji still wasn't used to being the best golfer in his foursome. He felt like an imposter, especially when he beat Vince. Almost every round he shot par and occasionally scored a sub-par round. Putting was still a problem for him, though. The strategy Vince suggested was to develop his driving power so his second or third shot was shorter. This would give Kenji a better chance of landing his second shot on par fours closer to the pin to assure a two-putt par, and in some cases, a one-putt birdie.

Every year the Makalei golf course held a club championship tournament. The winner of this tournament achieved a bit of notoriety and acclaim around town and certainly at the golf club. Whoever won had the bragging rights for that year and was the target among the next year's tournament entries.

The odds-on favorite to win this year was Jamie Fletcher. He was twenty-one years old and the grandson of John Fletcher, the major property owner in Kona. Kenji casually checked the bulletin board at the club that morning. Sure enough, Jamie's handicap was posted; he was listed as a scratch player. Jamie had a reputation for hitting massive drives. He had a golfer's build—six feet tall, lean, flexible, and at the peak of his strength. It was rumored that Jamie was learning how to be a smart golfer, but his wisdom wasn't yet perfected, because his ego whispered in his ear, *Hit it hard and long* on every shot, whether or not circumstances warranted that strategy. Sometimes Jamie's youthful exuberance and inexperience resulted in the ball landing in trouble spots or out of bounds—as opposed to playing it smart to tally up the lowest score.

A few months earlier at the clubhouse, Kenji had met Jamie and quietly cheered him on when he saw his handicap posted each week. They hadn't become friends but instead were friendly rivals. Kenji was surprised that John Fletcher seemingly had not passed along his hatred of Japanese people to his grandson. Kenji could honestly say that John Fletcher was the only person on the island he really disliked, if not hated. Their business dealings of the past, the lawsuit, and Fletcher's overbearing tactics had left a bad taste in his mouth. He had made a conscious decision not to spend time around such mean, spiteful people.

No one had told Kenji, or perhaps no one knew, that the heart of Fletcher's hatred stemmed from World War II. He didn't know that Fletcher's father had been one of the more than five thousand Marines killed in the Battle of Iwo Jima. Fletcher was reminded of this every time he saw the iconic image of the American flag flying over Mount Suribachi. His father had died on the slopes that led to the flag site.

In addition to the fiefdom that Fletcher had created in Kona, it was common knowledge that the only person he really cared about was his grandson, Jamie. Fletcher's son had attended an Ivy League school and, after living under his father's tyranny for twenty-odd years, had moved with his wife to New York City, leaving Jamie on his own in Kona. Fletcher's bigotry and business acumen were well known around the islands. Over time, he became very rich. He started in the real estate business just as the Kona area was starting to develop as a tourist destination. He specialized in commercial real estate. When he found a good buy, he'd leverage his other properties to the hilt. Over the years, he ended up owning most of the land and buildings along Ali Drive. He was a cantankerous SOB to everyone but Jamie; on him, he doted. Kenji didn't like John Fletcher, but he didn't spend much time thinking about him either, knowing it was a waste of emotional energy. Being a minority, he was used to racial bias. Occasionally he ran into a Fletcher type along life's path. Most of the time, however, he found that if you treated people with respect they responded in kind.

The club tournament was set for next week. Kenji and his usual foursome speculated about who would win and who the toughest competitors were, and the guys offered words of encouragement to Kenji to bolster his confidence. The round they played this week was a good omen as Kenji had scored under par, edging out Vince by three strokes.

* * *

The day of the tournament dawned clear and bright. "Just another day in paradise," the locals said. The temperature was a balmy seventy-two degrees, with light trade winds. Jamie Fletcher was surprised when he noticed Kenji listed on the tournament roster. "Hey, Kenji, we're going to play against each other today," he said. "I hope you brought your 'A game,' because my game is sizzling hot!"

"Yeah, well, I'm going out there," Kenji said, "and I'll shuffle along and do the best I can. Just remember — cunning and wisdom overcomes youth and enthusiasm almost every time." The gauntlet had been thrown down.

Jamie Fletcher and three other young Turks with low handicaps were in the first flight. Kenji's posted handicap was an eight, so he was placed in the third flight. He was the oldest golfer in his foursome and didn't know any of the guys in his group. As with most golf games, the camaraderie between the players developed early in the round. Kenji learned that two of the guys were from Kailua, and the third fellow was from Waimea.

Kenji got into the rhythm of the play quickly. He was the shortest driver but as usual the most accurate. Two teammates drove long but tended to end up alongside the fairway, occasionally in the rough. Vince cheered from the sidelines and gave Kenji a thumbs-up sign to keep his confidence high. This was Kenji's home course, so he had the added advantage of knowing the greens well.

Play progressed through holes one, two, three, four, and five. Kenji was shooting par golf. Not good enough to win, but he was quietly pleased with his performance so far. The others in the foursome started to pay attention to his score and couldn't help notice the accuracy of every shot. *How does he do that?* they wondered. *He's getting "up and down" on every hole.*

A little success goes a long way in golf. Kenji's breathing slowed, his laser-point concentration focused on achieving even more exact yardages. Even his putting was smoother. He sunk every putt within eight feet of the hole but missed a couple of ten footers for bogey.

By the seventeenth hole, Kenji had shot a lights-out game, at least for him. Vince and his cheering gallery noticed that he was limping. He was one over par with a 102-yard shot into the green. He followed his usual setup routine and let his mind go blank with the beautiful path to the green painted in his mind. The ball flew exactly where he had aimed, landed within three feet of the pin, and rolled to within a foot of the hole. After his birdie putt, his score was even par for the tournament.

Kenji got another birdie on eighteen and finished the tournament one under par. He was thrilled with his performance, whether he won or not. All the guys who knew him were amazed he had finished with such a low score in a competitive environment.

Yet the blonde, handsome heir of privilege, Jamie Fletcher, reigned as the champion, finishing two-under par, beating Kenji by just one stroke.

During the after-tournament barbecue, Kenji went over to shake Jamie's hand and congratulate him on his big win.

"Kenji, what a fabulous score you posted," Jamie said. "You almost beat me, you old dog. How about we play a game together sometime? I want to see how you came so close."

"That's a deal, Jamie."

On the way back to his table, Kenji noticed John Fletcher across the patio, glaring his disapproval. Apparently he didn't want his grandson talking with him or any other Japanese person.

Vince, even more excited than Kenji about the outcome of the tournament, was dancing around, reliving every hole of Kenji's success to anyone who would listen. He was so happy that Kenji had scored magnificently, which validated his coaching skills as well. He finally got Kenji off to the side, away from the crowd, and told him, "Kenji, I think this is the beginning of our plan. I mean, you played so great today, and the pressure of the tournament didn't seem to affect your game at all. You have nerves of steel! That's the key tipping point in my mind to see whether this whole idea has any merit. What do you think?"

"I agree," Kenji said. "I felt calm all the way through, though I did get invigorated with the competition. It just added another spark to the joy of golf, at least for me."

Once Kenji had returned home after dinner, he stripped off his sweaty clothes and limped into the shower to erase the tension of the day. As he was drying off, he noticed a red splotch on his towel — blood from his foot. He sat down on a chair for a closer inspection of his foot, suddenly despondent. *No, dear Lord, do not let my foot stand in the way of my plans,* he thought. *I promise I'll do something meaningful with the gift you've given me.* That night before Kenji went to bed, he got down on his knees and thanked his God for this blessed gift. He committed then and there to focus on doing something worthwhile with his gift as long as it was with him, fearing that like most everything else in his life that he had loved, it too would be taken away from him.

* * *

Jamie Fletcher, jubilant in victory, decided to celebrate his tournament win with his buddies at a bar on Ali Drive. After downing several beers and flirting with the local girls, the gang got bored and decided the action would be better among the tourists at one of the ritzy hotels up on the Kohala coast; the Waikoloa Marriott was their destination. There were usually lots of West Coast and Canadian girls at the bar looking for a party, especially this time of year — spring break from college. The guys were in for a huge disappointment. The "girls" turned out to be forty-year-old cougars, their older husbands already tucked in bed for the night—definitely not what they were seeking. After downing another round of beers, they were pretty drunk by the time they headed back to Kona while still hopeful for a romp with some local chickadees.

John Fletcher tended to spoil his grandson. Jamie was the first person he had really learned to love. When Jamie had turned twenty-one a few months earlier, Fletcher had gifted him with a new Mustang, brandishing the keys like a sword at Jamie's birthday party. Jamie was thrilled with this hot car, which was definitely a chick magnet, with a powerful engine. On their way back to Kona, he decided to find out just how fast his boy-toy car could go.

Jamie wasn't really a car buff, so he was unaware that starting around 1995, with the advent of computer ignition control, most cars had a rev limiter that cut the gas supplied to the engine at around one hundred miles per hour. When he hit this speed, his Mustang started to sputter. He was looking down at the instrument panel, distracted, when he topped a slight rise. A lumbering semi truck in front of them blocked their way. Jamie swerved to miss it, but at this high speed, his car skidded out of control and slid sideways down the highway for almost a hundred yards, then rolled down the embankment on the other side and crashed head on into a telephone pole. The young man in the passenger seat died instantly. Jamie and his two friends in the backseat were seriously injured. It took

two long hours before the ambulance got them to the Kona
Hospital.

* * *

The next morning, Kenji decided to forego his usual run,
opting instead to drive downtown for breakfast. Kona is a
small town, and news, especially bad news, travels fast. He
quickly learned that the boy who had been killed was from
Captain Cook and had gone to high school with Jamie. The
other two boys were from Kona. Kenji knew both of them
and their parents.

As the day progressed, the word got out that Jamie had
suffered a traumatic brain injury. The prognosis was grave.

Kenji wanted to give whatever support he could for
Jamie yet he knew that he was in the intensive care unit,
with no visitors allowed except immediate family. He even
felt a bit sorry for John Fletcher, not wishing this family
tragedy on anyone, even his worst enemy.

He put his thoughts about Jamie aside to focus on his
own issues. His foot was definitely infected. Even he could
see that.

CHAPTER 17

Kenji sat at his kitchen table with his right leg crossed over his left so he could study the three sores on the bottom of his foot. It was hard to keep a bandage on the area without bundling up his entire foot. The sores were way past the band-aid stage. Now panicked, he phoned Stu to try to get in to see him immediately. He drove to Stu's medical building and limped into his office. After examining the sores, Stu immediately called Dr. Jacobs in Honolulu to request a consultation. He left word for him at Queens Medical Center and at his office. Kenji sat in the waiting room dreading what lay ahead. Dr. Mark Jacobs was the primary care physician who had taken care of Kenji after his lightning-strike experience, and he trusted him. The doctor called back thirty minutes later, and after speaking with Stu for a few minutes, asked to speak with his patient.

"Hey, Kenji, how's the golf game going?'

"Hi, Doc. The golf game is great, but I'm having some trouble with my foot."

Dr. Jacobs suggested calmly, "Let's be proactive with this. Have Stu take some close-up photos with his digital camera and email them to me immediately and I'll call you first thing tomorrow morning." Since 170 miles and a $125 plane ticket separated them from Honolulu, it sounded like a good way to get a preliminary diagnosis.

The doctor's response to Kenji's photos of Kenji's foot wasn't good. He called early the next morning. "Kenji, I'd like to see you as soon as possible," he said. "When can you get over here to see me?"

The next day, Kenji was booked on the 7:03 a.m. flight to Honolulu. It was ironic that it was April Fool's Day, Kenji thought. Once inside the airport terminal, he called Lilly to let her know where he was headed. He had a nine a.m. appointment with Dr. Jacobs.

Try as he might, Kenji wasn't optimistic about the prognosis. Dr. Jacobs had cautioned him that he suspected there was damage to the blood vessels in his foot that might cause problems, but nothing definitive had shown up in all the tests they had run previously so he hadn't been concerned.

Kenji boarded the plane, took his seat, and settled in behind a newspaper to discourage conversation. He wanted some quiet time to think, uninterrupted. So many incredible things had changed in his life during the months since he had been struck by lightning that it was nearly impossible to wrap his head around it. In many ways this had been the most exciting and fulfilling time of his life. He was ranked second in the men's club at Makalei—no mean feat. He had developed close relationships with Stu and Ernie, which provided an unexpected richness to his life. He smiled thinking of Vince, his coach and golf mentor, twenty years his junior, almost becoming the son he'd never had.

Then there was Lilly. She was so different from Mia, but he had to admit that she was a joy, bringing a vitality to his life that he'd never experienced before. He had come to enjoy her raucous wit, her affection, and the way she challenged him to open up emotionally. They had entered into a relaxed, fun relationship that was very satisfying as far as it went. Kenji was getting more affectionate, which pleased Lilly, and truth be told, he enjoyed it as well. Lilly had hinted coyly, teasing him about a "sleepover," which surprised him as she proclaimed to be an ardent Methodist, which seemed a contradiction in terms. She had joined the Kona United Methodist church almost immediately upon her arrival on the island and went to services every Sunday. Kenji had even attended with her on occasion, impressed with Reverend Neely's sermons on love and forgiveness. His life was changing so fast—from Buddhist to Methodist? He wasn't ready to make that leap, but he was always excited to see Lilly, to spend time with her basking in the lightheartedness of her being. He desperately wanted to share an intimate relationship with her, but the gift the golf gods had given him unfortunately didn't extend to his love life. He was afraid of commitment, pure and simple. He didn't want to disappoint Lilly, but his reserved nature didn't lend itself well to intimate relationships. Even so, he admitted to himself that he was falling in love with her.

His mind was racing almost as fast as the plane on the short flight to Honolulu as he pondered his potentially serious medical situation. The frequency of the ulcers on his right foot and the tendency for them to get infected seemed to be increasing. Even though he was meticulous about keeping the wound clean and treated with antibiotic cream, he feared that he had delayed seeking professional treatment far too long. *Stupid, stupid, stupid,* he chided himself.

He sought divine intervention, silently saying his daily prayer. *Thank you God for giving me a new life. May I be worthy of the gifts you have given me. May I do your will. May I share the love you have given me with everyone I touch today. May I make a positive difference in the world today. Amen.* Today he could be forgiven for adding a postscript: *Lord, I pray for your grace and healing for my foot. Amen.*

He arrived at the doctor's office by taxi, lost in thought, not cognizant of the bustle of the city.

"Kenji, it's great to see you again. Aside from the foot problem, how are you doing?" Dr. Jacobs asked as he shook Kenji's hand.

"Doc, I can't tell you how incredible my life has been—one amazing adventure after another since I last saw you. How much time do you have?"

"I've set aside the entire morning to spend with you. It's not often we get someone in here who's been struck by lightning and lived to tell about it. Several of my colleagues would like to join us later. Is that okay with you?"

"Sure, that sounds great—whatever you think is best. I have another question for you. We have a confidential doctor-patient relationship. Is that correct?"

"It sure is, Kenji. Anything we discuss or anything I find is strictly between you and me, unless it's stated otherwise for ongoing treatment."

"Okay. Here goes—I have quite a story to tell you. After I got home and recovered, I went out to the golf driving range on a lark. This was only two weeks after seeing you the last time. That was when an amazing thing happened. I found out I could hit a golf ball perfectly every time."

"Really," Dr. Jacobs replied, somewhat skeptically.

"I swear to God. I play golf every week with Dr. Garner, and when I told him about this, he recalled a case in England where a man was struck by lightning and was able to become a high-level amateur concert pianist. The doctor on that case called the condition musicophilia. My foursome buddies figured I have a condition called golfophilia," he said with a laugh. "I haven't told anyone about this besides my golfing buddies and a lady friend. You'll be surprised to know that in March I won second place in our club's amateur championship. I beat some strong, healthy twenty-one-year-olds for that honor."

Dr. Jacobs listened intently as his patient spoke. As an occasional golfer, he was astounded by Kenji's story, yet he believed every word.

Kenji continued his tale. "The other thing I haven't told you about is that apparently I had a near-death experience, according to Stu. Ever since I got home, I've felt a great sense of peace and of being connected spiritually with a higher power. It's really great. It's such a peaceful way to live."

Dr. Jacobs smiled knowingly. He'd had other patients who had "died" and come back to life who'd shared similar experiences.

"Now my only problem is this foot," Kenji said. "I know you warned me about it and couldn't tell earlier whether I had any capillary damage from the lightning strike. The ulcers and the resulting infections seem to be getting worse, so I'm experiencing quite a bit of pain when I walk or run very far. It's especially painful at night when I try to sleep. I'm hoping you'll have a magic elixir or some kind of treatment that'll make everything all right."

Dr. Jacobs closed Kenji's file on his desk and leaned back in his chair. "That's an amazing story, Kenji, but let's deal with the situation at hand. Let's take a look at your foot and find out where we are. The plan is to get an MRI so we'll have a 3-D view of the blood vessels in your foot. Then we'll run some blood tests and gather some more information. After that we'll see where we stand. I'll need you to strip down to your underwear and take off your socks. You can put on this cute little paper dress so you can walk down the hall, with your bottom showing, to the MRI machine. But first let me take a look at your foot."

An alarm went off in Kenji's head, screaming, *Dear God, please don't let this be happening to me.* The qualified, noncommittal statement from the doctor sounded ominous. Kenji was under no false illusions about what might lie ahead, having spent several hours on the Internet doing research about the effects of arterial damage. The outlook wasn't good.

Dr. Jacobs carefully removed the bandages Kenji had put on his wounds then looked at each of the three sores. "Okay, we need to get a look underneath these sores," he said. "That's what the MRI will do. I'm going to be quite open with you. These wounds don't look good. They're clues that there has been some damage. But first I want to take a minute and give you the 'Blood Circulation 101' talk so you'll have a better understanding of what we're looking for, okay?"

"Sure," said Kenji, a bit reluctantly, anxious to get the MRI and a diagnosis.

"The human body is an amazing structure," Dr. Jacobs began. "The blood circulation system is composed of arteries, arterioles, capillaries, and veins. Arteries take the blood to the lungs to pick up oxygen and then send it out to the body. Then, in your foot, for example, the arteries branch out into a complex network and become smaller and smaller. The little ones we call arterioles. The arterioles in your foot are about half the diameter of a human hair, or about a fifteen-thousandth of an inch. There's a vast array of arterioles in your foot. Each one is connected to a metarteriole, which is a short vessel that links arterioles to capillaries. Each metarteriole has muscle cells that form a valve. This valve works like your anus sphincter to control the amount of blood that flows through the respective capillaries. In turn, metarterioles are controlled by hormones in your system, or in some cases by blood pressure medication."

Kenji sat on the examining table, trying to take in the barrage of information that was overwhelming him. A dull buzz started in his head, gaining strength until it sounded like a thousand foghorns blaring in unison. He shook his head trying to clear it, with no success.

"Now, Kenji, the capillaries are absolutely amazing." He was caught up in the doctor's wonder and excitement about how the human body worked yet confused by the medical jargon. "The capillaries are really small, about five to ten millionths of an inch in diameter. They're also thin, so oxygen, water, proteins, and lipids can diffuse from them into the intercellular fluid that surrounds the cell structures and feeds your cells. If you've ever used a soaker hose in your garden, you'll see that its action is similar to how capillaries work. However, in addition, they also support an osmosis action, which means they can absorb cellular waste such as carbon dioxide and urea after they've shed the oxygen and nutrients. The blood with waste in it is then taken into the veins, where it's filtered by the kidneys then returned to the heart. The artery systems are like city water works, and the veins are like the sewer system that takes the waste away."

"I'm not sure I follow you, Doc. This is a lot of information to assimilate."

Dr. Jacob's went on to describe the blood circulation process. "Isn't that the most remarkable story you have ever heard?" asked Dr. Jacobs. "The more I learned about how our bodies work, the more I came to believe in God.

There just has to be the work of a higher power involved in the development of these complex systems that most of us never think about."

Kenji, now more anxious than he had been in his life, attempted to respond intelligently. "So what most likely happened to me was that the instantaneous current caused by the lightning strike basically fried some of my arterioles and capillaries, is that right?"

"That's exactly what I'm thinking, Kenji. Since blood is a good electrical conductor, it's possible that the instantaneous current flow went through the small arterioles and damaged some of them. Then the current went through your flesh and out the bottom of your foot to your wet shoes and to the ground. Meanwhile, some of the current went through your brain, but, thank goodness for you, most of it traveled down your wet clothes to the ground."

Every nerve in Kenji's body was screaming out for answers, but he forced himself to sit quietly while impatiently trying to absorb the information that assaulted him.

"So where the arteriole is damaged," Dr. Jacobs explained, "the cells are starved for nourishment and eventually die. What most likely has happened is progressive. As some cells die, they interfere with healthy cells next to them. Also, this is what caused the ulcers that formed on your foot."

"Oh."

"I don't know if you know this, but your condition is very common here at Queens Hospital. The only difference is that yours was caused by an accident. Diabetes or heavy smoking causes most cases we treat. We average about thirty amputations per month. Nationwide about eighty thousand diabetics lose a leg every year."

Amputations? Why is he talking about amputations? Kenji's mind was reeling. *I'm not a diabetic. Why is he telling me all this? Dear God, please don't let them chop me into pieces like I'm a hunk of meat.* Kenji sat on the examining table, terrified yet wanting to get to the bottom line "So what does all this information have to do with me?" he asked.

"Well, first let's see if any of this is really your problem. After we get the pictures from the MRI, I'll get together with my team to review them. Let's head down to the imaging room for your MRI."

After the MRI, Kenji returned to the exam room, where he retrieved his clothes and quickly got dressed.

"Why don't you go down to the Starbucks in the lobby and get yourself a coffee or something. Let's reconvene in the conference room two doors down the hall in about an hour, after I confer with my colleagues. Will that work for you?"

"Okay. I definitely need a coffee right now. It's been a very stressful morning."

"Oh, and Kenji, is it all right for me to share your story about your newfound golfing skills with the team of doctors we'll be seeing after you get back?"

Feeling like he was on safer turf, Kenji replied, "Sure, that's fine. I just don't want the general public to know. With all the golf addicts out there, I don't want to turn into some sort of a publicity freak. I'm a very private person and prefer to keep it that way."

He took the elevator down to the lobby, ordered a decaf coffee and a muffin, not wanting or needing caffeine to jangle his already fractured nerves. He limped to the outdoor patio and dialed Lilly's number on his cell phone, desperately needing to hear a friendly voice of reason. "Hi, Lilly. It's me. I'm sitting on the patio outside Queen's Hospital, and I'm desperate to hear your voice."

"Hi, Kenji. What did you find out?"

"Nothing yet. I just had an MRI of my foot. A team of doctors is reviewing it while I'm sitting here in the sun drinking coffee. There may be severe damage to the capillary system. I'm supposed to go back up to the conference room to meet with the doctors in about an hour to get the prognosis."

"Oh, sweetie, I didn't realize your foot problem was that serious. I knew from time to time you were limping a bit, and you told me you get a sore now and then, but I had no idea it could be severe."

Kenji sighed. "Well, you know me. I didn't want to make a big deal out of it. I don't like having people worried about me. Though I hate to admit it, the foot has been giving me some pain lately, and the sores are getting worse, despite my home remedies."

He was relieved to be talking with Lilly. Just the sound of her voice calmed his churning stomach, though the muffin wasn't settling very well.

"I wish I was there with you," she told him. "You shouldn't have to go through this alone."

"That's silly. I'll be fine. And I'll feel even better if you can have dinner with me tonight. Are you free?"

"I'm never free, but I *am* reasonable," she teased, with a laugh. "I'll pray for good results on your MRI. Do you want to meet somewhere or do you want to come by my place?"

"I'll come by your place. Maybe you could order some sushi? It's been a crazy day so far, and I feel the need for comfort food.

"Consider it done. See you at seven then, and I'm sending a hug your way."

"Thank you, Lilly."

He flipped his cell phone shut, grateful that she was being so supportive. He finished his coffee, tossed the half-eaten muffin and his cup into the trashcan, then limped to the elevator to meet with the doctors and learn his fate. *Keep a positive attitude*, he told himself, even though he feared the news might not be good. Truth be told, he was scared as hell.

He entered the door to the conference room to see Dr. Jacobs and four other doctors, all young—in their early forties, he guessed. One was Japanese, which was strangely comforting. His suspicions had been accurate. The expression on Dr. Jacobs's face was not how you want your doctor to look.

After the introductions, Dr. Jacobs invited him to sit down then said, "Well, Kenji, unfortunately the news isn't very good. The MRI shows there's extensive damage to the tissue in your right foot. Our choices are very limited."

"How limited?'

"I'm sorry," he said grimly, "but I'm afraid we're going to have to amputate your foot."

Kenji thought he had prepared himself for whatever news the doctors would deliver but realized he had been kidding himself. The horrible knot in his gut he had felt so many years ago in the aftermath of his parent's death gripped him like a serpent, causing him to involuntarily giggle, not the reaction the doctors were expecting. He took several deep breaths before blurting the first thought that came into his head, "Will I ever be able to play golf again?"

Dr. Schultz answered the question. "Yes, Mr. Watanabe, I think there's a good possibility that you *will* be able to play golf after some rehabilitation. Orthopedics is my specialty, and I've treated quite a number of people who have lost limbs, mostly due to diabetes. Also, I've fitted prostheses to returning vets who were young and healthy and wanted to participate in sports."

Kenji, still in shock, with a crooked smile on his face, merely said, "Oh."

"At MIT and Brown University lots of new work has been performed in terms of the quality and usability of prostheses," Dr. Schultz said. "I know of one company that's building prostheses specifically for golfers. Kenji, you appear to be in top-notch physical condition, and all your vital signs are excellent. The next big question we face is how good the blood circulation in your leg is. Ideally we'll leave you with about half of the leg below the knee. This will give you the best ability to control the prosthesis."

The doctors' prognosis finally hit home with a giant thud. In moments of his gravest fears, Kenji had visualized that he might have to have his foot removed, perhaps at the ankle, and now they were telling him he would lose half of his lower leg or more. *This can't be true*, he thought. *Please, God, please don't let them cut off my leg.* Old feelings of loss overwhelmed him once again as if he were still a seventeen-year-old kid. He sat there unmoving, numb, wondering how he could live his life with only one leg. None of it made any sense.

"Why do you want to amputate my leg?" he asked. "I thought I had a foot problem?"

Dr. Jacobs rose from his chair to put an arm around Kenji's shoulders then bent down to gaze in his eyes and explain the situation. "Kenji, I'm sorry to just spring this on you. The reason for the mid-calf amputation is your blood circulation. The issue is distance. Your foot is farther from the pump, your heart. Experience has proven that in cases like yours foot-only amputations fail frequently due to inadequate blood circulation to the lower leg."

Suddenly angry and not wanting to hear one more word, Kenji stood up, eyes blazing. "I'll be damned if you're going to cut anything off me," he said. "I'm done." Without a further word, he limped out the door, down the hallway toward the elevator.

"Kenji, wait a minute!" called Dr. Jacobs, who rushed to catch up to him.

"No, you wait a minute. What are you guys, butchers? I came here for help, and all I'm getting are lectures on capillaries and a lot of other stuff I don't understand. You and your merry band of brothers can go straight to hell!"

The elevator doors opened, and Kenji got on, as did Dr. Jacobs. Kenji stood there, shaking uncontrollably, tears rolling like wet blobs down his face. Instantly recognizing that his patient had gone into shock, Dr. Jacobs put his arms around him to provide some warmth, embarrassed that he had rushed the dissemination of information and caused this mess.

"Kenji, listen to me. You're in shock. You need to get warm. Let me check you into the hospital to get you stabilized. I apologize for telling you all of this so quickly. I'm so sorry."

Dr. Jacobs punched the "up" button on the elevator as Kenji clung to him, shoulders heaving in sobs, his skin clammy and damp, not cognizant of the others in the elevator who stood staring. The doctor quickly led him to a private room and got him, still fully clothed, settled into bed with warm blankets and injected a strong sedative to calm him down. Even though he heard his name paged over the loudspeaker system numerous times, Dr. Jacobs didn't leave Kenji's side for several hours. His physician's oath kept running through his head: *First do no harm. First do no harm.* After the medication had done its trick, and Kenji had drifted off to sleep, the doctor hit "redial" on Kenji's cell phone. A woman answered the phone. "Hello."

"Hello, this is Dr. Mark Jacobs at Queens Medical Center in Honolulu. Who is this please?"

"Lilly Yamada. Is Kenji all right?"

"Yes, he's resting comfortably, but he had a minor meltdown earlier today, and I think it would be advisable if some of Kenji's family were here to give him some support. Are you family?"

"No, Kenji doesn't have any family, but he has several friends who fill that role. I'm one of them. I'll be there as soon as possible."

"Thank you. That will be very helpful."

Lilly hung up the phone and called Vince, telling him what the doctor had said. "Can you fly me to Honolulu?" she asked.

"When?"

"Right now. Kenji needs us."

"Meet me at the airport, and pack a bag," Vince said. "We may need to stay a few days."

Lilly quickly tossed a few outfits and her toiletries into a carryon bag and rushed out the door in less than ten minutes. Vince was already waiting for her at the airport when she arrived.

"What the hell happened to Kenji?" he asked.

"I'm not sure. I told you everything I know. What I *do* know is that he needs some support right now, so whatever prognosis they gave him must not be good."

They arrived in Honolulu in the midst of afternoon rush hour traffic. Vince, feeling frustrated and anxious, negotiated the rental car slowly toward the hospital.

"Kenji is such a level-headed, fun-loving guy," he told Lilly. "I can't imagine him having a meltdown or what prompted it."

"He's a lot more tenderhearted than he shows to the world," Lilly admitted.

"Yeah, I guess you would know more about that side of him. I always figured there were a lot of layers to his personality that he didn't share with us guys, but this is a real shocker."

They arrived at the hospital and immediately sought out Kenji's room, concerned and apprehensive, not knowing what they would find. They slipped quietly into his room to find him lying in a hospital bed, both side barriers in their full and upright position, his body covered with several blankets. They stood listening and watching for the rise and fall of his chest, both of them heaving a sigh of relief when he took a breath. *Thank God he isn't dead again*, Vince thought.

Lilly approached Kenji's almost still form, undid the latch to lower one side of the bed, and bent over. "Hi, sweetheart. How are you doing?" she whispered in his ear.

Kenji opened his eyes, wondering how Lilly had gotten there and why she had come. He struggled to sit up and rubbed his eyes as if to erase an apparition from his sight. Was he dead? Was she a ghost? Where was Mia? If these were ghosts, why wasn't Mia here? He was so confused.

"Hi, Kenji. It's Vince. How are you feeling, buddy?"

"Where am I?"

He felt loving arms wrap around him, gently rocking him back and forth. Lilly made soft, soothing sounds. "Shush, sweetie. It's going to be all right. Everything is going to be all right."

"Thank you, Mia Mouse," he mumbled as he drifted off to sleep again, unaware of his friends' startled expressions.

* * *

Early the next morning, Dr. Jacobs stopped by to see Kenji during rounds. "Oh, good," he said. "I see you're awake. How are you feeling, Kenji?"

"Like I woke up from a bad dream. I have a terrible headache."

"That's to be expected. I prescribed a strong sedative yesterday so you could get some rest."

"Thank you, I think. What happened yesterday? All I remember is getting on the elevator. Everything else is a blank, except I remember Mia, my dead wife, came to visit me."

"That was probably a side effect of the drug. I'm sorry, Kenji. It wasn't real. But your friends, Lilly and Vince, are here."

"Oh," he said, clearly disappointed.

"Do you remember our meeting in the conference room yesterday?"

"Vaguely. Listen, Doc, is there some way you can operate on my foot and remove the damaged tissue?"

"No, I'm sorry, Kenji. The capillary damage is far too great for that." He attempted to soften the blow as much as possible. "As I told you yesterday, you will be able to play golf again with the help of a prosthesis. When you're ready, we need to talk about a schedule for the next few weeks. Let me know when you're ready to talk about it, okay?"

"Let's talk about it now."

Dr. Jacobs, as gently as possible, restated the need for amputation and gave Kenji a short version of why it was necessary.

Kenji listened intently, not saying anything.

"We'd like to give you a complete pre-op physical, today, if you agree."

"Okay."

Encouraged by Kenji's apparent willingness to listen, Dr. Jacobs continued, "After the physical, we'll schedule a date and time for the procedure. You'll likely remain in the hospital for about five days so we can watch you very closely. After that we'll have to see you twice daily for another two weeks to monitor the healing process. In addition around that time, Dr. Schultz will start fitting you with prosthesis. He'll also teach you how to walk with it and gain the mobility you need to do the common things in life like take a shower when you have your prosthesis off."

Kenji felt numb, sad. He heard what the doctor was saying but felt helpless and unable to stop the amputation train that was racing toward a totally different life for him.

"You'll get a booklet that explains all of this. It includes some other information, like getting your bathroom modified with grab bars in the shower and things like that. Since you live in Kona, I suggest that you get a condo here in Honolulu for maybe a month or so to make it easy for yourself."

Easy? This whole amputation thing wasn't going to be *easy. This guy must be crazy*, Kenji thought. The hard truth is that this situation is my own fault. *I should have paid closer attention to my foot and had it looked at sooner.*

Ever pragmatic, Kenji asked, "What's the next step? What's the timing of all this, Dr. Jacobs?"

"We'd like to do the surgery as soon as possible. There's no reason to delay once the decision has been made. Your foot no longer works for the job it was designed for, and we want to amputate it as soon as possible. Let's do the physical today. Then I'll call you to schedule a time for the surgery. We need about three days' notice to reserve the operating room and fit the surgery into our schedules. Today is Thursday, so assuming you pass the physical, let's tentatively plan for next Tuesday. Hopefully one of your friends can be with you during the first few days that you're on your own in the condo. You'll need someone to help you get around or assist you in case you trip over something. The alternative is to hire a nurse's aide. We have a list of people we can contact if you prefer to do it that way."

"I'll see what I can arrange," Kenji said. "Strange, isn't it? This is almost like a genetic thing."

"What do you mean?"

"Oh, nothing much. My dad had his leg cut off too. A German hand grenade caused his injury during World War II. So, like father, like son, I guess."

"How did your father manage with his prosthesis?

"Fine, Doc, just fine. He never made a big deal out of it." He thought about his father's stoic, non-complaining nature, which brightened Kenji's outlook a bit. *Maybe this surgery won't be the end of my world after all*, he thought.

"So, Kenji, I've been dying to ask you, what does it feel like to hit a golf ball perfectly each time?"

"Awesome. It's totally awesome."

"Thanks for sharing. You've made life miserable for me and my golfing colleagues just knowing that we don't have your gift," Dr. Jacobs said with a chuckle. "Okay. Let's get started on your pre-op."

Dr. Jacobs examined his patient from top to bottom, looking for any additional signs of damage from the lightning strike, but he found nothing awry. A nurse checked Kenji's heart rate and blood pressure. He had to pee in a plastic cup and give a blood sample for more tests before another doctor came in to run an EKG.

Dr. Jacobs told Kenji what they were looking for with each test. "I'll get an orderly to take you down to X-ray to make sure your lungs are clear. You're the most interesting patient we've had in a long time. You're going to get the very best of our skills and care in the weeks ahead. Also, I'd like to schedule a round of golf with you about three months from now. I'll even fly to Kona to play it."

"You're on, Doc. Fifty bucks that I can beat you, peg leg and all?"

"I'm not taking that bet." He shook his head, laughing as he continued on to other patients, relieved that Kenji had agreed to the surgery knowing it would probably save his life.

About noon, Lilly and Vince peeked into the hospital room to see Kenji sitting calmly as he filled out forms.

"Hey, Kenji. How are you doing?" Lilly asked.

"Lilly, Vince, what are you doing here? They told me my friends were here, but I was zoned out on drugs."

"I decided it was time to take Lilly for a spin in the airplane, and here we are," Vince said.

"Well, your timing is impeccable. I'm having part of my leg chopped off next week, and I need to find a condo here for a month's recuperation. Want to go looking with me?"

Vince and Lilly exchanged quizzical glances.

Did we miss something? Lilly thought. *He doesn't look or sound any different than usual. Perhaps the doctor had overstated the 'meltdown situation.'* Still, she felt a twinge of doubt, or was it jealousy rearing its ugly head when Kenji had talked in his sleep to 'Mia Mouse'?

"Sure, let's go condo-hunting. Do you need a lift back to Kona this afternoon?" she said.

"That would be great. Thank you very much."

Kenji limped out of the medical center with his friends as he perused a list Dr. Jacobs's receptionist had given him with condos in the area that rented by the week or month. Lilly and Vince teased him and laughed, which was just the distraction he needed to keep from thinking about his devastating diagnosis. *Thank God Vince and Lilly are here to help me find a condo*, he thought. He wasn't going to make a decision today, but he wanted to get an idea of what was available and where it might be located.

They found a number of multistory condos within a mile of the hospital; they checked out both one- and two-bedroom units. Kenji secretly hoped that his friends would come to visit, and he wanted to offer his hospitality and a place for them to sleep. He tentatively decided on an upscale building; the condo of choice was spacious, with a large living room, a wall of glass with a sliding door that led to a spacious balcony with an extraordinary view of the Pacific, two large bedrooms, two bathrooms, and an elevator, which would come in handy.

"What do you think of this unit?" he asked Lilly.

It was furnished to his taste, tropical yet elegant. The furniture and appliances looked brand new, as if none of them had been used. He bounced rather awkwardly on the mattress in the master suite, grinning because it wasn't too stiff. He liked the feel of a softly cushioned mattress that enveloped its occupants. He sat for a moment as he took in the sun sparkling off the blue Pacific and noted the floor-to-ceiling view from the master suite. Lilly looked like she was about to say something suggestive but didn't, probably because Vince was having a bounce too, joyful as a kid. As thrifty as he was, Kenji rationalized that with all the misery that lie ahead the least he could do was stay in a comfortable home away from home.

Lilly replied, "It's lovely, Kenji. I could picture you living here. The view is fabulous."

While he was encouraged by her comment, he wondered whether she would continue to be so enchanted with the condo once the harsh reality of dating a one-legged guy set in. He planned to ask her if she could stay with him here for a week or so, but he was doubtful she would agree.

Later that day, they flew back to Kona, the conversation at a lull. Kenji remained silent, lost in his own thoughts.

CHAPTER 18

Over a quiet dinner that night with Lilly, he finally shared the details regarding what had happened during the day in Honolulu. She was shocked. She had no idea that his foot problems were so serious. She fought to maintain her composure as a feeling of helplessness welled up in her.

"Oh, sweetie. I'm so sorry. What do you think about all of this? What are you feeling now? What can I do for you?"

"I don't know," he confessed. "I feel sad, depressed, and totally bummed by the situation. I had a vague idea this could possibly happen, but I went on my merry way, playing golf, ignoring all the signs. It was such a jolt when Dr. Jacobs told me they'd have to amputate half of my lower leg instead of just my foot. I guess I just lost it. It still hasn't sunk in yet, but what choice do I have?"

Lilly reached across the table to touch his hand, wanting to reassure him. "It'll be fine, Kenji."

"The one positive thing I learned is that great progress has been made in the area of prosthetics, and there's a good possibility that I'll still be able to play golf. I remember my dad's prosthesis as a cumbersome, ugly thing, though he never complained, ever. I found out that three of the five doctors that were poking and prodding on me are golfers. They've assured me they'll do all they can to help me get back to golf. It would be really sad if I couldn't use my gift for something worthwhile."

"What happens next? When are you scheduled for surgery? Kenji, I'm serious. You tell me what I can do to help you through all of this. Being there for each other is what relationships are all about."

Kenji was so relieved by her last comment. He had thought that a beautiful woman like Lilly might not want to be stuck with a one-legged man. But now the nagging fear of her possible rejection was starting to dissipate. *She's not going to abandon me*, he thought. *She's made of stronger stuff than I gave her credit for.*

He outlined the next steps: surgery, rehabilitation, and spending a few weeks in Honolulu. He explained the sequence of events regarding fitting the prosthesis and his learning how to use it. Finally he mentioned that Dr. Jacobs had said that someone needed to be with him after he got out of the hospital. "Just in case I trip or something," he said with a smile.

How can he be so cavalier about something as horrific as losing part of his leg? Lilly wondered, but responded as calmly and matter-of-factly as possible, "I still haven't signed a lease for my new office, so I'm free to help you as long as you need me. Of course I'll help you, Kenji."

For a moment they stared into each other's eyes, silently acknowledging that their relationship had just deepened to a new level.

Kenji felt a lump in his throat, one of gratitude for this wonderful, beautiful creature. He wondered how he had gotten so lucky. *Thank you, God,* he thought. *Thank you.*

"You're amazing, Lilly. I can't thank you enough for being so understanding and supportive." Feeling the need for physical contact, he reached out to clasp her hand. He wanted to demonstrate the love he felt in his heart but was still unable to articulate it.

Lilly fought to keep a smile on her face even though her heart was breaking for this incredible man and the challenges he would soon face.

* * *

After Kenji got home that night, he checked his answering machine. Sure enough, there was a message from Dr. Jacobs to let him know the surgery was scheduled for Tuesday morning. Kenji immediately called Stu to tell him the news.

Stu wasn't surprised, since he'd been treating the ulcers on Kenji's foot and had some idea about what could happen. He had encouraged Kenji to seek further medical attention all along, as he was worried about his friend's situation. Kenji, however, had been so consumed with golf that he kept putting it off, saying, "It'll be all right. I need to focus on golf and develop my gift." Procrastination, as it turned out, had not been a winning strategy.

"I'll call Vince and Ernie in the morning and let them know what's going on," Kenji said. "The surgery is scheduled for next Tuesday, so I'll be missing out on golf for a while."

"I've been reading about the new prosthetics, and I think there's a good chance that you will be able to play golf once you get through this. Just know that I'll be praying for a successful outcome."

"Thank you, Stu. I'll need all the prayers I can get."

The next morning, Kenji asked Vince to meet him at Starbucks for a quick coffee before work. He needed to tell his friend and coach that he wouldn't be playing golf for a while.

After Kenji told him the news, Vince said, "That's okay. Whatever you need, buddy. I'll be there with you every step of the way." He chuckled softly. "That was a pretty insensitive comment, wasn't it? Even Kenji, however, couldn't help but laugh at the gallows humor.

The one who was totally astounded was Ernie. As Kenji outlined the course of action to him on the phone, Ernie was flabbergasted and asked whether he should come over and sit with him. "Do you want to talk about it?" he asked. "What can I do for you?"

What a sterling guy, Kenji thought. "That's not necessary. I'm dealing with it okay for now. I may have to hook up with you later, though. I'll probably be a total mess by the time I get through the surgery."

"You got it, buddy—whatever you need."

Kenji hung up the phone and sat at his kitchen table, depressed even though he had faked a brave outlook to his friends. He gazed out the window to admire the lush landscaping. He watched the birds lined up like miniature 747s to take their morning dip in the once-colorful tiled birdbath that jutted up in the center of the yard. His mom used to sit and watch the daily parade too, telling him after school about all the various species of birds that had come to call that day. How had his father managed being on his feet all day at the shop with his prosthesis? He never had talked about it. His leg must have hurt sometimes, but Kenji never once had heard him gripe about it. *I hope I can learn to be as pragmatic as he was,* Kenji thought. *He wouldn't expect any less of me. I've got to accept what is, not how I want things to be.*

Thinking about his father spurred Kenji into action. He limped into his office to fire up his computer and set about the tasks at hand. Ever practical, he began to put together a plan for the next six weeks. He did a budget and decided that, based on the number of trips Lilly would make to Honolulu, he would rent a car for the month. He phoned a car rental agency and worked out a deal so that a car would be parked in the lot at the airport, available for Lilly whenever she needed transportation. This would eliminate the need for her to fill out the paperwork as she came and went. Kenji was completely rational, making a dozen little decisions so he could feel some sense of control while tamping down the growing fear that gnawed at his insides.

Next he decided on the condo they had previewed and liked, phoned the leasing agent, made arrangements to rent the property, and checked that item off his list. *I'm getting really anal about the details,* he thought as he made out a shopping list of groceries to buy to have on hand at the condo. Dealing with the minute details was a coping mechanism for Kenji to keep his mind occupied. Energy vibrated through him as he thought through the details of his impending daily life in Honolulu; he wanted to make things comfortable for Lilly. The shopping list was getting longer and longer as he fantasized about their needs for food and supplies. He added toilet paper, coffee, steaks, rice, potatoes, and other fresh vegetables to the list. *I wonder if Lilly can cook,* he thought. He didn't have an answer to that one; it was a subject they never had discussed. He added papayas and mangos to the list, knowing they contained an enzyme to help speed up the healing process.

He looked through his closet and decided which clothes to pack. He purposely chose long, loose pants rather than shorts, not quite confident enough to face baring his soon-to-be stump of a leg to anyone, even Lilly.

* * *

On Sunday, Kenji and Lilly boarded the 7:03 a.m. flight to Honolulu. His surgery was scheduled for Tuesday morning at nine. He knew he had to go without food or liquids after midnight the night before surgery, so he planned on taking Lilly to a nice restaurant for a gourmet meal for the next two evenings. Hopefully they could relax in congenial surroundings and be distracted from frightening thoughts about the surgery.

Kenji had discussed with Lilly the probable sequence of events that would unfold in the next few weeks. He would be in surgery for one to two hours. Then it would take two to three hours for him to wake up in recovery. He should be assigned to a private room by midday, if Lilly would care to come and check on him.

"If I say something stupid, please don't hold it against me," he kidded her.

The doctor had told him he would be groggy and pretty much out of it most of the day; the throbbing pain would be calmed with heavy medication. He suggested to Lilly that she might drop in and see him on Wednesday and then go back to Kona since there wasn't much she could do for him during the first few days.

"You've got this all figured out, huh?" Lilly said. "Let's make a deal right now. You focus on getting well, and I'll come and go as I see fit, okay? I'm not going anywhere. I'm not going back to Kona any time soon. I know you're trying to have some sense of control over everything that's going on, but you can stop worrying about me. I'm a big girl and perfectly capable of making decisions and taking care of me *and* you." She said her piece lovingly but firmly.

Kenji smiled at Lilly's unabashed comments, thinking that she was so different from Mia, who would have
simply agreed to his plans. Lilly was so independent, and
surprisingly to him, her certainty comforted him.

After unpacking, getting settled in the condo, and making a trip to the supermarket to purchase supplies, Lilly
and Kenji worked side by side to put the groceries away.
I like this, he thought, admiring the efficiency with which
Lilly handled item after item, making logical decisions
about where to stash their purchases.

After everything was in order, they took turns shower-
ing and got dressed for an evening out. Kenji had made
a reservation for dinner at the restaurant at the Royal
Hawaiian Hotel, better known as the 'pink palace.' It was
one of the hotels lined up like soldiers at attention along
a stretch of Waikiki Beach. They strolled hand in hand
through the lush, green hotel garden that was splashed
with flowering hibiscus and bougainvillea.

"This is such a beautiful place," said Lilly, stunning in a
white flowing dress, the full skirt barely skimming the top
of her knees.

They stopped at the flower shop in the lobby, where
Kenji bought an orchid for her hair that she clipped on one
side of her shiny locks. Lilly insisted on buying a single
gardenia for a boutonnière that she tucked into Kenji's la-
pel. He had dressed with care as well, resplendent in dark
tan slacks and a crisp white shirt topped by a white dinner
jacket, but he wore no tie, as was the custom on the islands.

The hostess seated them at an outdoor table that overlooked the sea, the air fresh with the fragrance of flowers,

a soft sea breeze flowing in off the water. "Great choice. If the food here is as good as the ambiance, we're in for a treat," Lilly commented. "I haven't been here before."

"Stick with me, kid. There are a lot of wonderful restaurants in Honolulu. We'll make it our mission to try the best of them," he promised.

They ordered freshly caught mahi-mahi for their entree and a bottle of Champagne, as if to celebrate the loss of a leg was the most natural thing on Earth. Lilly looked particularly lovely this evening, and Kenji wondered what possibilities the night might bring. Lilly kept the conversation light, kidding about the two of them out on the town and away from the prying eyes of their friends in Kona. A string orchestra played dance music at the far end of the dining room while couples swayed to the lush sounds of violins. After dinner, even though he knew it would be painful, Kenji asked Lilly if she'd like to dance. The handsome couple made their way across the room, secretly enjoying the veiled looks of envy from other patrons. As they danced to "The Way You Look Tonight," the closeness of their bodies seemed to forecast the inevitable conclusion to the evening.

Later at the condo, much to Lilly's surprise, Kenji kissed her over and over again, gently holding her face in his strong hands and running his fingers through that lustrous hair that cascaded down her back. "Lilly, I love you. I love you," he murmured into her hair. "You're the most beautiful woman I've ever seen. I love you and I want you."

Lilly's body melted into Kenji's as they edged their way toward the master bedroom. She slowly took off his jacket, unbuttoned his shirt, and ran her gentle hands over the firm muscles of his smooth chest. Kenji unzipped her dress, and it fell to the floor in a heap of virtuous white chiffon as he ran his fingers down her throat, kisses exploring the golden skin, each little valley a mysterious adventure. A little moan escaped Lilly's lips as his hand caressed her breast. "Oh, Kenji," she said. "I've waited so long for you to make love to me."

He continued the exploration he had dreamed about so many times, their bodies tuned to the vibrations of their hearts like ancient islanders drumming louder and louder until the crescendo at last washed over them.

"You are spectacular, Lilly, my love," Kenji murmured in her ear.

"You're pretty spectacular yourself, darlin', more like a volcano," she teased, sated and happy.

"It's all those pent-up feelings finally bubbling to the surface," he said with a laugh.

They finally slept, spoon fashion, the warmth of their bodies giving them both solace.

* * *

The next day was Monday, one day before the surgery, and they agreed to do some sightseeing just to keep busy and to stay focused on each other rather than dwell on the horror that lie ahead. They toured the *USS Arizona* memorial, somber at the thought of those entombed below. "My dad saw the battleships get bombed." Kenji said. He pointed toward the northwest. "He was an eighteen-year-old kid hiking with his buddies in those hills."

Later they drove to the National Memorial Cemetery of the Pacific, known to the locals as the Punchbowl. More than thirteen thousand soldiers and sailors who had died during World War II had been laid to rest there.

In the late afternoon, Kenji wanted to show Lilly various aspects of the island, so he drove for an hour to the Turtle Bay Resort on the north shore of the island, which featured 21 Degrees North, the area's signature restaurant. The floor-to-ceiling windows overlooked the rolling surf, which was stormy at times. They ordered the five-course tasting menu in order to sample as many of the chef's culinary creations as possible. Lingering over dessert and coffee, the lovers spoke in hushed tones, giggling at times, about what they would do to each other once they returned to the condo. The unspoken yearning in their eyes spoke of their both wanting one more night of pleasure while their world still felt normal.

After driving back to Honolulu, they rushed into the condo, sexual desires simmering. They hurriedly tugged off each other's clothes the minute they entered the door. The throbbing need was visceral, taking them to new heights of pleasure. After cuddling for a while and whispering in the night, the need for intimacy surged again. They slowed down, the urgency over, as they made love the second time with quiet passion and great tenderness.

CHAPTER 19

Dawn and stark reality came early that morning. It was April 6, 1999, a day neither Kenji nor Lilly would ever forget. They packed Kenji's bag to take to the hospital. Somehow they were both serene in the knowledge that everything would be all right.

Lilly stayed with Kenji through the admitting process at the hospital while he filled out the mountains of paperwork. Most of it had to do with releasing the hospital from any liability. In addition to the typical forms, he had to sign consent forms for the surgery, a sobering task.

Once Kenji was assigned a room, Lilly discreetly left while he got undressed and put on the flimsy cotton gown that seemed to stay open in the back no matter how he tied the ties. He held it around himself as he sat on the edge of the bed. The nurse gave Lilly the "all-clear" signal to return to the room and handed Kenji a felt-tipped marker to draw a circle around his leg at the location where it was going to be amputated. This gave Kenji pause and made him wonder about the proficiency of the surgery team. The nurse was all business as she prepped him for surgery, hooking up an IV and shaving the meager hair off his right leg. She inserted medication into the IV line and told him he soon would feel relaxed and drowsy.

The anesthesiologist, Dr. Newman, stopped by, introduced himself, and explained his role in the surgery. Kenji nodded, feeling drowsy, not totally comprehending what was happening.

Just then, Vince, Ernie and Stu bustled into the room full of good cheer. "Hi, Kenji. We came to lend some moral support," they chorused.

He was surprised to see his friends, especially Stu whose free time was limited. He hadn't expected them to come but was grateful they had. It was all such a blur, but he felt better knowing they were there.

"Looks like you're ready to rock and roll," Stu said with a smile.

"Jus' call me Elvis," Kenji said with a giggle.

The medication had really kicked in and gave him a warm, pleasant sensation, which calmed his fears. Suddenly it was time to go. Two burly young orderlies dressed in surgical greens, with slippers on their feet, transferred him to a gurney and guided it out the door to the hallway. Lilly gave him a gentle kiss and squeezed his hand. "You'll be fine, sweetheart," she told him. "I'll see you in a while, okay?"

"We'll see you later, Kenji. We'll try to keep Lilly out of trouble—not a bad way to spend the day," Vince teased.

Kenji lay on the gurney, a goofy grin on his face, as if he were headed off for day at an amusement park. In a slurred voice, he mumbled something about a toucan's bright, colorful feathers.

"He's really out of it," murmured Stu. "Not to worry. This is all part of the drill," he informed the others. He noted the somber, far away look on Ernie's face, his warm brown eyes clouded in deep thought.

"Ernie, are you okay? We need to stay upbeat and positive for Kenji's sake."

"Yes, I'm fine. Sorry. My mind is whirring with algorithms."

The orderlies wheeled Kenji down a long corridor, the lights overhead passing in a blur. Once in the operating room, the orderlies lifted him onto the operating table in one swift movement.

Kenji had a picture in his mind of how the surgery room would look from having watched medical shows on television, all bright lights and high-tech equipment. He wondered about the regular old brown metal cabinets lined up against one wall, doors open, shelves stocked haphazardly with medical supplies. Not so high-tech after all. Dr. Schultz, the surgeon, came into the operating room, his hands held up as he air-dried them after scrubbing. He wore surgical scrubs and a green cap; a facemask hung around his neck. Smiling, he said, "Hi, Kenji. Are you ready for all of this?"

"Not really, but guess I have no choice."

The sound of classical music filled the room, twin operatic voices trilling in a triumphant melody. Kenji vaguely remembered the song from *The Marriage of Figaro*, which was featured in the movie *The Shawshank Redemption* and felt soothed, his spirits uplifted.

Dr. Schultz introduced the surgery team to his patient then told the group, "This is the fellow who was struck by lightning. He's quite a celebrity golfer but has a little trouble with his right foot, so we're going to get rid of it."

One of the attending surgeons chimed in, "Dr. Newman is going to give you an injection now, Mr. Watanabe. You'll go to sleep, and you won't feel a thing. Just start counting backward from one hundred."

Kenji looked down and mumbled, "Goodbye, leg! I'm going to miss you!"

This brought smiles to the surgery team. Out of nowhere, fear, like a thirty-foot wave on North Shore, assaulted Kenji's brain, causing tears to tumble down his face. He was already mourning the loss of his leg. *God, help me* was his last conscious thought as the anesthetic kicked in to carry him off to Never Never Land.

* * *

As a nurse tucked a warmed blanket around Kenji, he woke up shivering from head to toe. "Thank you," he said through chattering teeth. He surmised that he was in the recovery room; he had tubes running into one arm and oxygen flowing into him through a nose tube. He heard the beeps and noticed the little machine next to his bed, its lights blinking on and off, graphs curving up and down.

"Hi, Mr. Watanabe," the nurse said as she checked his pulse. "How are you feeling?"

"Okay, I guess. I'm really thirsty, though. Can I have some water?"

"Not yet, but I'll give you a teaspoonful of ice chips to take the dryness away. Later you'll be able to drink some water."

Kenji felt dopey and didn't really know why he was here. Over the next thirty minutes, his mind began to clear and then he remembered. He looked down, hoping against hope to see toes on two feet sticking up from under the light blankets. "Oh, my God. It's gone," he moaned as he saw only one mound under the blanket. He didn't feel any different, and he swore his leg was still there. He had read about phantom limb syndrome in the pre-op literature. It was a common condition that would likely be with him the rest of his life.

He was still groggy from the drugs, but as his head cleared somewhat he became determined to overcome his disability and come out on top like his father had. He murmured to himself, "Let the healing begin. I shall be the best amputation patient they have in the hospital. I shall do everything I am supposed to do. I will use a positive mental attitude to speed up my healing process, because there's a big, beautiful green golf course out there waiting for me." Nary a thought of Lilly crossed his mind.

The surgery had gone according to plan. When the orderly wheeled Kenji into a private room on the sixth floor, Kenji was still a bit dopey, as expected. Lilly and the guys were waiting to greet him. "Kenji, darling, how are you feeling?" she asked.

"I'm fine, but my foot hurts," he mumbled. He was surprised to see Lilly. *What is she doing here?* he wondered.

Lilly's heart was breaking as she watched the love of her life fight off his demons. *Toughen up. Be strong for him,* she thought as she peered at the empty space where his foot and lower leg had once been. She didn't have any doubts about being in a relationship with a one-footed, one-legged man. It didn't faze her in the slightest, as she knew Kenji was strong of character, body, and mind. Sure, there would be challenges along the way, but she knew in her heart that he—and they—would prevail. The tenderness of his lovemaking had erased any doubts she may have had. She chided herself for being silly and jealous of his passion for golf. Lilly was so in love with Kenji that nothing else mattered. She sat by his bedside holding his hand, thanking God that he had come through the surgery successfully.

Stu, Vince, and Ernie couldn't help the shock they felt seeing Kenji lying in bed with only one foot thrust up under the sheet. Each put on a brave face to cover their thoughts.

"Hey, Kenji. You'll be out playing golf in no time," said Stu.

The words didn't sink in. *Golf? I'm going to play golf? What the hell is he talking about?*

"No, I don't think so," Kenji said. "My golfing days are over. How many one-legged golfers have you seen at Makalei?"

"You'll be the exception," Vince said. "You'll be just fine."

He didn't believe them. He had steeled himself for the trauma that he was going to face, but hadn't considered some of the basic degradations of hospital recovery, including using a bedpan, especially for a bowel movement. *I shouldn't have had that big dinner last night,* he thought. *Stupid. Stupid.* He accepted the nurses' matter-of-fact ministrations to his body: washing and powdering, taking his blood pressure, checking his temperature, lifting his gown to expose his private parts. By nature he was a modest man. The poking and prodding made him feel bared, embarrassed, and out of sorts. His vow to maintain a positive outlook diminished at every turn.

Lilly excused herself from the room when the nurses or doctors came in, intuitively knowing Kenji would prefer it. She was there to be supportive, not to add to his discomfort. The first day passed, then the second. Her demeanor remained bright, upbeat, and positive, but serious too, as she knew he would need time to adjust to the trauma. *He'll probably get angry before he comes to accept this,* she thought. She feared his reaction to the loss was much like mourning the death of a loved one. On the third day, Kenji's anger set in.

"Goddamn it, why did this have to happen to me?" he asked, as the rage welled up inside. "I've got more important things to do than lie around in a hospital with one foot. This whole thing sucks!"

"You're right. It sucks," agreed Lilly. She knew from past experience that after having gone under general anesthesia patients aren't always very rational. Add in the pain medication that follows, and it's as if the self-control part of the brain isn't functioning and deeper feelings roar to the surface. *This too shall pass*, she thought.

"I've had enough grief in my life. How much more does God want from me? Does he want the other leg too?"

"No, I think one is quite enough," Lilly replied calmly.

"How the hell am I ever going to play golf again?" he asked her. "I'm not sure I believe all this happy horseshit the doctors have been telling me."

Lilly took a seat on the edge of his bed and held his hand in hers. "Sweetheart, I know you're feeling angry and impatient," she said, "and this whole thing is very frightening, but you have to keep the faith. You have a great team of doctors who've assured you that with prosthesis you'll be able to play golf again. They've said you'll be able to function just fine. This is the hard part, the waiting, not knowing. Perhaps the lesson you need to learn here is patience."

"I don't need to hear this, Lilly. In fact why are you still here? Why the hell don't you go back to Kona?" he lashed out.

"Nice try, Kenji, but I'm staying. You won't get rid of me that easily. You're cranky — I understand that — but I for one am going to rise above it." She smiled sweetly. "Is there anything I can get for you? Ice chips? A hot shower? A roll in the hay?" she teased, a glint in her eye.

Kenji couldn't help himself; he laughed out loud. "You're irreverent to the core — one of your better qualities,

I might add. I'm sorry I've been such a bear. I'm angry and upset, but please don't leave. As much as I hate to say it, I need you."

"And I need you," she replied quietly.

Kenji's anger slowly subsided, Lilly's constant upbeat demeanor helping to soften his fall from perfection. Both were avid readers, so Kenji escaped into light reading, anything to keep his mind off his new reality. His golfing buddies stayed until late in the day, encouraging him with words of support, filling him in on the gossip around Kona, and talking about their last golf outing and who had won the cash. They had tacitly agreed to keep the conversation light and cheerful while Kenji was in this first phase of recovery. "We're flying home, my friend, but each of us will come back to visit once you get out of the hospital," Vince informed him.

"Thanks for coming, guys," Kenji replied. "It means the world to me that you'd take the time out of your busy schedules to stay here with me."

"No big deal," Ernie said. "You'd do the same for any of us. We'll see you in a week or so, okay?"

Kenji wondered how the sleeping arrangements at the condo would work out but didn't say anything. "Awesome. That would be great. Safe travel, guys, and thanks again."

Each of the guys shook Kenji's hand, gave Lilly a quick hug, and departed.

* * *

Kenji was a bit of a celebrity in the hospital, Lilly noted. Doctors with varying specialties, none related to Kenji's case, often stopped by to chat. They mostly talked about golf, but the attention kept his spirits from sagging.

On the fourth day, the nurse and a rehab specialist with arms the size of tree trunks came in to get Kenji up and walking on crutches. Lilly excused herself to descend to the coffee shop in the lobby. She needed a break and wanted to give Kenji the space and time he needed to focus on the task at hand.

The surgeon came in twice a day to check on him and gauge the healing process. The nurses changed his dressings often, knowing this was a critical period when infections could occur. When the time was right, they would bind the stub in a pressure bandage to form it in preparation for fitting the prosthesis.

Kenji sat on the examining table, his stump in front of him. He was slowly getting used to the sight of his now deformed body. *Like father, like son,* he thought.

Dr. Jacobs leaned over and removed the dressing. "My goodness, look at you. I'm amazed at how fast you're healing. I'm going to write an order for you to get fitted with a temporary prosthesis today. If you can manage getting around with it, I'll get you out of here so you can heal at home. 'Home' means your condo down the street. You have to come back here to get your stump redressed twice a day, plus we'll start you on physical therapy tomorrow. How does that sound?"

"Terrific," said Kenji. "Is it okay if I take a shower?"

"Now you didn't hear this from me, but I've heard that some amputees have taped a trash bag over the stump, and it worked okay if they were very careful. They say duct tape makes a better seal than masking tape. Again, you didn't hear that from me. The hospital lawyer would cut out my tongue out if he found out I told you this. If you do get your bandage wet, get back over here immediately and get it changed, okay?"

Kenji grinned. "I didn't hear a word you said, Doc, and you've just made my day."

"You're doing fine," Dr. Jacobs told him. "You're in peak physical condition and you have excellent leg strength from all the walking you've done on the golf course."

"Thank you. I'm trying my best." Still, he wondered whether he was really up to the challenge that lay ahead.

CHAPTER 20

Seven days after Kenji's surgery, Dr. Jacobs released him
from the hospital. Kenji now would find out whether he
could learn to navigate in the real world. This was when
he would need Lilly the most. She would help him get in
and out of the compact SUV he had rented at the airport,
up steps, and into the condo complex. Thank God for the
elevator. By the time Kenji got to the living room of the
condo and slumped down on the couch, he was worn out
yet determined to take a shower to wash off the hospital
smell, as if to erase the whole experience. He had his
temporary prosthesis on, but he couldn't put much weight
on it yet. He needed to spend more time walking so he
could learn to balance himself.

"Lilly, I'm going to take a shower," he said. "Will you get a large trash bag and the duct tape for me, please?" He couldn't wait to get in the shower on his own.

Lilly had purchased a box of thirteen-gallon trash bags and a roll of duct tape just for this purpose. She grinned, a twinkle in her eyes. "Too bad they don't make super-size condoms. Those would be perfect for this application."

"Lilly, didn't you read the instructions that said you're not supposed to make fun of old, handicapped Japanese people?"

"Oh, my. I guess I just forgot, my sweet lopsided friend," she retorted.

Their relationship continued to grow stronger, more comfortable each day, even fun sometimes, despite the circumstances. Both of them had a quirky sense of humor, so their give-and-take sometimes took some weird turns.

"Okay, bag man," she said. "I'm going to get the shower turned on and adjusted for you. Then you're on your own, unless you want me to wash your back."

"I've been looking forward to this for days. I'll see you in about twenty minutes," said Kenji. "If you hear a loud crash, please come and rescue me," he said, only half kidding.

He made his way to the bathroom and carefully placed his crutches next to the shower, so he could reach them, and managed to get himself undressed by balancing on one leg. The traditional Hawaiian dress code of a loose shirt over a pair of baggy pants made that job easier. He reached into the shower, grabbed the safety bar and hopped in, careful not to slip.

Oh, God, this is really glorious, Kenji thought as the hot water cascaded over him, washing away the smell of disinfectant. He stood there, balanced on one foot for several moments, enjoying the almost sexual sensations. *I have to be careful not to get soap in my eyes,* he thought, *because if I have to close them, I could possibly lose my balance.*

Kenji carefully soaped up as much of his body that he could comfortably reach. He grabbed the bottle of shampoo from the built-in shelf and carefully balanced on his one leg while he scrubbed the hospital smell out of his hair. Everything went remarkably well until the rinse cycle. Shampoo got in his eyes, and he lost his balance and slid down to the tiled shower floor with a loud thump.

Lilly, waiting just outside the door like a mother hen guarding her chicks, heard the noise and rushed inside. "Kenji, are you okay?"

"Help me, please. I've fallen."

She opened the shower door to see Kenji, still slippery from soap, sprawled on the floor of the shower. She grabbed the handheld shower tool. "Let's get you rinsed off first," she said, "so I can get a hand on you."

Lilly was very strong for her size, and working together, they were able to get Kenji upright so he could reach the grab bar to pull himself to a standing position with her help.

Calamity averted, Lilly stifled a giggle, "Can you manage or do you want me to dry you off?"

"If you could do my back, that would be helpful. I can manage the rest, I think. I feel so silly for falling." He wasn't the least bit embarrassed in front of Lilly, though he was naked as a newborn baby.

He finished getting dried off and shaved off his whiskers in front of the mirror over the sink while perched precariously on his left leg — all without incident. He removed the baggie from his stump, pleased to see the bandage was still dry.

Kenji, with Lilly's help, passed all the tests of learning how to navigate with the prosthesis. They even giggled at times when some little thing went awry. It was helpful that he had very good balance. Several years ago he had taken yoga classes for a while and learned how to do the "tree" pose, which involves standing on one leg. After just a little practice, he could stand on one leg almost as well as a stork, which served him well, as he did his stork imitation in the bathroom of the condo. Lilly, amused at his description of this venture, kidded him, with a wicked gleam in her eye, "Well, I'll give you a little time, but we could have exciting times in that shower."

"Yes, those grab bars and the anti-slip floor do hold some adventuresome possibilities, don't they?" he replied with a grin.

Their close relationship had evolved to the point where they could joke about Kenji's new condition. Kenji, ever thoughtful, felt it was the best way to approach his "leg thing" so Lilly and his friends wouldn't feel self-conscious around him.

Their days passed in some contentment, which was strange, he thought, considering the circumstances. He discovered a lot of things about Lilly. Yes, she could cook.

In fact, she was a first-rate chef, having taken gourmet cooking classes in California, followed by more advanced training at Le Cordon Bleu during a holiday to France. The meals she prepared were not only delicious, but presented in a unique and creative fashion. Lilly's skills, knowledge, and expertise continually surprised him.

Every day they left the condo to work on Kenji's ability to get around on his own, with Lilly trailing along as a safeguard. There were also the twice-daily trips to the hospital for appointments with the doctor and physical therapists. They sometimes ventured to the post office; Kenji mastered the dozen steps up to the front door with some effort. By mid-afternoon he was usually exhausted, so he'd nap while Lilly, book in hand, sat on the balcony that overlooked the ocean, sometimes dozing in the sun.

Kenji promised a special treat for lunch one day, and both he and Lilly fell in love with the food emporium at Shirokiya's department store, which was located in the Ala Moana Center. As an island native, he knew about the store's history—Shirokiya had started as a dry goods store in Tokyo more than three hundred years ago. Opened in 1959, the current store is Honolulu's version of a Japanese department store food emporium. Different food stalls are dedicated to sushi, sashimi, tempura, saba, soba, and somen. People can come there often and never have the same meal twice.

"The next big job for this afternoon is to figure out where we're going to have dinner tonight. You deserve a night off from chef duties. And I'll be ready for some action after my nap," he teased.

Stu came to visit for a day during the first week, and Kenji invited him to stay at the condo. "Sorry, we can't offer five-star accommodations, but you're more than welcome to sleep on the couch."

Stu accepted this offer with aplomb, saying, "That's fine with me. It'll give us more time together." He was curious about Kenji and Lilly's relationship, but didn't say anything until Lilly left to buy groceries for the dinner she was planning for that evening. "It looks like Lilly's taking good care of you, Kenji," Stu said.

"Yes, she's a treasure,' he replied with a sly grin.

"So what's going on with you two? I didn't realize you two were so close."

"Close enough. So how's your golf game?" Kenji asked, purposely changing the subject.

They talked about golf and the news of the week, including Payne Stewart's win at the U.S. Open. He had beat out Phil Mickelson by one stroke. They agreed that the $625,000 first-place prize money was second in importance to securing a spot on the Ryder Cup team come September.

"I was happy to see Payne win, but I have to admit I started to cheer for John Daly after he birdied the first three holes," Stu said.

The two friends enjoyed the day, the conversation, and especially the gourmet dinner Lilly prepared that evening. The guys continued to talk over a brandy sipped on the balcony as the lights of Waikiki twinkled below. Stu flew back to Kona the next day, never once mentioning Kenji's new status as a one-footed man.

Kenji learned that Lilly was a master at card games—simple ones such as rummy and canasta—and that she was a steely-eyed opponent at poker, bluffing her way when necessary and coming up with a big hand when the pot was ripe with chips.

One night after a fine dinner that Lilly had prepared, they ended up playing gin rummy at the kitchen table. Lilly won as usual. "I can let you win if it would make you feel better," she teased.

"No, that's all right. I'm tough. I can take being beat by a woman," he retorted. "Though I think it's heartless, the way you continually beat a cripple. Have you no shame?"

"Cripple, my ass. Get over yourself."

They had fun playing cards, doing daily chores, and enjoying their forays out into the city, even though Kenji returned exhausted. They hadn't slept in the same bed since Kenji got out of the hospital; Lilly feared she might turn the wrong way in her sleep and injure him somehow. They did lie in his bed and cuddle at night before sleep. The kisses sometimes turned too passionate, which prompted them to back away from each other, and Lilly would retreat to the guest room. She wasn't concerned about it, knowing that when he was ready for lovemaking she would be the first to know.

Every day he told her how much he appreciated her, saying, "I'm so thankful for your good company and support throughout this whole process. Thank you so much for being here with me."

"You're more than welcome," she'd tell him. She basked in his daily praise, like a cat dozing on a sunny perch. *Kenji's such a great guy,* she thought. I don't care how many legs he has. He's definitely a keeper.

Vince and Ernie came to visit separately. The guys had agreed to spread out their visits, just one friend each week so as not to overtire Kenji.

Ernie arrived mid-afternoon looking tanned and relaxed in a business suit, carrying a briefcase and one garment bag.

"Great to see you, Ernie! Thanks for coming," Kenji greeted him at the door and motioned him inside. "Aren't you looking fine, all dressed up."

Ernie chuckled, "I just flew in from Canberra, Australia. I had a meeting with a prospective client."

"So what's going on out there in the big wide world?" asked Kenji, duly impressed.

"Opportunities, my friend, great opportunities. In fact, I've been thinking..."

"Oh, oh. That's always a scary thought," Kenji retorted with a grin as they settled themselves in the living room.

Ernie, usually subtle, dropped a bombshell. "Kenji, I think you're frittering your life away. You're too young to retire. I want you to come work with me."

Kenji laughed out loud, "Yeah, I can see it now. I can fold your tee-shirts, scour your bathroom, organize your store room, then what?"

"You have a lot of common sense and business experience. You have a deft touch at managing people. That's the expertise my company needs, a CEO I can trust, so I can concentrate on writing code for a new software application."

Kenji sat in stunned silence, finally replying, "No, I don't think so, Ernie. I need to concentrate on getting back to some semblance of normalcy in my life and playing golf. But thanks for asking. I am honored that you would even consider me."

It hadn't occurred to Ernie, single minded as he was, that his offer would be declined. "Just think about it, okay? Get back on your feet again and we'll have this conversation in a month or so. I really need you, buddy." Knowing that service to others was important to Kenji, he had saved his best closing argument for last. "This idea I'm working on could revolutionize how some countries provide an essential service to its people. It would be a good thing."

"Wow! That's a bold statement!" *Ernie never failed to impress,* thought Kenji. Tempting as the offer was, Kenji didn't need the money, but he was intrigued.

Ernie dropped the subject and reverted to common territory—golf. "I got an eagle last week, did I tell you? It was on the same hole at Makalei where you scored your first one." And the easy give and take conversation continued into the late hours, long after Lilly had retired for the night. Ernie departed the next morning on a flight to Oman, mission unknown to Kenji.

A few days later Vince arrived. He was amazed at Kenji's good humor and his fast healing. He was curious about the sleeping arrangements with Lilly, but was not emboldened to ask for specific details. Kenji wasn't so circumspect when it was Vince's turn on the couch.

"So tell me, Vince, how are you coming along with the redhead?"

"Ah, Kenji my friend, it's like I've died and gone to heaven."

"Really? That good, huh?"

"Better. She's awesome!"

"Tell me all about her."

They sat on the balcony, watching the sun dip into the Pacific, comfortable in each other's company, gossiping like two old maids at a church bazaar.

"A friend once told me that a gentleman never tells," Vince said, referring to a comment Kenji had once made when quizzed about Lilly.

"That's no fun."

"Her legs are really, really long, and that's all I'm going to say on the Sandy subject."

Kenji didn't press his friend for more information, knowing it wasn't his business to pry, while enjoying the sport of trying.

* * *

Kenji had had plenty of time to think about his progress during the weeks he spent in Honolulu. He considered the time a progression in his life. His stump was healing nicely, and soon he would be fitted for a permanent prosthesis. Then the real work could begin in rehab and on the golf course. He thought about the loyalty of his friends, about how lucky he was. Lucky? His leg was gone, yet he felt lucky. He treasured the wonderful, close bond that had developed between him and Lilly. *I'm in love with her,* he finally admitted to himself. *I never want to be without her.* Over the past few weeks, he had come to accept his new "normal" and click into a sense of gratitude. He had terrific friends and was blessed with the love of an exciting woman. There was a good possibility that he could play golf again—how well, he didn't know. Perhaps it really didn't matter if he had lost his gift for golf. Maybe he should consider Ernie's offer of employment more seriously. Before he dropped off to sleep on the last night in the condo, his final thought was, *What else could I possibly need?*

CHAPTER 21

On the flight from Honolulu to Kona, Kenji pondered how quickly time had passed over the last five weeks. He now had a semi-permanent prosthesis, and both the operation and his recovery had gone amazingly well, according to his new friend, Dr. Mark Jacobs.

His relationship with Lilly had blossomed into a loving bond. In some ways they were like an old married couple — but better because of the give-and-take repartee that occurred between them throughout the day. The two nights of lovemaking had been glorious, and his feelings for Lilly were strong and passionate, which was new ground for him. He and Mia had grown up together so getting married was more like a merger of the two traditional families. There was nothing traditional about Lilly.

He wondered whether the feelings he had for her were really what love was truly about. The high emotional walls Kenji had built around himself had crumbled under Lilly's tutelage and loving support. She didn't seem to mind a whit whether he had one leg or two, yet a part of him felt he was only part of a man, and he had yet to make love to Lilly since his surgery. God knows he wanted to ravage her body on a daily basis, but he couldn't visualize the mechanics. *She's a passionate woman*, he thought. *She won't wait forever.*

"You're awfully quiet. Are you okay?" inquired Lilly.

"I'm fine, just thinking about my father and how he handled his one-legged-ness," he said with a smile. "Maybe remembering how he was can help me gain my equilibrium."

Knowing Kenji needed his space from time to time, Lilly retreated to reading her book.

Kenji thought about his father and what a good man he had been. He hadn't amassed great riches during his lifetime, but he had lived a rich life. He had been faithful to his wife and son, to his business, to his friends, and to his country. He had built a life, a family, and a business, and throughout the years, Kenji had never heard him once utter a complaint or mention his lack of a leg. *I love you, Father*, Kenji thought. *I wish I had told you that when you were alive.* The regret stabbed like a knife.

From 24,000 feet, Kenji thought the Pacific appeared bluer today, and the puffy clouds more dramatic than he could recall. He was adjusting to life as an amputee with some amount of grace. He experienced the phantom-limb pain occasionally at night, but with his strength and balance, he was adapting to the demands of going through life with one leg missing.

He firmly believed the adage that the first twenty-one days of any life experience—marriage, divorce, or even the death of a loved one—are the toughest. He had conquered those twenty-one days, with some frailty, yes, but he had survived. Now he would have to accept life as it was. A tumult of feelings assaulted him: gratitude for excellent doctors, his joy with Lilly, painful regret for not having tended to his sore foot sooner, and the happy prospect of seeing his Kona friends once again.

Vince, Stu, and Ernie were waiting at the Kona airport to greet the travelers, leis in hand along with a big sign they had obviously hand-painted that read, Welcome Home, Kenji. Lilly and Kenji chuckled, pleased at the sentimental gesture. Kenji was on crutches, his semi-permanent prosthesis in place, and walking almost normally, with only a slight swinging of his right leg providing a clue that all was not perfectly normal.

"You're managing quite well with your new leg. I'm impressed!" exclaimed Vince. "I have a rehab regimen all worked out for you, which we can talk about over dinner."

"The therapists at the hospital really made me work hard," replied Kenji, "but I'm anxious to hear what your recommendations are."

"Dinner at my house tonight, seven o'clock, Hawaiian attire," said Ernie, "that is, if you're up to it, Kenji—you too, Lilly. It wouldn't be much of a party without you. Stu and Gloria are coming, and Vince is bringing the infamous redhead."

"So we finally get to meet Vince's girlfriend? I'd show up just for that," joked Kenji. "Will this evening work for you, Lilly?"

"Sounds lovely," she responded with a devilish smile, knowing the guys would instantly like the tall, witty red-headed Sandy, her tennis chum.

"So who's *your* date for the evening, Ernie?" Kenji inquired.

"I have a date with a barbecue apron, but there may be a few surprises." He winked at Lilly.

After stowing the couple's luggage in the trunk of his car, Stu looked at Kenji inquisitively as they left the airport.

"You can drop us off at my house. Lilly is going to be staying with me for a while, until I get back on my feet again," Kenji instructed, sensing that Stu was looking for directions. Lilly and Kenji smiled at each other like cats that had just gobbled a plump canary.

Kenji and Lilly arrived promptly at seven o'clock, ahead of the other guests, to be greeted by Ernie, who welcomed them cordially. "I can't wait to show you the grounds." He motioned them to follow him as he led the way around the beautifully landscaped estate, flowers a riot of color. He pointed out half a dozen kangaroo's paws bushes, imported from Australia, stunning against the black wrought iron fence that surrounded the property. "I don't want to wear you out on your first night home, Kenji, but you have to see my library. I'm a bit of a collector," Ernie admitted sheepishly yet proudly.

His large estate home was stunning. Lilly noted the high ceilings, the open architecture, each room filled with eclectic furnishings evidently collected from the world over that were somehow made cohesive by the peach and off-white color scheme. They were odd color choices for a man, yet very cool and a bit exotic, continuing to add to what Lilly dubbed, "The mystery about Ernie." The library lived up to his hype, housing hundreds and hundreds of books from floor to ceiling on shelves made of koa wood, which lent a striking contrast to the mellow color of the walls and Persian rugs. Ernie carefully took a few books off the shelves and proudly showed off his first editions. "Not bad for a homeless kid, eh?" he whispered to Kenji.

"Not bad at all, my friend."

The others guests arrived in clumps. Lilly greeted Sandy with a hug and introduced her to Kenji and the others.

"Kenji, so lovely to meet you. Any friend of Lilly's is a friend of mine."

Kenji was duly impressed by her statuesque frame and friendly nature.

After all were assembled, Ernie donned a large black chef's apron and led them to the back terrace to get everyone settled with drinks from a bar built into an elaborate barbecue area spacious enough to seat a couple of dozen guests.

"Welcome home, Kenji, and you too, Lilly," Ernie said with a smile as he raised a glass.

He was a gracious and attentive host, chatting with everyone individually, asking questions, pouring

Champagne for several rounds of toasts—some ribald and funny, others sweet and sentimental. They feasted on jumbo shrimp and lobster tails, smooth, creamy risotto, and asparagus that had just the right amount of crunch. This disparate group sat at a long glass-topped table, comfortable in cushioned swivel chairs, happy to share one another's company. The evening was one of celebration and renewal. After an hour or so, Kenji realized he hadn't once thought about his missing foot.

After coffee and dessert, Vince pulled his chair over to Kenji's and shared details of the rehab plan he had worked out. Kenji, grateful for his friend's knowledge and expertise, agreed to start sessions the next morning.

Everyone looked at Ernie expectantly as they heard the sound of the doorbell chime softly. Ernie excused himself and walked through his mansion to admit the latest visitor.

"Who can that be?" Vince asked, curious that someone would come to call at such a late hour.

Kenji laughed. "He said there would be surprises."

Ernie walked out onto the terrace, his hand resting protectively on the back of a tall, slender young Eurasian man who appeared resplendent in an all-white European tailored suit. "Hey, everyone. This is George," he said as a wicked grin sliced his tanned face. He didn't offer any additional information about his guest, preferring to leave everyone to speculate.

* * *

The rehabilitation center was a beehive of activity when Kenji arrived the next morning. He wasn't driving yet, so he relied on Lilly to chauffer him to appointments. With great effort he managed to complete the complex regimen Vince had set up for him, working each area of his body to build flexibility, strength, and balance. Then came the walking lessons; he attempted to take steps sans crutches while holding on to bars that were parallel to the floor. *Not as easy as I thought it would be* thought Kenji, though he was determined to complete the task and trusted Vince's plan.

"Just five more steps," encouraged Vince. "You can do it. Just stay focused."

Kenji took the steps and then inched gingerly toward a chair to rest. "My stump is starting to hurt," he said.

"That's normal. It'll subside over time as you build up your muscle tone. You did great today, my friend. I'll see you Wednesday, okay?"

"By the way," Kenji said, "I really enjoyed meeting Sandy last night. She definitely lives up to your hype. I can see why she and Lilly have become friends—they're both irreverent to the core."

"You have no idea. You have no idea." Vince was as coy as a virgin at her first dance.

Kenji noticed a young man, slender of build, ashen face, across the room working with another therapist. "Vince, is that Jamie Fletcher? He sure has changed! "

"Yes, he's been coming here since his release from the hospital. He suffered a brain injury in that car crash so he's learning how to walk and function all over again. Do you want to go over and say hello?"

"Sure," said Kenji as he retrieved his crutches and made his way across the room. "Hi," he said as he approached Jamie. "Do you remember me?"

Jamie looked at Kenji, a crooked smile creasing his rather dull looking face. "You're Kenji, the golfer, right?" he asked, speech slurred. "I beat you."

"Yes, you did. I used to be a golfer — now not so much. I had part of one leg cut off as you can see."

"Too bad. I don't play golf now either."

Kenji couldn't help notice that Jamie was talking and acting like a much younger person, perhaps age ten or so. "Well, then, let's make a pact, Jamie. Let's both work real hard so we can play golf again, okay?"

"Okay."

"Good! See you!"

"See you!"

Kenji thought about his chance meeting with Jamie. *The poor kid. Here he is in the prime of his life reduced to a mere shadow of his former self, once a muscular good-looking young man full of confidence and talent. I wonder what I can do to help him? I must remember to ask Vince.*

On the way home, Kenji asked Lilly to stop by the bookstore. "I want to pick up a copy of a book called *The Inner Game of Golf*. I ran into Jamie Fletcher at rehab today, and I want to do something to help him recover."

* * *

The next day, Wednesday, Kenji struggled through his exercises, taking ten steps without his crutches.

"You're making steady progress. Keep up the good work," Vince encouraged him.

"Thank you. As you well know, patience is my strong suit," kidded Kenji. Then, true to his character, he asked, "What can I do to help Jamie?"

"He needs to work on his motor skills, vocabulary, speaking, and relearning just about everything."

"Can he still read?"

"Yes, but only for short spans of time. The brain injury makes it hard for him to concentrate for very long."

"Okay, I have an idea," Kenji said. "I bought this book about golf for him yesterday, and I'll ask him to read to me. Then when he loses focus, I can read to him. Would that be helpful?"

"Sounds like an interesting idea. It sure can't hurt."

Kenji crutched his way over to Jamie, who sat on a chair looking dejected. "Are you finished for today?" Kenji asked him.

"Yes, I'm done."

"Come on. Let me buy you a juice, okay?"

"Okay."

After they were seated on stools at the health drink bar, Kenji ordered two glasses of fruit juice. "Jamie, I brought a book for you on golf. Would you read some of it to me, please?" he asked, handing the book to the young man.

Jamie stumbled through the first two pages then got a bit agitated, twisting his hands and picking at his clothes.

Recognizing the signs of frustration, Kenji reached for the book. "Here, let me read a couple of pages to you. Can you listen for a few minutes?"

"Okay."

That's how it started. Kenji talked with Jamie about golf, and they took turns reading back and forth and discussed the mental aspects of golf. More important, Jamie's verbal skills improved over the next few weeks to the point where he could read seven or eight pages at one sitting. He started to smile more, and according to Vince, he began to work harder at his rehab exercises. He seemed to listen attentively while Kenji read to him. Kenji wondered whether any new connections in his brain were forming. Meanwhile, Kenji was so focused on helping Jamie that he went through his own exercise regimen faithfully, not complaining about even the more difficult aspects of his recovery. He felt stronger every day and walked more easily now without crutches.

The doctors in Honolulu phoned to tell Kenji it was time to be fitted for his permanent prosthesis. After that process was completed, he took the next step toward independence and had his car fitted with hand controls, so now he was free to come and go on his own.

During Kenji's recovery process, Lilly had been very helpful and nurturing, but he knew she was anxious to open an office in Kona, so after discussing the situation it was agreed that Lilly would move back to her condo to resume her independent life and career. "Don't get too independent, though," Kenji teased. "I have plans for you."

"Oh, really? And what might those be?"

"It won't be long before I summon enough courage to make love to you again — that is, if you'll help me figure out how to manage it. I may have to buy a copy of the *Kama Sutra* to find a workable position," he teased. "I love you, Lilly. Thank you for being so patient with me."

"You're welcome. I love you, too, darlin', but I plan on getting my business up and running while you get your courage and positions sorted out, okay?" She smiled, hopeful he would visit the bookstore very soon.

CHAPTER 22

While the notion of playing golf again was always in the back of his mind, Kenji focused on learning to live with one leg, helping Jamie in his recovery, and spending time with Lilly. He could walk pretty well with his prosthesis, and life was getting back to what he called "a new normal." He was conflicted about living alone; he enjoyed the solitude but missed day-to-day life with Lilly. Outwardly he presented a confident, cheerful demeanor. The rational part of his brain told him it was time to move on with his life. Emotionally, fear paralyzed him from taking the next step.

Kenji opened his journal to write a letter to Mia. A long time ago, he had learned that this exercise helped to clarify his thoughts and feelings. He had started this journal shortly after Mia had died. At that time he felt as if his world had collapsed, and writing to Mia offered him a safe haven. Back then it had never occurred to him to think of any other woman taking over the role Mia had played in his life. It seemed they were destined for each other from the very beginning 'til death do them part. It was no wonder that the loss of Mia was such an overwhelming tragedy in Kenji's life. His folks had been gone for years now, and he hadn't really had any close friends besides Mia at that time. Since her passing, writing in his journal became his way to express his feelings and keep his love for Mia alive. It offered some salvation for a shattered soul.

> *Dear Mia,*
>
> *It has been several weeks since I last wrote to you. A lot has happened, so this will probably be a long letter. As I mentioned in my last letter, I went to Honolulu to get my right foot checked. As I had feared, they had to amputate my leg just below the knee. I didn't take my journal with me because of security reasons; I couldn't bear to lose it.*
>
> *Here's the latest. The leg is gone, and I have a prosthesis. I seem to be doing okay with the whole thing so far. The operation, the healing stage, and then the fitting of the prosthesis took almost five weeks. My car has been fitted with hand controls so I don't have to use my prosthesis leg for the accelerator and the brake.*
>
> *My new friend, Lilly, whom I mentioned to you in an earlier letter, came to Honolulu to help me during my recovery. In the process we have become good friends and lovers. Does that shock you? She is lovely and I am smitten,*

drowning in her lush body. Is it love? I don't know for sure. I have never felt this way about anyone besides you, the lure of her body is like a thirst I cannot quench, but I don't trust these feelings.

I am determined, Mia, to make the very best of my situation. Things happen in life that we don't understand, but indeed life does go on. It's my goal to become a positive example for anyone else who might have to undergo such an operation. While doing research and listening to the doctors who took care of me, I've learned that many thousands of people have leg amputations every year — either from accident, war, or predominantly from diabetes. I want to be a positive influence for those people and to be sure to conduct myself in a way that would make you and my folks proud.

To be totally honest, I've been going through tough times, though I haven't spoken with anyone about it, not even Lilly. I try to put up a brave, cheerful front. The doctors told me ahead of time that there might be an adjustment period. In fact they said it would likely be several stages of adjustment. As it turned out, they were right. My plan was to set a high example, but privately I was, and still am, to a certain extent, uncertain and insecure. Vince, my physical therapist and friend, told me, "It's normal to grieve your loss." He told me to expect a number of stages, including denial, anger, depression, and finally acceptance and hope. I hate to admit it, but dark thoughts have ruled my nights these past few weeks. Hopefully I'm finally getting over the depression part.

The big question right now is whether I'll ever be able to play golf again, and if I can, will I still have my gift? Vince and I were beginning to put together a plan for a way I could use my golfing gift to help charitable organizations and other people, but that may have been pie-in-the-sky thinking.

Soon I'll be going to the driving range to find out what's going on with my golfing abilities. I'm trying not to worry about it, but I do. Truthfully I'm scared and deeply saddened that now I am only part of a man. This happened at an especially bad time. I haven't forgotten the promise you made me make to you that last day – that I would find someone to love. I think Lilly is that person, but now I don't know what to do or even what to feel. Is it love or just lust? I enjoy spending time with her. We're compatible on a day-to-day basis, as we discovered in Honolulu. I tell her "I love you" because I think that's what she wants to hear. She isn't anything like you, Mia Mouse. She is very independent and really doesn't need me. "What would she want with a one-legged man?" I ask myself. Maybe the big question is, "Will I have the courage to trust someone other than you?"

I think of you every day, and treasure the memories of our years together. Your love gives me strength.

Goodnight my love,
Your Kenji-san

That night before Kenji went to bed, he reread what he had written to Mia, feeling the loss of her as if she had died yesterday. He looked at the single foot causing the lump in the sheet and, shoulders heaving, wept. He rolled over and hid his face in the pillow; he didn't want Mia to see him cry. He was grieving the loss of his leg even though it felt as if it were still there.

* * *

Lilly phoned the next morning. "Hey, good looking, what's cooking?"

"Not much."

"Good. I just bought these luscious giant sea scallops at the fish market, and at this moment I'm making a divine secret sauce. Dinner is at seven, if you're available," she announced gaily.

Lilly's good cheer was an antidote to the previous night's indulgence into self-pity. "Yes, of course, that sounds terrific," he said. "What wine would you prefer?"

"A crisp Chardonnay would be lovely."

"See you at seven, then."

Kenji hung up the phone, suddenly cheerful, determined to get his head on straight, to get his life figured out. "Man up," he muttered to himself. "Today is a bright new day."

That morning he spent an hour with Jamie talking and reading and noted the excellent progress Jamie was making. *I wonder if it's time for both of us to get to the driving range?* he thought. Just then John Fletcher stormed into the rehab center and yelled at Vince, "What the hell is that son of a bitch Kenji Watanabe doing with my grandson?"

Vince just looked at him and smiled. Furious that he hadn't received a response, Fletcher left, murmuring, "That SOB has no right to see my grandson. This isn't going to continue."

Jamie evidently had told his grandfather that Kenji had been reading with him and spending time helping with his verbal communications skills.

Vince apologized to Kenji. "Sorry about that. That little outburst caught me totally by surprise."

"Knowing him, he'll probably take out a restraining order against me."

Having heard the interchange, Jamie piped up, "Grandpa doesn't like you, Kenji, even though I told him you were helping me."

"He doesn't like Japanese people, Jamie. It really has nothing to do with Kenji personally," Vince explained.

"I told him I want to play golf with you," Jamie told Kenji.

"I've been meaning to talk to you about that, Vince. Would it be okay for Jamie to go to the driving range with me?"

"Hey, it's okay with me, but John will be really pissed off if he finds out."

"Don't worry about that. I'll just ask him," Kenji replied, grinning at the thought of how that conversation would go.

Later that afternoon, Kenji sat in his home office, thinking about the best way to approach John Fletcher. *Just be honest*, he told himself. He picked up the phone and dialed the number.

"Hello. John Fletcher here."

"Hello, John. It's Kenji Watanabe. Don't hang up. Just hear me out, okay?" There was silence on the other end of the line, so Kenji continued, "We both want the best for Jamie. Have you noticed the vast improvement in his verbal skills, his ability to read for longer periods of time, his increased attention span?"

"Yes, I've noticed the improvements," he responded gruffly.

"We've been reading *The Inner Game of Golf* together, and he asked me to take him to the driving range. He was such a gifted golfer, with a great swing and unbelievable timing. I wonder if he still has that swing somewhere down deep in his subconscious. Anyway, he wants to try golf again, and I'd like to help him. Is that all right with you?"

"I don't want him playing golf with no goddamn Jap!" he yelled, and the line went dead. John Fletcher had hung up.

Kenji sat for a moment, thinking, *Okay, that's about what I expected. Time to figure out plan B.*

* * *

John Fletcher spent a restless night, tossing and turning in his sleep. The next morning, he had calmed down a bit and started to think rationally about the situation with his injured grandson and analyzing the pros and cons of that bastard's request. *Maybe Kenji's help is actually aiding Jamie's recovery,* he thought. *But I don't want him tending to my family. He has no right. Still, the doctors said that brain injury patients recover at varying rates, depending on the time and effort put into regaining the skills they lost. And they don't really know which skills can be revitalized until they try each one.*

Jamie had told him that Kenji spent at least an hour with him every time he was at rehab. *How much time have I spent with him?* he thought. He was ashamed to admit that he hadn't devoted any time to Jamie's recovery other than to drive him back and forth for his appointments at rehab and doctors' offices. He never had sat down with him to read a book, even when Jamie was a little boy. For the next two days, John Fletcher thought long and hard, going back and forth, considering all aspects of the situation with Kenji. He did some research on the Internet and talked again to Dr. Jamison about the value of human interaction with people with brain injuries. Finally he made a decision and placed a call.

"Kenji, this is John Fletcher."

"Hello, John. What can I do for you?"

"Well, I know you've been spending time with Jamie, and his doctor seems to think it's having a positive influence on him. If you want to take him to the driving range, you have my permission." Without so much as a thank-you, he hung up the phone.

A smiling Kenji wet his index finger on his tongue, lifted it in the air, and made a checkmark motion. *Round two, Kenji-san.*

CHAPTER 23

For two weeks, Kenji and Jamie had been going to the driving range together. While each of them had their own challenges, it was amazing how well they could drive the ball on occasion. Vince said it was muscle memory that allowed the unlikely twosome to hit the ball a good distance with a driver. Kenji was learning how to position the club and maintain his balance in a somewhat awkward-looking swing. His results were good, but only some of the time.

Jamie was the miraculous one. He teed up a ball, driver in gentle hands, aimed at the flag two hundred yards out, and took an easy, flawless swing. It was the most beautiful thing to behold, seeing the ball soar through the cloudless sky to plop down then roll another twenty yards past the flag. Jamie jumped into the air, pumping his fist and yelling, "I can still do it! I can still do it!"

Kenji gave him a high five followed by a hug. "Wow! That was awesome! What a drive! Hit another one."

He took some photos of Jamie in full swing with his digital camera, planning to download them into his computer then send them to Jamie later in the day as a surprise. *I must remember to send copies to Jamie's doctor and Vince as well,* he thought. Photos of Jamie's astonishing ability to hit the ball might be helpful to them as they continued to help guide his recovery.

In no time, Jamie and Kenji went through a large bucket of balls, going in reverse order from a driver down to a pitching wedge. Not every shot hit its mark, but there were plenty of victories that day, especially for Jamie and some for Kenji. The ravages of physical deficiencies held no real power over either of them as they swung away, hopeful optimism ruling the day.

"It was a great day," Kenji said, "but now it's time to go home."

"Okay. I can't wait to tell my grandfather about my swing."

"I'm sure he'll be pleased."

"When can I play a real round of golf?" Jamie asked.

"I don't know. You'll have to ask your doctor and Vince what they recommend."

"I want to beat you again," Jamie said with a crooked smile.

"You probably will, son. You probably will."

They loaded their golf clubs into the trunk of the car, and Kenji drove up through the hills above Kona to John Fletcher's magnificent estate, stopping at the large ornate double gates to enter the security code that Jamie had meticulously memorized. As they proceeded up the long curving driveway lined with hibiscus of every hue and interspersed with huge pots of white orchids, Jamie asked, "Can we go to the driving range again tomorrow?"

"Not tomorrow, but the day after, okay?"

"Okay. Thank you, Kenji."

"You're welcome. We can go after we do our exercises at the rehab center."

Kenji popped open the trunk so Jamie could retrieve his golf clubs. He gazed up at the ten-foot-tall solid mahogany front doors, hand carved with an elaborate pineapple design. *Odd that*, he mused. The pineapple is a symbol of hospitality, and he doubted that John Fletcher, as cantankerous as he was, had had even one guest come to visit in the past ten years.

"Bye, Kenji. See you!"

Kenji waved goodbye as he noticed a slight movement of the drapes behind one of the ground-floor windows. *The old man is watching us*, he thought. *Good. We'll see what the next time brings.* It never occurred to him that the ongoing feud with Fletcher, one-sided though it was, could ever be completely resolved.

Kenji and Jamie continued to go to the driving range three days a week. They both worked very hard — Jamie to improve his concentration and attention span, and Kenji to find solid footing. Kenji laughed out loud as he thought about that phrase — solid footing indeed. His balance continued to improve, but his right leg hurt like hell with the shift in weight that was necessary to execute a cohesive golf swing. *Where's the magic now?* he wondered.

CHAPTER 24

It had been more than three months since his surgery, and Kenji decided it was time to get back on the horse and play an actual round of golf. The usual Wednesday foursome was elated at his return to the group. "Hey, Kenji. Welcome back!" they exclaimed.

"Thank you. It's so good to see you all!" he said as he clasped his hands chest high and executed a perfect Japanese bow as a sign of respect.

While feeling confident in his ability to function on a daily basis, Kenji felt self-conscious about his artificial leg. He had flushed with embarrassment when he noticed people staring at his peg leg as he walked along the street in downtown Kona dressed in Bermuda shorts. He felt uncomfortable with the unwanted attention, so he started to wear long pants even when the air was steamy with humidity. Strangers to the golf club weren't aware that Kenji only had one leg; therefore they weren't awed that he was a handicapped golfer. Some women at the club, tourists probably, glanced up in approval as he walked through the pro shop dressed in khaki-colored long pants and a muted red Captain Cook Hawaiian shirt, making an appealing fashion statement. Even though he was a man of humility, he wasn't immune to these veiled glances that helped bolster his self-confidence, or unaware of his bronzed good looks.

Kenji was happy to be at the cooler elevations at Makalei. Even with help and advice from his friends, his first golf outing wasn't stellar; he finished with a final score of 115. The somewhat positive experiences at the driving range had caused him to be more hopeful about his return to the golf course. *So much for setting unrealistic expectations*, he thought.

He felt heartened and grateful, however, that he could still play golf. The bad news was that it would take a lot of work to get back his game of the recent past, and it was obvious that he needed to devise a technique that would allow him to be consistent. On some shots, when his balance was steady, he could see the red pathway in the sky. *Thank God. The gift is still there!* he thought. During the round, Vince suggested they play the Waikoloa Beach course the next day so he could help Kenji develop a new swing style. Of course he agreed. The one thing that was consistent was that Kenji's putting was still awful. *I have to learn to read the greens much, much better*, he thought. *Agh! I have so much work ahead of me.*

The next day dawned in a golden blaze, a precursor to the hot day to follow. Kenji wasn't pleased at the prospect, knowing that heat wasn't a friend to a sweating stump. He rode out to Waikoloa Beach with Vince and Ernie hoping for a cooling breeze at least on the holes that nestled alongside the ocean. When they arrived at the clubhouse and checked in at the pro shop, Vince and Kenji took one cart, and Ernie loaded his clubs and camera equipment into the other. Ernie had asked if he could come along today, mysteriously indicating he might have some ideas that could help Kenji. "I have a special camera I want to use during your swing," he'd said, "if that's okay with you."

"Sure, you're more than welcome to join us," Kenji had told him. "I need all the help I can get. If you've got some real solutions for me, all the better."

The threesome teed off. Kenji struggled with his follow-through on the long shots, due to lack of flexibility of the ankle of his prosthetic leg. He was having difficulty completing his turn, which resulted in his shots going all over the place. He sacrificed one ball to the lava gods on the first hole, not an auspicious beginning. When they arrived at the second tee, Ernie unpacked his tote bag, which held a big camera with a long lens. He also had brought a professional photographer's tripod.

"That equipment is impressive," Kenji said. "What kind of camera is that, Ernie?"

"It's a high-speed camera that'll allow me to look at your swing frame by frame. It's similar to the special cameras they use at PGA tournaments to show a player's swing in very slow motion. I want to study the

linkage between your body movement and the action of
your prosthesis, especially your right ankle during the
follow-through."

Throughout the game, Vince suggested different tactics
for Kenji to try in an attempt to achieve more distance and
accuracy. Kenji had trouble letting his mind go blank and
getting into the mental zone, so the red path didn't show
on many shots. However, some setups worked better than
others, and occasionally he got a good shot. Those good
shots were the ones he filed away in his subconscious to
replay when faced with a similar shot.

Ernie filmed only Kenji's shots with the driver, not
wanting to slow the play or interfere with Vince's coaching. By the end of eighteen holes, Kenji was exhausted —
from the heat, from the 112 shots he had made, and from
the frustration of not having an easy, consistent swing. *My
game has gone to hell*, he thought, and wondered whether it
would ever come back.

On the way back to Kona, Ernie was quiet. Finally he
said, "Kenji, I think I might be able to modify the ankle
joint on your prosthesis to give it a little more flex. I know
a little about material characteristics and think there might
be something that'll work. My idea is a dual tension that
holds the ankle flex as it normally is when you walk but
has a hysteresis point so it'll reduce the tension it needs on
your follow-through. How much does it cost for a new leg
if I screw up?"

"Well, this one cost eight thousand dollars, but if you
think you can do something that'll help, let's go for it. I'm
game, and I have a dollar or two stashed away, so I can

afford to replace this one if you break it. And hopefully I can count on Lilly to feed me," he teased.

They agreed on a date when Kenji would revert to crutches and surrender his prosthesis to Ernie for the modifications. Kenji already was plotting ahead in his mind. *I'll ask Lilly to stay over for a few days while Ernie has my leg*, he thought, *and I must remember to buy her some flowers and get food in the house so she can dazzle me with her gourmet cooking.* Ever the good and decent man, Kenji was thinking like an old-fashioned, traditional Japanese head of the household.

As soon as Kenji got home, he phoned Lilly at work. "Hi, Lilly. How are you today?"

"Terrific! I'm just finishing up some paperwork, and then I'm out of here."

"I know it's last minute, but are you free for dinner tonight? I thought we could eat in—there's this new sushi place that delivers. I know how much you love sushi. I've been out at Waikoloa Beach most of the day with Vince and Ernie working on my golf game, so I'm exhausted, but I'm desperate to see you."

"Really," she responded with skepticism. "Since when have you ever been desperate to see anyone?" Not giving him time to reply, she quickly agreed to come over for dinner.

Just as he hung up the phone, it rang.

"Kenji, I know you and I have had our differences over the years, but I want to thank you for what you're doing for Jamie."

Kenji was stunned. Never in a million years did he think he'd hear the words "Thank you" coming out of John Fletcher's mouth.

"You're welcome," replied Kenji, wondering where this conversation was leading.

Fletcher continued, "I want to apologize to you for all the years I've been an absolute asshole and thought less of you—and, in fact, thought bad things about all Japanese people. I just can't believe the goodness in your heart that would let you nurture my grandson despite all the things I've said and done to you through the years."

Kenji remained silent.

"Are you still there? Don't you hang up on me!" Fletcher shouted, reverting to form.

Kenji's mind was racing. *Could this be real?* he wondered. He was astounded to hear words of appreciation coming from this hard, bitter, grizzled old man. "I accept your apology, John, and I'll do whatever I can for Jamie to make his life better."

"Thank you, Kenji," replied Fletcher before gently placing the phone into its cradle.

After John Fletcher hung up, he did something he hadn't done since he was a child. He wept. He wept away the bitterness. He wept away the prejudice. Finally, after drying the tears from his face with a used handkerchief, knowing that a complete transformation at his age was impossible, he vowed that he would become less of an SOB, and at least make an attempt to treat people fairly. This was new territory for the old man, but he had learned a valuable lesson from Kenji Watanabe; reaching out to help others had seemed to help Kenji. *I wonder if helping others can help me, too,* Fletcher wondered, selfishness continuing to lurk in his thoughts. *Well, we'll see about that. No sense getting too carried away with this generosity shit. I do have an opportunity to redeem myself with Jamie, though. That's the important thing. Spending time with him is a good place to begin. Who knows, perhaps I can even begin to truly like Kenji Watanabe – or not.*

CHAPTER 25

Kenji knew Ernie was very intelligent and suspected his IQ to be in the upper ranges. When Ernie offered to modify Kenji's prosthesis, he was convinced that his friend truly was a genius, an out-of-the-box thinker kind of genius.

The modifications Ernie had made thus far had helped Kenji's golf game tremendously. It was like night and day, the before game versus the after game. Golf was fun again; the halo of light showing the pathway to the target was back like a gift from God, perfect in every way. Kenji once again was tearing it up on the golf links, until he got onto the greens. It dawned on him that to be successful at putting he first had to do the work to master that part of his game. He reread *Putt Like the Pros*. He learned that statistically putting represented 43 percent of his game, so he practiced a smooth stroke, over and over again until he developed a feel for each putt. He studied the different types of turf typically used on the golf courses in Hawaii and learned how to take more information into consideration. Was the putt against the grain of the grass or with the grain? Was there a hill or sea that would affect the curve of the green? He obsessed over putting. He practiced his follow-through. He practiced reading the greens until he could visualize the line to the cup. He practiced positive visualization of the ball rolling toward the hole then into the cup. He put in the work; he put in the time; and magically it all came together.

Wearing his prosthesis became less of a challenge. He and Vince were now in the fine-tuning process. Ernie suggested to Kenji over dinner one evening that he wanted to mill off a little bit of material from the flex joint that he had invented just for him. He assured Kenji that this action would increase the flexibility but still preserve the strength he needed for normal walking.

"Did you know that before sophisticated structural analysis software, this was the way they designed the wings on airplanes?" Ernie said. "I read an article about this. They'd design the wing to be very strong. Of course it also would be heavy. They then put hydraulic jacks under it and flexed the wing vigorously. Then they'd remove some material. When the wing broke, they'd add some material back, and that was it. That's basically what we're doing here — trial and error."

"So far it seems to be working well. Of course I would like more flex if possible, as long at it doesn't make it too floppy for walking."

"Okay then. Let's do it. Drive out to my office, and we'll tweak it a bit more," Ernie suggested as they finished dinner and paid the tab. Some business acquaintances motioned to Kenji as they were about to leave.

"I'll be there in a few minutes, Ernie."

Kenji stopped to say hello and chat for a few moments with some people he knew from one of the charity organizations he supported. After exchanging pleasantries, he excused himself, telling them he had an important appointment, and drove to Ernie's office.

Ernie's company was housed in an office complex on the north side of Kona. Kenji pulled into a guest parking space. The front of the building was dark, but he saw a light glowing from Ernie's office. The front door was unlocked. *That's weird*, he thought. He opened the door and entered the reception area. As he rounded the corner moving toward the light, he saw a tall muscular man standing in front of the executive desk with a gun pointed at Ernie's head. Instinctively Kenji bent over low and bounded into the room with the intent of startling the intruder, who turned rapidly, sensing motion behind him, and fired his gun simultaneously. Kenji dove to the left as the bullet hit his lower right leg, and he landed softly on the thickly cushioned carpet. The intruder's mouth dropped open in surprise. When Ernie saw his friend on the floor, he felt a deadly rage and instantly reverted to the street-brawler mentality of his youth.

He vaulted across his desk with lightning-fast speed and hit the intruder with a perfect knockout punch at the point of his open jaw, causing him to collapse to the floor in a heap. Ernie's blow was a classic knockout punch that causes the mandible nerve in the mouth to redirect blood flow from the brain to the intruder's stomach. The resulting shortage of blood and oxygen to the brain caused instant unconsciousness. Ernie picked up the gun and rushed to Kenji, who was trying to get upright.

Totally uncharacteristic for Kenji, he blurted out, "What the fuck was that? That bastard shot me in the leg!" His heart was racing like a high-speed train.

Ernie pulled up Kenji's pant leg to ascertain the damage. There was a clean hole through the calf of Kenji's prosthesis about the diameter of an index finger. It appeared that Kenji was okay, even though he was shook up and looked scared as hell.

Ernie thrust the gun into Kenji's shaking hand. "Keep this guy covered while I go back to the shop to get something."

Kenji looked puzzled and confused. This was the first time he had ever held a gun. He had no idea what he would do if the intruder woke up while Ernie was gone.

Fortunately, Ernie was gone only a moment and came back with some long cable ties. The guy was still unconscious, and Ernie went over to him, undid the man's belt, and yanked his pants and underwear down around his ankles. He put two cable ties close to each ankle and effectively made a hobble out of the guy's pants. Then he rolled him onto his stomach, tied his hands, bent the intruder's knees backward, and tied his bound hands to his hobbled feet. He attached the man's handcuffed wrists to the cable ties on the intruder's ankles. This is what is known on the farm as "hogtied" he explained. The intruder was entirely disabled. Ernie used his foot to roll the intruder onto his side.

Ernie quickly stepped to his desk then opened a drawer to retrieve a box cutter and a pair of rubber gloves. He sat cross-legged on the floor about two feet from the intruder. Just then the intruder groaned, and his eyes fluttered open. The first thing he saw was a hulk of a man a few feet from his face, glaring at him. Feeling cool air on his skin, he glanced down, shocked to see he was naked from the waist down. That's when he noticed the box cutter in Ernie's hand.

"Now, you son of a bitch, start talking! Who are you and what are you doing here? Why did you break into my office? What are you after? Talk now or face dire consequences," Ernie commanded in a sinister tone of voice, as he swiped the air with the box cutter.

The intruder looked confused. After a moment, Ernie reached down and put on the rubber gloves. At the sound of the final snap, as Ernie finished putting on the gloves, it dawned on the intruder that it was possible he was going to be castrated. He mumbled incoherently, tears rolling down his cheeks.

Suddenly Ernie realized the intruder probably didn't understand or speak English.

Kenji remained in a sitting position on the floor holding a weapon he didn't know how to use. He looked up to see two burly men rush into the room, guns drawn.

"Hold on, Ernie, and drop that knife!" Both men were holding leather cases open to show gleaming gold FBI badges. Ernie tossed the box cutter aside, and said, "What the hell are you guys doing here?"

It slowly became obvious to Kenji that his mysterious friend knew exactly who these people were.

The FBI agents holstered their guns. "Ernie, I'm sorry to tell you this, but it appears that the North Koreans have found you."

"Shit," Ernie said.

Kenji followed this conversation, looking back and forth between Ernie and the two FBI men like he was watching a tennis match. "Ernie, what the hell is going on? Are you in trouble?"

Ernie glanced at the agents and said, "Well, guys, do you want to tell my friend what's going on or should I?"

"First things first," the biggest of the agents growled. "What's your name, sir?" he asked Kenji.

"I'm an innocent bystander. I don't have anything to do with any of this."

"That may be so, sir, but you *are* holding a weapon."

Kenji quickly placed the gun on the floor, which the second FBI agent, a pocked-face taciturn individual, kicked across the room.

He looked at Ernie for guidance and saw him nod his head, so he replied, "Kenji Watanabe." The agent wrote his name in a little black-covered notebook. He directed a comment to his partner, "Jerry get numb nuts here cut loose from Ernie's hogtie, put some regular cuffs on him, and for God's sake pull up his pants. Load him up. I'll be out in a minute."

He then focused his full attention on Kenji, and used his most serious, gravelly tone. "Sir, what's going on here is that Ernie has a contract with the US government for some of his proprietary software used on GPS satellites. This *was* a non-classified project, but it seems your buddy here has software that's so advanced that our for-once enlightened government put it on the export control list. This means it can't be sold to foreign governments. Agents from some of these *foreign*..." He stressed the word as if it related to dog shit stuck on his shoe. "...governments are attempting to steal it. That's where we come in. Ernie's facility in California was ransacked a couple of years ago, and his customer, the US government, alerted the FBI about the break-in. Since then, Ernie here has had extra company trailing him around at all times, even though he chooses to ignore us and our advice about his personal safety." The agent quickly glanced at Ernie to gauge whether he had heard his last comment.

Ernie nonchalantly ignored him.

He continued, "Now, Mr. Watanabe, since you were a witness to the events of this evening I'm going to take you down to our office to sign a debriefing statement. This whole project has just been classified as a national secret. It's nothing to be concerned about, sir. There are just some bureaucratic items we need to attend to."

The burly one didn't appear in the mood to answer questions, so Kenji sat on the floor in stunned silence, eyes downcast, not even attempting to rise to his feet. After a few seconds, he glanced at Ernie hoping for guidance. Ernie sat in a chair off to the side of his desk, looking kind of bored with the whole affair.

"Mr. Watanabe, follow me to our office in your car."

It was not a request.

Kenji looked at Ernie and asked, "Will my leg still work?"

The FBI agent looked confused but wisely did not comment.

Ernie finally joined the conversation. "I'm sorry you got caught in the middle of this, Kenji, and, yes, your leg should be okay. Please come back here after your debriefing so we can talk."

Kenji struggled to his feet, gingerly testing his prosthesis by putting weight on it and shifting from side to side. "Looks like it still works. Okay then. I'll see you in a little while," he said, as the agent led him out of the office.

The debriefing meeting was approaching two hours when Kenji's lack of patience asserted itself. "I'm not involved," he exclaimed. "I'm an innocent bystander. I'm leaving now!"

It seemed that Mr. Burly, as Kenji now thought of him, had other ideas. He described the dire consequences that Kenji faced if he spoke a word to anyone about the events that had transpired that evening. The top-secret nature of things meant that he came under all of the laws and national security requirements of any citizen who might have a secret level clearance or higher. By the time the agent was done verbally pounding him, Kenji felt like the wrath of God had come to Earth, exactly as the agent had intended.

It was almost midnight by the time he got back to Ernie's office. Ernie sat at his computer typing away, nonchalant as ever. Kenji noticed a light from the adjacent office and glanced through the window to see a slim figure, also hunched over a computer. He recognized Ernie's mystery guest from the dinner party. *Ah, so George works here too,* he thought.

"Hey, Kenji. How did the debriefing session go?"

"I'm not in jail, though truthfully, they scared the shit out of me with all their mumbo jumbo about top-secret clearance and the penalties that'll rain down on my head if I breathe a word to anyone. Trust me — I'm not saying anything to anyone about anything."

"My apologies," Ernie said. "I'm so sorry you stumbled into this mess. I've gotten so used to living in a world where espionage and corporate theft is a daily occurrence that I don't think much about it anymore. I'm actually happy to have these government types watching over me, though it does present a challenge to my love life," he said with a grin.

"Since when do you have time for a love life?"

"Actually, I don't, but I really enjoyed the look on all your faces when George showed up at my door a while back. Did anyone speculate about my being gay?"

"Not a one, but they all thought you had great taste in men." Kenji laughed, thinking back.

"Fortunately George came in tonight after all the commotion. He's working on some new algorithms."

"I see," Kenji said, even though he didn't understand what the relationship between Ernie and George truly was, and his friend didn't seem to be in the mood to elaborate.

"Kenji, let's get serious for a moment. Apparently a lot of people think I create pretty special software. Unfortunately some of these people are very dangerous and

don't concern themselves with my good health. You now
know more about my life than just about anyone. I can't talk
about my work because of the top-secret clearance. But between you and me, I'll be glad to have a confidant in whom
I can share a few things now and then. And if tonight's
events haven't totally freaked you out, you could always
come be my CEO," he said, a sly grin lighting up his face.

Kenji sat there trying to absorb everything Ernie was
saying. Finally he shook his head. "You're one crazy son of
a bitch to get mixed up in all this. But, hey, we all have to
make a living, right?"

"Come on. I know it's late, but let's go get a coffee. I'll
make sure you get a decaf so you won't be up all night
worrying about bad guys lurking outside your window.
Oh, and by the way, it's not a good idea to talk about any
of this stuff in any public place. All my good FBI buddies *and* the bad guys have access to excellent listening
devices."

"Talk? I'm not going to talk at all except maybe about
the weather and golf, and maybe we can gossip about
women. That's it. That's the sum total of my verbal
repertoire."

"Good fellow," Ernie replied, clapping him once on the
back as they left the building, both calling over their shoulders, "Good night, George."

What Ernie and the FBI hadn't shared with Kenji was
that the government customer was the National Security
Agency. After the honchos at NSA evaluated the software
Ernie had developed for the oil industry, they could see
immediately how the basic architecture was suited to

analysis of the communications signals they collected from all over the world. Ernie was put under contract immediately and had received a top-secret clearance. He was still pissed off at the way they had treated him in years past, so the price they paid for his special skills was very dear. He chuckled every month when he reviewed his bank statement, noting the hefty automatic deposit to his account.

Initially the guys at NSA had been upset when Ernie moved his operation to Kona, but it actually had worked out well for both parties. He was a long arm's reach from his customer at Fort Meade, Maryland, so from the outside it wouldn't appear that he could be an active contractor. Meanwhile the FBI had assigned a team of six people to watch over Ernie because he was a valuable resource the government needed to protect. This duty in Hawaii quickly became a plum assignment for agents, especially during the winter months, when they laughed about the poor schmucks stationed in Washington, DC, having to deal with the snow and cold weather.

Later the FBI informed Ernie that the thief he had cold-cocked was one of two North Korean agents, a technical guy who wasn't adept at firing a gun. The FBI rounded up the other spy that night, and early the next morning, before daylight, the handcuffed hostages departed on a military plane with an armed escort. There would be no leaks on this case, and the Department of Justice would quietly deal with the matter.

Ernie relaxed a little, but only a little, forever wary, wondering which country's spies would find him next, try to steal his software and do him harm.

CHAPTER 26

Kenji and Vince sat side by side at a table for four in the bar area at Splashers, each having ordered a beer to steel their nerves before the upcoming meeting. "What's this lunch all about?" asked Vince.

"I have no idea," Kenji said. "John Fletcher called me this morning and asked in that charming way of his if you and I were free for lunch. He said he has something important to talk to us about. Maybe it has something to do with Jamie."

"Intriguing, to say the least. I've been hearing some talk around town that he's a changed man, though that's kind of hard to believe."

Kenji responded with a grin. "Don't sell old John short. He actually said 'Thank you' to me a while back. I was so

shocked you could have knocked me over with a feather.
Let's give him the benefit of the doubt and hear what he
has to say. The gossip is that he recently wrote several big
checks to some local charities."

"Really? Now that's interesting. He's a very rich
man—God only knows how rich—so he can well afford
it. I'm just not convinced he's changed all that much. You
know what they say, 'Once an asshole, always an asshole.'
I wonder if this supposed renaissance may be due to
Jamie. Sadly, Jamie probably will never function at a high
level due to his brain injury. Certainly he can have a full
life and get along okay, but he has some loss of function
that affects his memory and learning ability. It's amazing
how that kid can still hit a golf ball. I'm still in awe over
that."

"He's a terrific kid, despite his spoiled upbringing."

The two friends sat sipping their beers, curious about
what the day would bring. Kenji asked, "So will Jamie be
able to take over his grandfather's empire once old John
bites the dust?"

"Probably not. But hopefully John has set up a trust
and named a guardian to look after Jamie and the money.

"I hope so too. This whole thing reminds me of Scrooge
in *A Christmas Carol*. Perhaps there's hope for redemption
for John after all."

Just then, Kenji saw the Fletchers—the gnarled old man
and the mentally challenged grandson—slowly head up
the stairway into the restaurant. The hostess guided them
to the table John had reserved, even though Splashers typically didn't take bookings.

Jamie grinned when he saw Kenji and Stu. "Hi, guys! We have a surprise!"

Fletcher frowned at his grandson but didn't utter a word of disapproval. The two shook hands with Kenji and Vince, who sat down across the table from them.

The waitress came by and took their order. "Thank you, gentlemen. Your orders will be up in a few minutes." It was almost one o'clock, and the noontime rush was subsiding as people headed back to work.

"Jamie, how are you doing in rehab?" asked Kenji.

"It's going slow," he admitted. "I get frustrated when I can't do things."

"Actually, you're making great progress. You just need to keep working at it. Listen to your therapists. They'll keep you on track," said Vince.

"At least I can still hit a golf ball. I didn't forget how to do that," Jamie said proudly. "Grandpa got a tutor for me. He's going to teach me about property management!"

"That's a terrific idea!" Vince said.

"I'm alive and kicking, so thank you all for your help. Especially you, Kenji. You've been very good to me. I'm happy to see the sun come up every morning, right, Grandpa?"

"That's right, son. You're doing just fine," said Fletcher with a newfound tenderness in his voice.

Those kind words touched Kenji. Evidently Fletcher had decided not to mourn what Jamie had lost through his brain injury. Instead they would celebrate the here and now and the little victories that Jamie could achieve by fighting back.

Kenji could see the pride in John's eyes while Jamie was talking. It had been a challenging journey these past few months. He had let go of the aspirations he'd had for Jamie before the accident. He'd had long conversations with the therapists at the rehab center and focused much of his energy on doing research regarding traumatic brain injury. Only time would tell if Jamie would one day be capable of taking over his empire. Meanwhile he had put a plan in place, with his attorney as overseer, to ensure that Jamie's future needs would be met.

The waitress served their lunches, and after taking a few bites, Fletcher looked across the table at Kenji. "Listen, I've got something really exciting to tell you," he said. "At least I hope it'll be exciting for you. I happen to have a financial interest in the Toyota dealership in Honolulu. For the past three years, we've purchased a silver sponsorship to the Hawaiian Open golf tournament. It's been a good advertising opportunity for the dealership. This coming year, Sony has signed on to be the sponsor of this prestigious PGA tour event, so it'll be called the Sony Open. Typically, one of the managers or the top salesman is chosen to be the amateur who gets to play with the pros on the Wednesday before the tournament starts. Well, it turns out, all the people there know what happened with Jamie and about your role in his recovery, and they unanimously decided they want you to be the amateur golfer representing the company this year. So, come January eleventh, you and three other amateurs will be teeing off with one of the pro golfers."

Kenji was speechless. He sat dumbfounded, his mouth slack as he tried to formulate a response. After what felt like an eternity, he looked at John and Jamie. "Wow!" he said. "I don't know what to say. I never, ever thought I'd have the opportunity to play in a public event at this level. I'm overwhelmed!" He fought back his tears, knowing Fletcher would consider such a display unmanly.

"Grandpa, it was worth it just to see the look on Kenji's face," Jamie said with a giggle.

Vince finally recovered from his astonishment. "What a great opportunity! Just to hang out with some of the best golfers in the world is really exciting."

"Yeah, that's right," John beamed. "And Vince, you know Kenji's going to need a caddy, and I suspect you'd be the natural choice."

"Vince, can you believe this? You and I playing with the pros, just like we belong there," beamed Kenji.

"You do belong there. You're one of the best golfers on the Big Island, and you haven't been playing very long. I'm confident you'll do well and do a great job representing our company and the community of Kona," said John. "Having a one-legged Japanese golfer representing my company— there's some irony in that statement," he added, the scruffy whiskers on his face covering a wry grin.

"Thank you very much, John. I promise I'll do my best. So what's the next step?" asked Kenji.

"You'll play a practice round at Waialae the Sunday of the tournament week. Then Tuesday night they have what they call the draw party. It's a reception where you get to meet the guys on your team and where you'll be assigned a team number. There are fifty-two teams. Then there's a drawing to select a team, and each team has thirty seconds to pick the pro they want to play with. Meanwhile the pool of pros will be diminishing, and you guys may have to pick another pro if your favorite is chosen before your draw. Then on Wednesday, you play the Pro-Am. This is an important part of the week because the money raised is a big chunk that the tournament earns for charity. Every year this golf tournament contributes over a million dollars to more than a hundred nonprofit organizations."

"Part of the money comes from the TV sponsorship," Fletcher went on, curiously enthusiastic. "The tournament is seen in over a hundred and fifty countries and four hundred and fifty million homes. I learned this at the presentation the Sony Open people gave to sponsors. It was impressive to say the least. They say the tournament's economic impact for Hawaii is about forty million dollars each year. Now, Kenji, don't get all big headed on us," Fletcher cautioned, a twinkle in his eye. "They don't televise the Pro-Am nationally. ESPN does spot coverage, and the local TV stations usually have a camera crew roaming around to get shots for the evening news."

Kenji sat there smiling, trying to process all the information. *Thank you, God*, he thought, *for this opportunity to use the gift you have given to me.*

* * *

Vince, with his shattered dream of playing on the PGA tour, was stoked about his upcoming involvement in the Sony Open, even if it was as a caddy/coach. "This is such an awesome opportunity for you, Kenji! I can't believe we're actually going to the Sony Open, and the irony is that we're going on John Fletcher's dime. Life doesn't get much better than that!" he blathered on and on.

"Calm down, Vince. It's just a golf tournament," Kenji replied.

"It's not just any old golf tournament. It's the Sony Open. Do you realize all the guys who'll be there? Davis Love III, Corey Pavin, Curtis Strange, Mark O'Meara, Ernie Els, and John Huston, just to name a few. In fact Huston set the tournament record last year with an overall score of two hundred and sixty. Let's see—divide that by four rounds. Geez, that's an average of sixty-five shots a round. We've got our work cut out for us. Hey, buddy, what's going on in that head of yours?" asked Vince, knowing that when Kenji got quiet something usually was bothering him.

"I'm okay, just excited," Kenji said. Deep down, however, he was scared as hell, but he couldn't quite figure out why.

Upon arriving at home, Kenji phoned Lilly and told her his big news about playing in the Sony Open. She was thrilled for him and asked if she could attend the event. "Of course. You'd better come. You can place a horseshoe of flowers around my neck in the winner's circle," he teased, but he didn't mention anything about his fears.

Later he sat down and wrote Mia a long letter. He told her how profoundly moved he was that John Fletcher had arranged for him to play in the Pro-Am tournament. John's orneriness and meanness through the years had caused both him and Mia times of stress. He also shared that he had a feeling of foreboding about the golf tournament that he didn't understand.

That night, the mysterious ways of the mind revealed the reason for Kenji's feelings. His dream was vivid. He was on that school playground with that football all those years ago, and he was running in the wrong direction. He suffered through the agony of the humiliation the older boys heaped on him after the misunderstanding. He woke with a start. *God, I haven't consciously thought about the incident in years. What is getting triggered in my head?* he wondered.

* * *

The next morning, Kenji did something he thought he'd never do. He called a therapist and asked for an appointment. The time was set for two o'clock that afternoon. Sandy Jones was a highly recommended marriage and family therapist in Kona. She also happened to be Vince's stunning redheaded girlfriend and had been for some time, so Kenji knew her socially.

When Kenji arrived at Sandy's office, he noted the soft pastel furnishings, cushioned chairs strewn with teddy bears of all sizes that created a warm, friendly environment. She was striking in a tailored white pants suit topping a silk blouse, the color matching her startling green eyes. Sandy greeted him with a warm hug. "Kenji, I was surprised to hear from you. Come into my office and have a seat. Can I offer you a coffee or soft drink?"

"No, I'm fine. Thank you for seeing me on such short notice."

"You're welcome. Now tell me what's going on with you."

Once seated, he talked as if the floodgates to his soul had opened. He told Sandy about the Pro-Am deal John Fletcher had offered him, though he suspected Vince had already shared this bit of information. He rambled on about how thrilled he was about getting to play with one of the top hundred golfers in the world and what a big deal it was for regular golfers like him. Suddenly his demeanor darkened as he talked about his feeling of foreboding that he didn't understand until he'd had that dream. For the first time in his life, Kenji shared with another human being, besides Mia, the details of his childhood incident.

"Sandy isn't that the weirdest thing you've ever heard? Here I am fifty years old, and that little incident still comes back to haunt me."

"Not at all, Kenji. This is a common occurrence, actually more common than most people think. One of the reasons is that for many kids school is their first exposure to the give-and-take of the real world. They've lived in a protected environment, especially if they're the only child in their family. Kenji, I bet in your family no one talked openly about their feelings. Am I right?"

Kenji thought for a moment then responded, "Yes. You're right on. We talked about the weather and how business was going and who we saw that day, but never our feelings."

"Well, there you go," Sandy said. "The healthy way to deal with your incident at school would have been to share with your parents what had happened and how badly your feelings had been hurt. If you could have talked about the incident back then it wouldn't have been so traumatic, especially if your parents had provided some comfort and nurturing."

"Let me tell you a similar story," Sandy continued. "Dolly Parton, the country-western singer, ultimately made a lot of money because of a schoolyard incident where kids made fun of a coat her mother had sewed for her at home. She loved that coat, and the hurt of this incident stayed with her for many years. When she was a successful music-recording star, she wrote a song about that day called 'Coat of Many Colors.' The record sold millions of copies. What a way for her to reclaim her power."

"As an adult," Kenji said, "I look back on my schoolyard incident and it seems so simple. It was such a short-duration event that it seems silly to me that it has affected my life at all."

"Let me ask you a question," Sandy said. "Which feelings are triggered when you think of that incident?"

Kenji thought for a moment then said, "Shame and embarrassment. Those boys hurt my feelings."

"That's good. You identified the feelings. Did you do anything to be ashamed about?"

"Not really, because I didn't understand the rules of the game."

"And you were embarrassed because...?"

"Because I did something stupid."

"But you didn't know the rules, so how can your actions be considered stupid?"

"I guess they can't," Kenji replied.

"The key to overcoming an issue like this is to number one, recognize the feeling, and number two, decide whether the feeling is valid. If the feeling isn't valid, then the decision is yours. You can take your power back or stay mired in the negative feelings.

"You make it sound so simple."

"It *is* just that simple, Kenji." She smiled, impressed that he could so easily get in touch with his feelings.

"Since I'm here, there is something else I need to discuss with you. As you know, I've been spending quite a bit of time with Lilly. Frankly, I'm having difficulty sorting out my feelings for her. I like her a lot, and I think, but I'm not sure, that I'm in love with her. I think about her all the time. She makes me laugh too. But this is the only time I've had feelings for a woman other than Mia, my wife who passed away, and frankly, it scares the hell out of me."

"What's the worst thing that Lilly has ever done to you?"

"I can't think of anything," Kenji said. "She's always very supportive. I mean, we've had a few disagreements, but it was usually my fault because my priorities were screwed up."

"If Lilly hasn't done anything bad to you, where is the fear coming from?"

"Get real," Kenji said. "Here I am a one-legged man, obsessed with golf, having nightmares about a dumb incident from my childhood."

"Does the fact that you lost a leg bother her?"

"Not at all. She teases me sometimes, but it's all in good fun. She doesn't hurt my feelings."

"Does your obsession with golf bother her?"

"Not that I'm aware of."

"So what is *really* bothering you about Lilly?"

Kenji shrugged. "I don't know. Perhaps it's because she's so independent. She doesn't need me," he confessed. "What if she gets bored with me? She's so gorgeous that men would be lined up around the block just to get a date with her. She told me once that she prefers the company of men."

"So do I, truth be told, so we won't hold that against her. Has she been dating other men?"

"No."

"Would you prefer to be in a relationship with a compliant woman who has no interests beside you?"

"Sounds boring."

"My point exactly. Kenji, listen to me. Lilly already has made her choice of men. And that man is you. You enjoy your time together. She makes you laugh. She's supportive and affectionate. I know that's true. Vince and I have seen the two of you together. You always look so happy. Kenji, you're so special and so is Lilly. The ball is in your court. Either make a commitment to her or free her up to be happy with someone else."

"Wow! Once again, you make it sound so simple."

"It is, Kenji. Let me ask you one final question. What is the worst thing that could happen to you?"

"A lot of bad things already have happened to me. My parents were killed, Mia died, I got struck by lightning, and I lost part of my leg. The worst thing that could happen to me now is if Lilly left me."

"Is that likely to happen?"

"Probably not."

"If it did happen, how would you handle it?"

Kenji thought for a moment before answering. "I'd probably go on living my life, playing golf and spending time with my friends." The stark realization finally dawned. *I'd be okay*, he thought. *Everything would be all right.* All of his fears suddenly vanished like ghosts into a foggy night.

"Thank you, Sandy. I think I've just seen the light."

That day, Kenji embarked upon a new journey. He brimmed with self-confidence about Lilly, about golf, about life in general. *Take your power back. Take your power back*, played like a familiar song in his head. Even the Sony Open held no sway over him. It was just another competitive challenge, and he relished any challenge.

CHAPTER 27

It was Sunday morning, and Vince had picked up
bagels and cream cheese for a breakfast meeting with
Kenji to go over a plan for the Sony Open. The day was
stifling hot, the air thick with humidity even at this
early hour. Vince pulled his car into the driveway of
the house where Kenji had lived since early childhood.
If this house could talk I wonder what stories would it tell?
Vince wondered. The notion of continuity and stability
appealed to him.

Kenji opened the door dressed in white shorts and a
pink tie-dyed muscle shirt, his prosthesis in full view.

"Vince's bagel-delivery service for you, Mr. Watanabe."

"Good morning, my friend. Happy to see you!" he greeted his guest with a wide grin. "Come on in. The coffee is hot."

The two sat at the kitchen table sipping coffee and slathering cream cheese on toasted bagels, "God, Kenji did you ever think we'd be sitting here planning a strategy for you to play in the Sony Pro-Am?"

"It's no big deal," Kenji kidded him. "Just another tournament."

Vince was concerned about Kenji's rather muted reaction to this momentous opportunity but was encouraged by his good spirits. He had to admit it was still shocking to see the artificial limb fully displayed. He hoped that if Kenji had any reservations about the tournament he would talk about them. Vince, a huge PGA fan, a groupie, couldn't wait to hang out with the pros.

"You've got to understand," Kenji said, "that I'm not in this for the notoriety unless it'll somehow help others."

"I've got an awesome idea for you. Assuming you do really well in the Pro-Am, I could visualize starting a Kenji Watanabe charity golf tournament. I know all the guys in the men's club at Makalei would support it. Once your photo hits the Honolulu newspapers, the publicity would attract players from all over the islands. What do you think?"

"I've got a better idea. We could call it the One-Legged Open," teased Kenji. "But we're getting ahead of ourselves. First, what are your thoughts on competing in the Sony tournament? What's our plan of action? What should I be practicing on? I may be kind of anal about preparation, but that attitude and mindset has worked for me so far."

"Here are some of the things I've been thinking about. One is the issue of the wind. Some of the holes could have significant wind conditions, especially in the afternoon. Part of our plan is to include strategies for dealing with the wind and practice playing in windy conditions. That means that we'll likely spend some time at the Waikoloa Village course, since that'll give us our best chance of playing in the wind."

Vince continued the strategy session with facts. "Waialae is a short par-seventy golf course at 6,627 yards from the white tees. There are some tricky things to consider. Some of the fairways are narrow, which shouldn't be a problem for you. Your visualization gift will serve you well on this course. But if we're really serious about this, I think we should fly to Honolulu and play the Waialae course a few times so you can get a feel for it and also get a feel for putting on the greens. They're probably lightning fast."

"Will they let us on at Waialae?" Kenji asked. "It's a private country club course."

"Not to worry. A friend of mine runs the pro shop there. Once we tell him you'll be playing in the tournament, we won't have any problem getting a tee time. The other advantage to this scheme is you'll get experience playing with strangers. You may as well get used to the extra pressure we all feel when playing with people we don't know. The key is to be able to stay relaxed and not let the pressure of the event, the gallery, and the probability of TV cameras interfere with the way you normally hit the ball or how you'll think about your next shot. The second area where we need to spend time is reading the greens and putting. The greens and the fairways at Waialae are Bermuda grass. Since I'll be your caddy, it'll be my responsibility to give you detailed reports on the grain and the slope of each putt that you'll have coming up. The purpose of the weeks of practice ahead will be to focus on consistency and to get repetitive shots at the right distance."

Determined to make a good showing at the tournament, Kenji meticulously took notes as his coach outlined their strategy.

"The Sony Pro-Am is a best-ball tournament," Vince continued. "You play your own ball on each hole. At the completion of the hole, the lowest score among all team members serves as the team score. Club selection will be critical and probably different from your usual game. You'll want to practice your mid-iron shots just in case and know the exact yardage for each club."

"I already have a good handle on that," Kenji replied, calm and confident.

The thought occurred to him that Vince was making this more difficult than it needed to be. *Is it possible he's trying to make me feel intimidated?* he wondered. *Is he jealous that it's me playing in the tournament and not him?* Grateful for Vince's input, he dismissed the idea as irrational.

"Since we only have twelve weeks to prepare," Vince told him, "I suggest we make some assumptions. First, all the amateurs will be feeling the pressure of playing in such a prestigious event. The one place where pressure shows up most is on short putts. Everyone understands when you miss a twelve-foot putt. Even the professionals only make fifteen to thirty percent of putts from this distance. But everyone expects you to make putts of three feet or less. The pros make eight-five to ninety-five percent of these. The effect of these high expectations is tough on amateur golfers, and in tournament situations, it's easy to muff short putts. My idea is that we make you the short-putt specialist. This means most of our putting practice will be for short and medium distance, say six to eight feet.

"Okay."

"The other thing I need is for you to be totally honest with me about how much exercise you can tolerate. I know you're doing really well with your new follow-through to accommodate the fact that you don't have total flexibility in your prosthesis. We just have to be sure that you don't run the risk of abrasions on your stump with a heavy practice and playing schedule. You have to be the guide on this and set your own pace, okay?"

"I understand," Kenji said. "I'll be careful. I promise."

"You should work on developing a consistent putting stroke. I'll give you some routines that we used when I was in college. The third area of focus will be your ability to put the ball close to the pin. This will ultimately affect your score more than anything else. I'll put together two or three different case situations on which we can base our training. The idea is to have the fewest surprises possible when we're actually out there playing a round. What do you think so far?"

"Everything sounds good, Vince. As always, you bring so much common sense to the game of golf. This is a great plan! It makes me sadder than ever that you were injured and couldn't pursue a career in the PGA. You would've been a huge success."

Vince, suddenly quiet, was lost in his own thoughts of his glory days playing golf. *This sucks*, he thought. *Why didn't Fletcher choose me to play? This is my dream, and all I get to do is caddy for someone else? Life isn't fair.* Vince usually wasn't a selfish person, but anger welled up inside him like a churning volcano about to erupt.

They had been discussing their strategies so intensely that Vince hadn't noticed the time. He stood up abruptly. "I've got to leave. I have an appointment at eleven. Let's go to Waikoloa Village tomorrow. Ernie wants to play too. Is that okay with you?" he asked, effectively hiding his dark, jealous thoughts.

"You bet! I'm eager to get started," Kenji replied enthusiastically, as he walked Vince to the front door.

The excitement was building now that the plan was in place. Could Kenji maintain his composure under pressure? He took a few deep breaths to slow his heart rate, knowing that his Zen-like concentration would contribute more than anything else to his success. His only nagging concern was his leg. Would it withstand the rigors of this practice schedule?

CHAPTER 28

It was a combination of events that got Kenji in trouble with Lilly. The Waikoloa Village course was busier than usual due to a late-morning tournament. Vince, Ernie, and Kenji had to wait around until two o'clock to even tee off. To top it off, play was very slow; it looked like it would take five hours to get through a round. Kenji had made arrangements to take Lilly out to dinner at the Kona Inn that evening to celebrate her birthday. The dinner reservation was set at seven. He had purchased a beautiful three-carat diamond engagement ring, hoping that she would love the elegant pave setting. Tonight was the night that Kenji planned to embrace the future wholeheartedly by asking Lilly to accept his hand in marriage. He had it all planned with the chef at the restaurant. Kenji would get down on his left knee to propose; that would be the signal, and when she accepted, the chef would deliver the birthday cake ablaze with candles. He couldn't wait to see the look on her face when she opened the blue velvet box. He also planned to pick up a bouquet of flowers on his way home to present to Lilly, knowing she loved fresh-cut flowers.

It was a little after seven when Kenji finally got back to his car and had a chance to call Lilly. "Hey, beautiful. How are you? I'm sorry, but I'm running late. In fact I just got off the course at Waikoloa Village, so by the time I get back to town, shower and change clothes, it'll be at least eight o'clock. I'll pick you up about eight thirty, okay?"

Silence. He could almost hear Lilly fuming on the other end of the phone. After at least thirty seconds of dead silence, she responded, unable to keep the anger and hurt out of her voice. "Just skip it, Kenji. Since you're so late, I'm not much in the mood to celebrate tonight."

He talked fast, apologizing and was just getting into a plan to make it up to her when she interrupted, "Kenji, I've got another call coming in. Call me tomorrow." He heard the click of the line going dead.

Wow, he thought. *She really is pissed off.* He never had heard Lilly talk to him or anyone else so curtly. He couldn't blame her, though, and he felt uneasy about having made her so angry. He was disappointed as well; all his fancy plans had gone up in smoke. He dialed the number for the restaurant, cancelled the reservation, and left a message for the chef to put his proposal scheme on hold.

Kenji planned to call Lilly first thing in the morning and set up another date. A belated birthday celebration at a gourmet restaurant near the Waikoloa resort complex would be just the ticket. This was one of the best restaurants on the Big Island, and he knew Lilly loved the cuisine there. He and Vince ended up settling for Big Macs when they got back to Kona—a small consolation. He had a feeling of foreboding for the remainder of the evening, but he'd make up for tonight's debacle first thing tomorrow morning, he rationalized.

The call Lilly got was an emergency. Bill Mason, the new owner of her business in Southern California, tearfully told her that his wife and business partner, Joan, had been killed in a car accident. Lilly's consulting contract still had two months to run before it ended. Bill asked if she could come right away for an emergency board of directors meeting to help get some of the legal documents sorted out in the aftermath of this tragedy. She readily agreed.

Lilly phoned Kenji from the airport before she left. "Hi, Kenji. Sorry I cut you off last time. I'm at the airport, headed for Los Angeles."

His first thought was, *She's leaving me.* "What happened? Why are you going to L.A?"

She told him what had happened. "Sorry I was short with you earlier, but I was upset because you obviously put playing golf higher on your list of priorities than celebrating my birthday."

"No, I'm the one who's sorry for missing our date. It was my fault."

"Kenji, frankly I'm concerned about your having become so obsessed with this whole golf thing. I hope you don't push yourself too hard and end up injuring yourself. There, I said what has been bugging me, so I won't say any more about it."

She sure is upfront about her feelings, Kenji thought. *Will I ever be able to do that?* "Honey, I'll be okay," he told her, "and I'll pay attention to what you just said. In fact there's something I planned to talk to you about tonight before everything got screwed up. When will you be back?"

"I don't know. We have a board meeting set up for sometime tomorrow morning. I'll know more after that. I'll call you when I can. Oops, they just called my flight. Talk to you tomorrow. Bye."

Kenji felt terrible. He was getting used to feeling connected with Lilly. *I love this woman,* he thought. *I want to marry her. I don't want to live the rest of my life without her. I like not being lonely.* The more he thought about it, he realized that Lilly was right. Golf had become his number-one priority. *Why can't she understand that? Do I have to make a choice between golf and Lilly?* If he did have to make a choice, he wasn't completely sure which one he would choose.

Lilly hadn't planned on falling in love with Kenji, but she had. Her original Kona plan was to build a single life, make some friends, and along the way figure out what might be fun to do for the next few years. *So much for plan A*, she thought. She had fallen in love and opened an office in less than a year. Her business was acquiring new patients every day, which prompted her to hire two employees, a receptionist, and a personable young fellow who helped customers choose frames for their new glasses and fit them properly.

She had fallen for Kenji almost from their very first meeting. He was such a gentleman—a very attractive gentleman. And she was secretly pleased to be in a relationship with someone of Japanese descent. Her parents must be smiling down from heaven. Enough of those white guys. After the hearty, too self-assured, arrogant men she had dated on the mainland, Kenji was a breath of fresh air. She adored his quiet sense of self, the little things, his courteous manner, his reticence, plus the fact that he had a clean fresh scent tinged with some exotic spice that stirred her senses. He was constant. She could count on him—except when it came to golf. Then all bets were off. Her thoughts went back to Honolulu and the month they'd spent together living under the same roof. She couldn't help but smile as she remembered their passionate yet tender lovemaking before his surgery. The feelings were magical, stirring passions she hadn't felt in a very long time.

Where did it go awry? Was it her fault? Was she too independent? Kenji had been very supportive as she set up her new business practice, offering suggestions and advice. Was she too forward? He seemed to enjoy her sometime ribald sense of humor and frank, open way of speaking. Sometimes he seemed totally enchanted with her, but then at times he'd distance himself from her. Or was he just happy to have a beautiful woman on his arm, a trophy to show off to his friends? *What did he want to talk with me about?* she wondered. The entire situation frustrated her.

Even so, their time in Honolulu had been miraculous despite the trying circumstances. Kenji had just lost part of a leg and had major adjustments to make both physically and emotionally. He was brave and amazingly upbeat and positive. Lilly was so proud of him. Another quality she loved about Kenji was his tendency to consider the welfare of others and to help whenever possible.

For some reason she remembered something that happened when she was a little girl. Her parents had gotten a puppy from the dog pound as a birthday gift for her. The puppy was cute but scared, apparently having been mistreated by its previous owner. Lilly was very gentle with her new charge and after a few weeks had finally won its trust. *Maybe that's the tack to take with Kenji,* she thought. *Just be gentle, patient, and loving.*

* * *

When Vince called to decide on a meeting place before the drive to their agreed-upon practice session at the Big Island Country Club, Kenji wasn't in the mood to play golf or practice or even see anyone. "Sorry Vince, but I'm going to have to miss today," he told him. "I don't feel well."

"What's wrong?" asked Vince. "Do you have the flu? Is your leg bothering you?"

"No, I just feel off." He didn't want to bare his heart broken soul to Vince, at least not now.

"You take care of yourself, Kenji. Our mission today was to work on your sand shots since this club has the best sand traps on the island. We can catch up later. Call me if you need anything, okay?"

* * *

Lilly sat through the board meeting in Los Angeles, anxious to be done and fly back to Kona. The meeting went on and on, and it was clear that they wouldn't finish before lunch. After three grueling hours, the group decided they needed a break and walked to a Chinese restaurant down the street. After Lilly had ordered, she excused herself and stepped outside to call Kenji. She only had a little battery power left on her cell phone, so it would have to be a short conversation. His phone rang and rang and rang, and finally the call went to his voicemail. She tried to tell Kenji what was happening, but before she got more than a few words out of her mouth, the connection cut off as her cell phone died.

When Kenji came out of the bathroom, he noticed he had a new voicemail from Lilly. Her message got cut off after a few words. Kenji was in a state of panic and paranoia as the hours slowly drifted into sunset; he considered every possible negative scenario. Suddenly the phone rang, and he thanked God it was Lilly.

"Sorry I didn't get to call you again earlier," Lilly said. "Our meeting just broke up. What's going on with you?"

"Oh, I'm just hanging out today. I had a voicemail from you earlier today, but I couldn't make sense of it."

"My phone ran out of juice when I called. Listen, Bill is going to drop me off at the hotel after dinner, and I'll call you from there. Will you be around?"

"You bet. I'll be waiting for your call." He was so relieved he felt like crying. *Man up, Kenji,* he thought. *Lilly called. That's a good sign.* Perhaps all was not lost after all.

CHAPTER 29

It had been three days since Vince and Kenji had arrived in Honolulu on a tropical December morning. They had played Waialae the first two days, making detailed notes on every hole of the course. Kenji's game was in top form, the visualization gift continuing to work well, the putting and chipping still a challenge but improving. He was getting better on the iron shots onto the greens with the ball landing within ten feet of the pin on most holes but not all. After the second day, Kenji was feeling some pain in his stump. That evening they lounged in Kenji's room at the hotel having a beer. He excused himself to go to the bathroom and took off his prosthesis. The stump was red and sore but not bleeding, so he wrapped it up with gauze, reattached the prosthesis, and flushed the toilet.

He didn't share the information about the soreness with Vince.

He came out of the bathroom and suggested, "Let's order dinner from room service. How about a couple of nice T-bone steaks?" He knew that would appeal to Vince, who typically relished a good cut of beef.

"That sounds great!" replied Vince. "Are you sure you don't want to go out? There's a great steak house down the street. I'm buying!"

"You go on if you'd like, but I'd prefer to kick back and have a glass or two of Cabernet Sauvignon and a nice steak right here."

"That's fine with me. Are you okay, Kenji? I was worried about you drowning in the bathtub. You were in there so long."

"I'm okay, just a little tired," he said, not wanting to raise any red flags about his leg, knowing Vince was more excited about the Sony Open than he was.

They ordered dinner then talked about each hole on the course. "Tomorrow, our strategy is to work on putting," Vince told him. "The rest of your game is fine, but I want you to practice putting from ten to fifteen feet out just in case you need that range in the tournament."

Kenji gratefully agreed, knowing he'd have an easier time putting than playing eighteen holes of golf with his sore stump. The day of the tournament was getting closer and closer, and he wanted to be in peak physical condition for the event. He'd have a couple of weeks to rest at home and then enjoy the Christmas holidays with Lilly and his friends.

He and Lilly had patched things up when she had returned to the island from Los Angeles. Both were a bit wary, but as the days passed they fell back into a comfortable routine, though neither was inclined to delve deeper into the misunderstanding. Kenji had decided not to propose marriage just yet, rationalizing there was no rush. Truthfully he was still feeling a bit gun-shy and wanted to let some time elapse while he focused on preparing for the Sony Open. He wondered how Lilly would react to his golf game in the midst of TV cameras, the huge gallery of people expected to attend, and all the hero worship toward the pros. Lilly never had seen him play golf, so she truly didn't understand its alluring appeal.

Day three in Honolulu went according to plan. Kenji's putting from longer distances improved with practice, and Vince seemed pleased with the results. It had been an enjoyable experience for the most part, but Kenji was anxious to get home. They drove to the airport, dropped off the rental car, and proceeded to the terminal. "I see you're limping a bit," Vince remarked. "Does your leg hurt?"

"Just a bit. I'll be okay," cutting off further discussion about his leg.

Kenji had purchased a bottle of Lilly's favorite fragrance, Chanel No. 5, one of his Christmas gifts for her. He had also found a buttery-soft leather suit for her at an upscale department store in Honolulu, where there were ample choices. The suit was the color of extra-ripe peaches, a terrific color to highlight Lilly's skin tone and dark hair. It had a short tight skirt and a tailored jacket. He couldn't wait to see the looks on the mostly staid Rotarian faces when she wore it to a future meeting. He knew Lilly would get pleasure from the stunning outfit and the accompanying admiring stares.

They boarded Vince's plane for their flight to Kona and arrived without incident.

Lilly and Sandy were in the main terminal to meet them. "Hello, boys! Have a good time?" they asked as hugs were exchanged all around.

"Yes, we had a great time, though of course we missed you desperately," came the joint reply.

"Yeah, right," the girls retorted.

They went to their respective cars and drove off into the safety and security of Kona. Kenji was happy to be home.

Lilly invited him to attend Christmas Eve church services with her, and he gracefully agreed, even though he didn't consider himself Christian. Lilly had been attending church since her arrival in Kona and enjoyed the people, the music, and sense of community. She had made several friends there, in addition to Sandy and Vince, who also attended regularly. Earlier in the week, Lilly had extended an invitation to the threesome to spend Christmas Eve at her condo. She had been brought up on the old adage "A way to a man's heart is through his stomach," so she planned an elegant gourmet dinner, Peking duck complete with authentic trimmings. As they lounged at the table after enjoying the repast, Kenji smiled tenderly at Lilly. "Thank you, sweetheart. That was an awesome meal."

"You're very welcome," she responded, knowing she had hit a home run.

Then they opened presents, a full range of silly and practical items—fun golf items for the guys, a light sweater, a computer accessory, an expensive bottle of wine; mostly clothes, jewelry, and perfume for the women. Lilly was thrilled with her gifts, especially the suit, which she modeled while dancing around the room gleefully. Kenji had chosen wisely.

After church at midnight—although it seemed a bit irreverent after hearing the story of the birth of Jesus—they all trooped back to Lilly's condo for a nightcap. They sunk into her cozy white plush sofas, brandies in hand, talking about the sermon and all the things for which they were most grateful while toasting to a Happy Christmas.

Kenji and Lilly celebrated Christmas Day at his home, just the two of them watching old movies, laughing and teasing. He had purchased the *Kama Sutra*, which they reviewed page by page; they laughed hysterically at some of the sexual positions only a contortionist could possibly achieve. Lilly was relieved Kenji was thinking about the subject of sex, while Kenji was happy to see that her bawdy sense of humor was still intact.

Kenji made a momentous decision that night. If there was any hope for a future with Lilly, he knew he had to open up and share his history. "Lilly, this is a journal my father kept. It would honor me if you read it. Perhaps you'll understand me better if you know more about my family," he said as he handed the tattered pages to her. The cover was obviously homemade, with childlike drawings of island scenes, the pages tied together with a sturdy ribbon. The inside pages were neatly handwritten.

Taro Watanabe's Journal

December 7, 1941

The world changed today, and the future for my family and me is very uncertain. This morning, Japanese airplanes bombed Hawaii. Most of the bombs fell on Pearl Harbor and Hickam Field.

I was hiking in the hills northwest of Pearl Harbor with two of my friends when the devastation began. We could not believe what we were seeing, the carnage exploding before our eyes. We were terrified and immediately set out for home to make sure our families were okay. People were in the streets milling about and talking excitedly in the village we passed through on a dead run. We couldn't help notice the dirty looks that came our way.

When I finally reached home, my parents were frightened, and when it was confirmed that it was Japanese airplanes dropping the bombs they felt ashamed that people of their homeland would do something like this to America. My father loved America. He had worked hard and was able to open a barbershop after having spent years toiling in the sugarcane fields. He was proud of his business and grateful for the opportunity that America offered. My mother was a picture bride and worked in the home of our landlord as the housekeeper.

We huddled together indoors as we saw armed soldiers patrol our neighborhood.

December 8, 1941

A neighbor kid showed me a copy of the newspaper. An article estimated that four hundred people had been killed in

*the bombing. There were rumors that Japan also had invaded
Guam and the Panama Canal. The newspaper told people
to fill their bathtubs with water in case the waterworks had
been poisoned or damaged, so we filled the galvanized tub on
the back porch. All people were instructed to stay inside, and
a total blackout and a curfew was announced.*

*Defying the edict, my buddy and I walked into Honolulu
and tried to enlist in the Army today but were refused. The
Army sergeant told us we were considered enemy aliens and
suggested we get off the streets. I'm eighteen years old and a
senior in high school. I want to fight for America.*

*Japan declared war on the United States and Great
Britain. Military law is in effect, and an Army general is
taking over as military governor of Hawaii. All residents
must be fingerprinted and carry ID cards. Civilians are pro-
hibited from carrying more than two hundred dollars.*

*The general population is frightened, and many think
Japanese residents are spies. We try to stay home and out of
sight.*

*All ROTC students at the University of Hawaii formed
the Hawaiian Territorial Guard. They each received a rifle
with five bullets and were assigned to guard vital installa-
tions such as bridges and waterworks.*

January 5, 1942

*Japanese bank accounts have been frozen, and no bank
will cash my father's checks. No one is coming into the shop
for haircuts, so our family is running out of money. Also,
many stores will not sell to us. Only Japanese shopkeepers
honor our meager business.*

When politicians in Washington, DC, discovered that the Hawaiian Territorial Guard was comprised of Japanese, the two-thousand-man unit was disbanded, and all members were classified as 4C, enemy aliens.

Conversely, there are 1,300 Nisei Japanese in the Hawaiian National Guard. They were mobilized within hours after the December 7th attack. Initially their rifles were stripped from them, but they were returned almost immediately.

January 15, 1942

I quit school and was allowed to join the Hawaiian National Guard. My parents are proud of me.

June 5, 1942

I'm leaving. Last night all 1,432 of the Japanese members of the National Guard were loaded onto the USS Maui. The ship will head east, we think, while zigzagging to avoid Japanese submarines.

June 12, 1942

The ship steamed into the harbor at Oakland, California. We disembarked and boarded a train. We are now in the 100th Infantry Battalion, United States Army. I am now an American soldier.

June 16, 1942

We arrived at Camp McCoy somewhere in Wisconsin today. We marched to a field and set up tents. There are four of us in each tent.

July 17, 1942

The other soldiers don't like us much, but we're separated so there aren't any fights. We have been training hard, and I am becoming a lot stronger. I have learned to shoot my rifle and qualified as an expert marksman, which is the best. Many of my buddies are also experts.

We compete with the white soldiers in several sports and win a lot of the time, which fuels their dislike of us. All of us try harder to win each game — I think to honor our families and heritage.

October 4, 1942

We are still in tents, and it is starting to get cold at night, bone-chilling for us islanders.

January 6, 1943

We boarded the train headed for Camp Shelby in Mississippi. I hope it is warmer there.

July 10, 1943

It's hot and humid here, with lots of bugs and snakes. We've been on field training and war games in Louisiana. All of us are eager to go fight the Germans.

There have been fights with new Japanese soldiers coming into our unit from the mainland. Their families are in internment camps, and most are angry about this situation. They're pretty snotty with their precise English and show disdain for us islanders. Our guys love to gamble, and we do get loud after a beer or two. They call our English "pidgin."

We grew up around kids whose parents were Portuguese, Chinese, Pilipino, or from other islands in the Pacific, so we combine words from several languages. We all sound fine as far as I'm concerned.

The fights between the mainlanders and the islanders have become a distraction and are pissing off the officers. The commander decided to haul some of us to visit a detention camp in Rohwer, Arkansas. About fifty of us were told to wear Class A uniforms for the three-hour bus trip. We were rowdy and loud on the trip, yelling at each other and singing. The camp was a real eye opener. There are about 8,500 Japanese Americans there. Over half are US citizens just like me. The older ones came to the mainland from Japan in the early 1900s.

We learned there are ten relocation centers in America with about 120,000 Japanese Americans interned. Just after the attack on Pearl Harbor, panic ensued. There was pressure from the military to intern all Japanese on the West Coast. The Justice Department disagreed. President Roosevelt finally sided with the military and signed Executive Order 9066 in February 1942, which authorized the relocation of all Japanese with one-sixteenth or more Japanese blood. The first evacuations began in late March 1942. After notification, residents were given six days to dispose of all possessions they could not carry.

The military considered evacuating all the Japanese from Hawaii at this time, but calmer heads prevailed. It was pointed out that the Japanese represented over one-third of the population, and the economy of the islands would be severely affected if they were interned.

Placing 120,000 Japanese Americans in relocation centers was a horrid decision. Camp conditions are awful; crowding and lack of privacy take a hard toll, especially on the women, married couples, and the elderly. The people were more cheerful than we'd expected, considering the circumstances. They did everything they could to show that they were good citizens. They were especially proud of the bountiful gardens they had planted outside the fence. They showed us the chickens and pigs they were raising, which made them self-sufficient for food. This is a big deal, since a lot of food is rationed. Many told us how proud they were of us and asked us to fight hard for them. Their hospitality and kindness touched me. The captain introduced us to four families who had sons in Company B. Most of us knew these guys. We were very quiet on the bus ride back to the base.

The commander's scheme worked. The inter-fighting stopped, and we gained a healthy respect for our mainland counterparts. We also found a renewed sense of mission to be good soldiers for all the people of our culture and especially be outstanding American citizens.

August 11, 1943

Today we leave for Camp Kilmer, New Jersey, and then move on to a staging area in Oran on the north coast of Africa.

September 19, 1943

We arrived in Salerno, Italy, today. It's twenty-five miles south of Naples. This is it. We're now in a combat zone. It's time to go to work and earn our pay.

September 29, 1943

We went into battle today. It was the first time I ever saw dead people up close, the horrors of war. Four of my buddies were killed today; several others were wounded. After five days of off-again, on-again fighting, we drove the Germans back twenty-five miles and seized control of the town of Benevento, about forty miles north of Salerno. We've had almost no sleep and no hot food for days. I am sick at heart to see my friends mutilated and slaughtered. I feel numb, partly from lack of sleep, but more likely from witnessing the carnage on the battlefield.

January 8, 1944

I will never forget Monte Cassino, a beautiful hill town with a monastery on the top. It was a key location in our march to Rome. It's really cold here. Yesterday Company B tried to reach the wall where my Company A and Company C were located. They set off smoke grenades then started their advance across the open field. When they reached the halfway point, a gust of wind blew the smoke away, and they were trapped in the open. Only fourteen of the 187 soldiers reached the wall. Despite my hardened numbness to battle, the bile rose in my throat and I threw up again and again until there was nothing left. My thoughts were of the parents of the boys I had met at the Rowher Relocation Center. Combat conditions are getting much worse and the cold weather saps one's strength. My goal is to just put one foot in front of the other and try to stay warm, alert, and alive.

February 8, 1944

We were pulled back to San Micheli for a night, and then we were ordered to take Castle Hill. The tree cover is sparse, and the Germans are dug in.

The battalion moved out at 0500 in the dark. At 0616 hours, 350 men were ordered up the hill. I am in Company A. We were inching forward when the machine guns started. Company C took the brunt of the fire.

"Okay, guys, this is it. Let's go!" commanded our sergeant. I saw an embankment fifty yards ahead. That was the first objective; it would offer some protection while we regrouped. We ran, zigzagging back and forth to present a difficult target for the damn Germans. I made a dive for cover in a shell crater. Bobby Suzuki was lying on his left side, blood oozing out of a wound. Just then a German hand grenade landed between us. Without thinking, I lunged for the grenade and made an off-balance throw over the embankment, then fell on top of Bobby just as the grenade exploded. A large piece of shrapnel shattered my right shinbone, dazing me in the process. Somehow Bobby rolled over and wrapped his belt around my upper leg, before falling back groaning from pain. At first my leg felt numb, but later the pain was excruciating. The battle raged on for another two hours before medics finally came to rescue us.

April 10, 1944

I am on my way home with an artificial leg and a Bronze Star medal in my duffel bag for having saved Bobby's life. I also got a Purple Heart in place of the lower half of my right *leg, which was tossed into a trashcan at the field hospital. I can walk pretty well after lots of practice. The pain lessens every day.*

On my way out of Italy, I heard the 100th had eight hundred casualties. We were 1,300 men when we landed. Now only 521 remain. The newspapers refer to us as the Purple Heart Battalion. I was lucky to get out alive.

They combined our outfit with the all-Nisei Japanese 442nd Regimental Combat Team, the most decorated Army unit ever, with over 18,000 individual decorations. My Purple Heart was one of 9,500, and my Bronze Star one of the 4,000 the unit would receive. I still have nightmares about the carnage I witnessed. I see the faces of my fallen comrades every time I go to sleep.

May 15, 1944

It is so good to be back in Hawaii, though I feel guilty for not being with my outfit. I am actually pretty mobile with my prosthesis, and I could work in a support role of some kind. But the Army told me that the guys in our outfit already had done more than their share. I visited the families of all the guys we lost in Company A and told them how brave their sons were. The only good thing to come out of this war so far is that people in town treat my family and me a lot better now. Maybe there is hope for the future.

May 1, 1945

I haven't written in this journal for a while or felt the need to do so. However, the German forces in Italy finally surrendered. There was not a lot of news coverage about the war in Italy, especially after the Normandy invasion. About 300,000 military and 155,000 civilians were killed in Italy. Although my unit, the 100th, was in France and Germany, most of our casualties were from the Italian campaign. Our losses are not counted in the above figures.

May 8, 1945
VE Day. The Germans surrender. The war is over in Europe.

August 15, 1945
The Japanese nation surrendered after the US dropped atomic bombs on Hiroshima and Nagasaki. The war is finally over, thank God.

Now the task at hand is to heal our wounds, both physically and mentally, while rebuilding from all the damage that was done. War comes at a high price. Estimates place the loss of life for WWII at about sixty million. Of this, twenty-two to twenty-five million were military, the rest civilians.

This is my last entry in this journal. My parents arranged for my marriage to a nice girl, and we are moving to the Big Island. I put a down payment on a small clothing shop in the town of Kona. I think airplanes will help grow the tourist business in Hawaii in the years ahead, so hopefully we can make a life for ourselves.

Lilly finished reading Taro's journal and gently set it aside. "Unbelievable!" she said. "That's quite a history, Kenji. Thank you for sharing it with me. I have almost a complete mental block about history classes in high school and college. I had no idea how bad it was for the Japanese Americans during the war. I can't even comprehend that sixty million people died, and worse yet is the knowledge that that horrendous number didn't sink into my consciousness."

"I know, Lilly. I feel the same way. How can we learn from history if we put a tragedy of this magnitude out of our minds? We probably have both felt the prejudice against the Japanese from time to time, but I can't imagine how my father handled it knowing that almost everyone he saw each day hated him."

"Thank God that times have changed for the better. Sharing your family history with me was quite a leap of faith. Thank you, Kenji," she said as she crossed the room to give him a hug. "Your father was so brave and the insights he shared as such a young man were more than impressive. Now I see where you get those same qualities. It's in the genes; you're brave, insightful and so intelligent, which makes me love you even more. Thankfully, we can celebrate the changes in attitude about lots of things, especially prejudice against our race."

The Sony Open was just three weeks away. *Will we all be celebrating again then?* she wondered.

CHAPTER 30

Kenji and Vince flew in Vince's plane to Honolulu on a
Sunday in January and checked into the luxurious Hyatt
Regency Hotel on Waikiki Beach, splurging because of
the occasion and knowing the women would join them
the next day. They had a late dinner while reviewing their
game plan.

The next morning they drove the rented Lincoln Town
Car to Waialae to play one last practice round. Vince
coached his student on every hole, suggesting the best
angle into each green, and helped read the greens for putts.
The wind reached a fierce howl on the back nine, causing
one of Kenji drives to land in the deep rough.

"Not to worry," Vince told him. "You need to practice
this type of shot since you rarely hit the ball any place but

the fairway." Kenji hit down on the ball with a lofted club and watched the ball fly back onto the fairway. "Good job!" exclaimed Vince.

They dressed in slacks and sports jackets for the Tuesday night draw party, anxious to find out which PGA professional would play with Kenji's foursome. They met the other team members. Roland Johnson and Sammie Yee were from Honolulu; Jake Windsor was from Calgary, Canada. It was really an exciting event for all of them, players and caddies alike.

The next drawing was to assign the pros to teams. Each team got to select which pro they would like to play with. The first team drawn had a selection from the entire list of fifty-two PGA pros; Kenji's team was the ninth team to draw. Their team had agreed ahead of time on their top choice, Ernie Els. As luck would have it, they got him. Els, they discovered, was a good-natured, friendly fellow and very courteous to the foursome of awed amateurs. They had chosen wisely.

Later that evening, Vince and Kenji drove to the airport to pick up Sandy and Lilly for a happy reunion. Vince didn't react when Lilly went to Kenji's hotel room; he knew Lilly would help keep Kenji calm and focused. Stu and Gloria along with Ernie were coming in the next morning, each excited to see their friend Kenji compete.

The big day finally arrived. The morning air was a cool sixty-eight degrees, perfect golfing weather. The two couples met for breakfast at the hotel dining room. Vince's demeanor was calm; Kenji was uncharacteristically anxious, fiddling with the silverware, taking tiny sips of water, squirming in his chair, and not talking or eating much.

"At least eat a banana, Kenji. You'll need the potassium for your legs by the time you reach the back nine. In fact take one with you, and I'll stuff it in your golf bag for later," suggested Vince.

Vince wasn't overly concerned about Kenji's nervousness, figuring this was perfectly normal. When an athlete trains for a big event or someone has to make a speech in front of a large audience, the nervous system tends to work overtime before the event starts. Vince was confident that Kenji would go into his Zen-like state sooner or later.

They were due to check in at Waialae in one hour. All they had to do was load up Kenji's clubs and drive to the course, which was only about two miles away.

Kenji and Vince were excited to be in Honolulu again and grateful for the opportunity to participate in the prestigious event. Vince was tickled to be part of it, even as a caddy. Sandy had sensed trouble brewing, and he finally had admitted his anger about the unfairness of the situation. She talked him through it, in her typical no-nonsense fashion. As a result, his anger had subsided over the past few weeks, and he was content in his role as coach and now caddy. The time he had devoted to training and coaching Kenji had been fulfilling. He enjoyed the mentor role, but upon reflection he was happy that he had chosen a different path for a career.

"Well, Kenji," Vince said, "my only comment to you this morning is don't be surprised by the adrenaline rush you'll feel when they announce your name on the first tee. Just remember to keep your swing nice and easy, and maybe dial it back a bit to compensate for the rush. You can't help feel the tension and the pressure — hordes of people, TV cameras, the noise and spectacle of the event. You're not at Makalei anymore," he teased, relieved to see Kenji laugh at his adapted reference to *The Wizard of Oz*.

There was a hubbub of activity when they arrived at the check-in desk, volunteers scurrying around and the amateur golfers trying to appear cool and calm. The atmosphere was electric, palpable. They checked in to get tee assignments; they would go off the first tee at exactly 9:24 a.m. "If you have any questions or concerns, ask one of the volunteers in the blue shirts," they were told. "They'll either help you or get you connected with somebody that can. We want this to be a fun event for you, and it'll be our job to help you do that."

"Thanks a lot," said Kenji. "It looks like you guys have done a great job."

Vince purposely decided to play the alpha dog role to get Kenji calmed down. "Let's go to the driving range so you can get loosened up a bit, then we'll hit the putting green for a while. I'm going to be an observer and stand off to the side so you can gather your thoughts. You're very skilled at knowing how to relax yourself, so that's all I'm going to say on the subject."

"You got it. Who would believe that a fifty-one-year-old amateur golfer who up until a year ago had never held a golf club would be playing in this PGA event? And a one-legged one to boot." Kenji smiled at the irony of the situation. "I'm going to relax, have fun, and cherish every moment."

Meanwhile, Lilly and Sandy strolled around the tented areas soaking up the festive atmosphere. They scoped out where they could sit in the bleachers, opting instead to follow Kenji from hole to hole to ensure he could see a friendly face in the gallery if he ever looked up.

Their tee time finally arrived, and the foursome gathered at the first tee with Ernie Els. Vince and Kenji had met the other three players and their caddies the night before, so they just shook hands, attempting, without much success, to appear nonchalant and confident.

Ernie Els was trying his best to put them all at ease, joking around and talking about how much he enjoyed playing this tournament in Hawaii. He talked about the role of PGA professionals and the need to be a good public relations guy because they each represented the profession of golf to the public. This was a difficult role if the guy tended to be shy; for others it was a natural part of being friendly. The way pros acted and interfaced with the amateurs and the spectators was a vital component in building the reputation of professional golf in the hearts and minds of the fans. It was also one of the reasons that professional golf raises more money for charity than any other sport, he told them proudly.

They were up next. One group was going off the front nine; another was going off the back nine. They were scheduled to get through the round in about four hours. Kenji was thrilled when he heard the announcer say, "On the first tee representing Allen Toyota of Honolulu, please welcome Kenji Watanabe from Kona, Hawaii." Even though Vince had cautioned him about this, Kenji was hit with an overwhelming rush of adrenaline and felt his hands start to tremble. *Shake it off,* he told himself. *Focus, focus, focus!*

Heart pounding, Kenji bent over to tee up his ball. Then he backed off, took two practice swings, and stepped up to address the ball. He looked down the fairway, 331 yards from the hole, the flag that seemed to be waving at just him. He visualized where he wanted the ball to land, took a deep breath, relaxed as he saw the red path to his spot, then swung his driver, making perfect contact.

He was surprised that he felt so confident now that he had made his first shot. He barely noticed the polite applause from the assembled gallery. Vince picked up the bag and said, "Good shot, Kenji. You're out about two hundred and twenty-five yards. You're right on the money!"

The white flag signified that the pin was in the middle of the green so Kenji had 106 yards left. A light rain last night had softened the greens but only a little. Based on practice putts this morning, the greens were about medium fast. Vince estimated there would be about a twenty-foot roll. "Use your wedge and choke up a little bit then target your landing about two feet onto the green," he advised Kenji.

This would be where all of the practice, plus Kenji's special gift, would pay off. Kenji could control his distance within a few feet. Then there was the luck factor. Sometimes you got a lucky bounce, sometimes you didn't. Kenji was feeling lucky, and out of the corner of his eye, he noticed Lilly in her bright red blouse, walking along with Sandy and what were probably Ernie Els's fans hoofing it to the green.

"Keep your rhythm, Kenji, and don't rush. After all this is just another golf game," Vince counseled.

When it was his turn, Kenji stood behind the ball and chose his line to the pin. He picked a blade of grass about six inches ahead of his ball on the sight line. He fixed his grip on the pitching wedge. For a ninety-yard shot, he would choke down about an inch. He softened his grip and totally relaxed as he focused on the red pathway that showed the flight of the ball. Kenji then set up over the ball and lined up the face of the wedge with a blade of grass in front of his ball. He looked at the pin, and then back at his ball, then let his mind go blank. He swung with a natural follow-through to the pin. The ball took flight and tracked perfectly, landing exactly where it was supposed to and started to roll toward the pin, veering left a little. The ball stopped pin-high about three feet to the left.

"Good shot, Kenji," Vince said.

Kenji didn't reply, his mind in deep concentration, his competitiveness kicking in. A strange thought flitted through his mind. *Wouldn't it be the cat's ass if I won this thing? No, don't think, just focus on the next shot.*

Ernie Els didn't say anything to Kenji on the way to his ball. Kenji could tell he was in a concentration zone. Ernie used a sand wedge and aimed his ball right of the pin about ten feet. He hit a draw. He landed about ten feet short and right of the hole, then grinned in satisfaction as the ball rolled to within nine inches of the pin. Kenji could tell that having the power and distance to hit higher lofted clubs to the green resulted in a lot more control since the ball wouldn't roll as far after landing. Yes, there was a lot more to this game than it first appeared. Kenji knew he had the benefit of having learned a great deal about golf from Vince. His only question now was whether his leg would hold up after walking eighteen holes — which was about five miles. Because of the prosthesis, it took about fifty percent more energy for him to walk than a two-legged person. This meant Kenji would walk the equivalent of seven-and-a-half miles today.

The other three amateurs missed the green completely. One was over the back and two were off to the right.

Els and Kenji each scored a birdie; Ernie said he thought they would need to be twenty-one to twenty-two under to win, so they'd need a couple of eagles (two strokes under par for the hole) plus birdies and some luck along the way. As Vince had told Kenji, this was a best-ball tournament. Each played their own ball, and they used the best player's score on each hole.

The second hole was oriented north-south. It was a three par that ended at the edge of the Pacific Ocean. Fifty-foot palm trees soared over the green on the left and right, framing a stunning view to the ocean. It was one of the signature holes at Waialae. Kenji recognized the scene from a brochure for the golf course. The view actually relaxed him, and he was eager to take his shot. It was 196 yards from the championship tees and 171 yards from the white tees. Sand traps guarded both sides of the green and another at the right rear, but it was a clear shot through a narrow opening from the front. Ernie Els pulled a nine iron out of his bag. Kenji had never seen anyone hit a nine iron two hundred yards. Els's shot flew straight and true and landed with a couple of little bounces within twelve feet of the pin.

Kenji was up next and 170 yards for him meant a four hybrid. He knew he'd get about a ten- to fifteen-foot roll if he could land the ball on the green. The green had a tear-drop shape with the small part of the tear facing toward the fairway and slightly to the right. He needed to land near the front edge of that small protrusion. This was a difficult shot. He talked with Vince about strategy, and Vince agreed the four hybrid was the correct club to use. If he veered left even a little, the ball would land in the sand. Vince pointed out, "Remember, this is a best-ball tournament, and Ernie's ball is already on the green, so go for it!"

Kenji methodically went through his pre-shot routine. He didn't rush it and stayed calm. When he stood over the ball, the red path appeared in his mind's eye. He swung smoothly, and the ball tracked perfectly. It hit the exact spot he had picked and trickled to within a foot of the pin. His playing partners all gave him a high five. Vince quietly said, "Great shot, my friend."

He tapped in for another birdie and gave Lilly a little smile on his way to the third tee. He could literally feel her support from twenty yards away.

As they were walking over to the third tee, Els fell in step with Kenji. "I noticed you don't use much leg action," he said. "I'm amazed you can hit it so far."

"Yeah," Kenji replied, "that's because I have a wooden leg. Actually, it's made of titanium and plastic. Rather than try to figure out how to move just my left leg, I found out by trial and error that if I turn my body and keep both legs perfectly still I can hit better. I give away distance by doing it that way, but it helps the accuracy."

"That's the damnedest thing I ever heard of," Els said. "Well, if the last two shots are any indication of your golf game, keep up the good work! I'm proud to play with you. You set a great example for others who might be in a similar situation."

Kenji smiled. "Thank you. That's very kind. Since I lost my leg, it's been kind of a mission in my life to set a good example. I've had a lot of help along the way."

Kenji started to have trouble on the ninth hole. His stump was feeling tender around the sides where his leg connected to the prosthesis. This had happened before when he had over-exercised. He wasn't used to walking eighteen holes. Why hadn't he practiced this to build up his stamina? *Dumb, dumb*, he thought. On the twelfth tee, he slipped a couple ibuprofens out of his pocket so Vince wouldn't notice and asked him for a bottle of water. He concentrated hard on keeping all the weight off his right leg when he was standing, even though doing so was harder on his hip.

Their team was scoring well. After fourteen holes they were fourteen under par, thanks mostly to exceptional play by Ernie Els, who had scored an eagle on a five-par hole, and Kenji's dead-eye accuracy into the greens. But they did get a bogie on one hole.

Els pushed his tee shot off to the right on the fifteenth hole, his first miss. Roland and Sammie both missed the fairway to the left. Jake was in a sand trap. Now it was up to Kenji to get a good shot since none of them had landed in the fairway. He went through his usual setup routine and visualized the pathway in the sky. He relaxed and hit his shot. It was tracking perfectly down the center of the fairway, but something happened when it landed; it bounced high and right and landed off the fairway on a down slope. "Damn, must have hit a sprinkler head," Vince said.

Once they got down the fairway, they discovered a cell phone lying there. "It must have fallen out of someone's bag, and my ball bounced off it," Kenji rationalized. Jake wanted to smash it with a three wood, but cooler heads prevailed. The grass was about three inches deep at the spot where Kenji's ball came to rest.

Hole fifteen was 415 yards, tee to green. "You have a hundred and eighty yards to the front of the green, Kenji, and the pin is back right," Vince told him. "I think you need your three hybrid or a three wood. What do you think?"

"I've got some grass behind the ball, so the distance is going to be a guess and some luck. I think the hybrid would be best."

It was an awkward stance due to the slope. Kenji was first to hit since he'd had the shortest drive. There was a good chance one of the other four would get a good second shot, but Kenji's goal was to birdie every hole. So far he had missed only two.

He had difficulty setting up because of the lack of mobility of his ankle. His stance was awkward, and it was difficult for him to keep his balance, but it was a vital shot. He concentrated hard and carefully picked his line to the green. Vince told him where he thought the ball needed to land. The green sloped away from Diamond Head. This meant Kenji had to aim to the right of the pin. Kenji's competitive juices were flowing. He let his mind go blank and then he saw his guide. He focused on keeping his stance steady with a big shoulder follow-through.

The big follow-through did two things. First, it guided the ball down the path perfectly; second, the torque where the stump met the prosthesis broke a large blister that had formed. Kenji fell awkwardly. Vince rushed to his side and helped him get up. He could tell Kenji was in a great deal of pain.

"Are you okay, buddy?"

"No, I really hurt my stump. Just stand there a minute so the others can't see me until I can regain my composure. I'll be okay in a second." After a few moments, Kenji turned and limped back onto the fairway, heading toward the green.

Els came over to walk with him. "You doing okay, Kenji?"

"I'll be all right, but my leg hurts a little right now."

One of the marshals, having seen Kenji fall, pulled up in a cart and asked, "Sir, are you okay to continue playing?"

"Yes, I'm fine. I'm fine. No big deal."

The marshal, taken back by this abrupt answer, quickly drove back to his monitoring position off the fairway.

Lilly and Sandy were walking down the cart path from the fifteenth tee and missed seeing Kenji take a fall, but Stu, Gloria and Ernie witnessed it all from the sidelines. Stu, his face frowning with concern for his friend, suspected that Kenji had injured himself.

When Kenji got closer to the green, he saw his ball was within eight feet of the pin. Jake made his putt for yet another birdie for the team.

Kenji feared his quest for a low score was in jeopardy. He was becoming a better putter, but an eight-footer in tournament play wasn't an easy putt. Vince told him the grain pointed to the west, so he should allow for a three-inch break to the right. Kenji set up and forced himself to put aside the pain and relax. He stroked through the ball down his target line. The ball tracked perfectly and curved toward the hole as it got closer and closer. It dropped in for another birdie.

"Great putt, Kenji!" his teammates cheered.

Kenji smiled his thanks through his pain. It felt like someone had taken a ball-peen hammer and struck a blow to his stump, but he masked it well to his teammates. Only Vince could fathom how much trouble he was in. He was trying with all his might not to limp, fearing the officials would force him to quit. *Only three more holes to go,* he thought. *I can do this. If my dad could spend two hours in a bomb crater with his foot blown off, surely I can finish a simple round of golf.*

Channel 9 KGMB TV had a camera crew set up on the sixteenth green. The cameraman noticed Kenji approach with a bad limp; he zoomed in and noticed what appeared to be blood on the pants of his right leg. *This is great,* he thought, ever mindful of the TV news mantra "If it doesn't bleed, it doesn't lead!" He got on his cell phone to the station hoping to get some background information on this player.

Vince walked close to Kenji and said, "Your leg is bleeding through your pants."

"Damn! Stay on my right side and try to shield the view from the spectators."

Lilly saw Kenji limping, "Sandy, Kenji's hurt!" she cried out.

Sandy also saw him limping and noticed Vince was walking unusually close to Kenji's right side. "What the hell is going on?"

Jake walked up to putt first. He dropped it from fifteen feet. His line was close to Kenji's, and he got a good read for his ten-foot putt.

Kenji cleared his mind and willed himself to mask the pain. His stroke was smooth, and the speed was right on; it dropped in for yet another birdie. *Only two holes left,* he thought. *I can do this.* How had his father possibly endured two hours with a missing foot while a battle raged on around them?

As he limped off the sixteenth green, he noticed two young men on the sidelines, both obviously veterans. One had a full left-leg prosthesis; the other had lost both legs and had prostheses but was on crutches. "Win this one for us, Kenji!" one of them called out. How did they know his name? Forcing himself to smile, he gave them a thumbs-up signal and a slight nod.

"Two more holes, Kenji. Are you going to make it?" asked the vet on crutches.

"You bet!" Kenji replied rather abruptly.

Stu's group, now including John and Jamie Fletcher, followed Kenji's team on every hole. As a doctor, Stu immediately knew Kenji was in trouble, seeing the limp and the close proximity of Vince shielding his right side. *Should he alert the marshall?* He wondered. He saw the interchange with the vets and decided, against his better judgment, to do nothing.

Els nailed his tee shot on hole seventeen. It was a draw that curved left to follow the natural dogleg shape of the fairway. He already had one eagle and now had a chance for another one.

Vince showed Kenji the layout book of the green. They studied the slopes. Today's pin placement was close to the front of the green and a little right of center. The green sloped away from the center. It was a tough pin placement. Vince normally would suggest the five iron, but it appeared that Kenji was hitting with almost all of his weight on his good leg. He couldn't get his full distance with a shoulders-only swing. "Let's go with the four hybrid," Vince said. "You need to land about two feet short of the green and just let it dribble on. Maybe choke up a little."

Kenji trusted Vince's judgment implicitly, but he was in so much pain he wasn't putting any weight on his right leg. On the last hole, his awkward stance had cost him about five yards. When he lined up and set his grip, he didn't choke up; he'd need to make full contact with this club to make the shot.

Despite the fierce pain, Kenji went through his normal setup routine. He teed up his ball then limped behind it to get the line. He picked a spot just in front of his ball for an aiming point then relaxed his mind. The red pathway showed, clear as ever. He took a deep breath and set up over the ball, let go, and swung with a full-turn follow-through. The pain was excruciating. He bent over for a few seconds to gather his wits then lifted up just in time to see his ball hit his exact spot. Vince's advice had helped him nail it; the ball landed, bounced once, and dribbled down a foot past the hole.

"Vince, you're one magnificent bastard," Kenji quietly spoke in his ear.

Vince grinned, knowing Kenji was exactly right.

A large crowd had started to follow them after the news spread like a virus about the wounded golfer. In addition to Channel 9, ESPN had two cameras following Kenji. One of the cameramen noticed first. "Hey, this guy is wearing a prosthesis."

The ESPN cameraman said to the on-site talking head, "Get a hold of a producer at the studio. Tell them we got something hot here. This guy has only one leg, and he damn near made an eagle on sixteen. The Channel 9 news crew was close by and heard the comment about the leg. Their cameraman zoomed in to ascertain whether the story was fact or fiction. When Kenji was standing normally, his pants leg covered the leg and foot area. But when this cameraman did a close-up on Kenji's face, it triggered a memory. "Oh, my God. I think this is the same guy who got struck by lightning a year or so ago. We did a story on him when he got out of the hospital. Get the station on the phone and have them look in the archives for the golfer-lightning story," he exclaimed to his reporter.

Meanwhile, Lilly could see the pain on Kenji's face. She, and the rest of Kenji's cheering gallery, was worried, fearing the worst possible scenario. Even John Fletcher looked concerned. Whether his worry was motivated by selfishness or true concern for Kenji, was open to question.

For the first time in a golfing situation, Vince was uncertain of what to do. He could visualize the wound Kenji had. He knew that damage was being done to the exposed flesh on the lower part of his stump. But he was reluctant to interfere with the personal battle he could see was going on inside Kenji. He sensed this was a lot more than just a game of golf for him.

Eighteen was the longest hole at 509 yards from the championship tees and 475 yards from the regular tees. It was also the narrowest fairway on the entire course. There were identical sand traps, left and right of the fairway, at 250 yards. Ernie nailed another beautiful shot; it sailed 310 yards and rolled out to 320. That left a 155-yard shot to the green. If Ernie could get a good second shot, there was a chance for another eagle. An eagle might just win the round for their team.

Kenji remembered back to when he was about six years old and had fallen on the sidewalk and seriously skinned his knee. It had been very painful. His mother had worked with him and taught him how to meditate to overcome his pain. He was a little boy, and it was hard for him to concentrate his mind in a way that was necessary for this meditation work, but now he recalled his mother's words and thought about them. *Ohmm. Ohmm. Ohmm.* The words had a soothing affect.

Then unbidden thoughts of his dad came into his mind. As Kenji was growing up, he never thought much about the fact that his dad only had one leg. He overheard his parents talking with friends about how he had lost his leg in battle in Italy during World War II. It wasn't until he uncovered his father's journal after he was gone that he knew in detail what had happened to him that day. He thought of the pain his dad must have felt as he lay in a shell crater with a tourniquet around his thigh to prevent him from bleeding to death. *My dad was a hero in that battle,* Kenji thought. *He saved another man's life. That took real courage. How much courage does it take to finish a simple round of golf? Not much. Not very much at all.*

He glanced at the spectators and saw Lily with tears running down her cheeks and her hands clutched in front of her. He gave her the thumbs-up to help relieve her worries. He grinned at his friends on the sidelines. He was so grateful they were all here to lend moral support.

Kenji's drive went about two hundred yards. He was losing his strength. *Don't quit. Never quit. Don't quit,* played in his mind as he limped up the eighteenth fairway. *I'm almost there. Just keep putting one foot in front of the other.* He repeated the mantra again and again to keep his mind off the pain.

When they got to the ball, Vince called out the distance at about 275 yards to the pin.

"Kenji, it's your call," he said. "Normally this would be a three wood, which you've been using to hit two hundred yards. But anything that'll leave you a hundred yards or so would be good."

On the walk up the eighteenth fairway, Kenji felt faint, little sparkles of light flashing through his head. *Oh, oh, the next thing is a fade to black,* he thought. He gulped down some water and took several deep breaths to fill his diaphragm with air and stave off unconsciousness, at least for the moment. This was the last full swing he had to take today.

"Give me the driver, Vince. I've practiced a little with it off the fairway and actually hit some pretty good shots. The ball is sitting up a bit, so I know I can hit it."

It was a big gamble. The club head had to meet the ball and the ground at precisely the same time. This tactic was too risky for most golfers, even the pros. Kenji would take that gamble; he had to get inside a hundred yards if he wanted to get close to the pin on his third shot. Vince had had him practice lots of sixty- and seventy-yard shots, but he needed 205 yards from this shot and he knew he had only one full swing left in him.

Vince threw his arm around Kenji's shoulder in support. "Go for it, baby!"

God, what a courageous guy! Vince thought. His respect for Kenji had always been high; now it soared to new heights. He was humbled by his own pettiness as he remembered the anger he had felt at being a mere caddy. *I'd walk through hot coals for this guy just to prove I'm worthy to be his friend.*

For the past six months, Kenji had been using an extra-long driver to make up for the lack of strength in his right leg. He was good with it, but it made the odds of making an accurate shot off the fairway even tougher.

The ESPN spotter told the announcer that Watanabe was going to use his driver for the next shot. The announcer was on live feed saying, "What is this guy thinking? It's a huge gamble hitting a driver off the fairway. No way will this one pay off, folks." The camera zoomed in on the club head as Kenji went through his setup.

"Ten bucks says he'll muff it," said the cameraman.

The spotter replied, "You're on."

Kenji, fighting off nausea and stabbing pain, kept his same routine and pacing even though this might be the most important golf shot he'd ever make. "This one is for you, Dad, and also for the wounded vets, and Jamie," his whispered.

When he set up over his ball, he noted that at this moment he didn't feel any pain. The red pathway was there and he swung. He hit it perfectly. The ball took off in a low trajectory that never got more than fifteen feet in the air, but it was a bullet and dead straight. It hit and rolled at least thirty yards.

The huge crowd following him went crazy, yelling, "Kenji! Kenji! Kenji!"

His teammates were jumping and dancing around. Ernie Els ambled over and gave him high five. "Kenji, that's the best damn golf shot I've ever seen!" he proclaimed.

Kenji just smiled.

He looked out at the crowd and saw the two vets. He gave them a wide grin then pointed at his ball and then to them. They understood that the shot had been for them. The ESPN cameraman didn't catch the interchange, but the Channel 9 guy, lens focused on Kenji, didn't miss a thing. He had the studio on his headset now and asked, "Did you guys pick up on that little interchange?"

"We sure did. See if you can find out who those guys are and try to get an interview after the game is over. This could be a real story. This Kenji character is the same guy who got hit by lightning last year. We have footage from an interview with him at that time."

Kenji's adrenaline was pumping full force now. He felt no pain. In fact he didn't feel anything other than euphoria. That last shot was the best shot he'd ever made. It looked like he was out about seventy-five yards. If he got lucky, he might make another birdie.

"We're almost home, Kenji," Vince encouraged. "Hang on, my friend. You're killing it!"

His pitch shot landed on the green then bounced once to stop within four feet of the cup. The huge crowd was cheering as he limped onto the green. Vince handed him the putter. Kenji looked at Vince with a crooked smile of thanks, winked, and sunk his birdie putt. The crowd went wild, screaming "Kenji, Kenji, Kenji!" He had scored the best game of his life. Ernie Els and his teammates rushed to congratulate him with high fives and bear hugs on such a spectacular round. Vince, holding Kenji up to take the pressure off his leg, whispered, "That's the best goddamned round of golf I've ever seen, my friend."

They wouldn't know the final scores for a couple hours until the last teams finished their rounds, but Kenji thought they might be in the running with their nineteen under-par score. Ernie Els, his golfing hero, was very optimistic that their team would win.

Like sharks after prey, the Channel 9 camera crew had been tracking Kenji's every move. The raw footage was being sent to the station wirelessly, with an editor furiously piecing together today's images with the background story. This was a real-life drama, a fifty-one-year-old amateur golfer, one legged at that, shooting the round of a lifetime while practically bleeding to death in front of their eyes; they tended to exaggerate the details a bit to add drama to the story.

Channel 9 had dispatched their top reporter to the golf course when they saw the story unfolding. The cameraman and the reporter scrambled through the throng in an attempt to get an interview, the ESPN crew in hot pursuit. Kenji stepped off the green, ignoring the media, to give Lilly a big hug. "I love you, Lilly," he said. "I love you with all my heart."

"Oh, God, I love you too, Kenji. That was the bravest performance I've ever seen," Lilly cried into his shoulder.

"This might take a little while. Will you wait for me?"

"I'll be right here, sweetheart."

Though he was limping badly, Kenji felt like he was floating on air as he slowly made his way to the scoring tent.

The media broke through the crowds to pepper him with questions "Mr. Watanabe, how does your leg feel?"

"Are you all right?" "Was this the best score you've ever posted?"

"My leg hurts."

"Why did you continue to play when it is obvious you were injured?"

"I can't talk now. I have to go in and post my score." And Kenji hobbled off to the scoring tent, leaning on Vince for support before the reporters could pose more questions.

"Well, it looks like we'll have to wait until Kenji Watanabe is through in the scoring trailer. We'll try to get you more information and the whole story the minute he comes out. That was quite a performance today," the reporter enthused into the microphone on camera for a live feed.

The media folks had to wait a while, but they noticed two paramedics enter the scoring tent, which only added more fuel to the unfolding drama. It was twenty minutes later before Kenji exited on crutches wearing a pair of sweatpants with the right leg pinned up.

The media sharks swarmed in for a feeding frenzy. "Mr. Watanabe, how in the world did you play such a great round with only one leg?" a reporter asked him.

"It was no big deal. I come from a one-legged family."

Confused by this response, they asked, "What you mean?"

"My father didn't have his right leg either. The difference is that he left his on the side of the mountain in Italy during World War II. He got his foot and lower leg blown off and lay in a bomb crater for two hours before he was evacuated. I figured if my dad could handle all that and survive, then the least I could do was finish a simple golf game. This round was in honor of my dad, who was an exceptional man. Oh, and there are a couple vets in the gallery who inspired me along the way. This was also for them and my young friend and sponsor, Jamie Fletcher."

"Thank you, Mr. Watanabe, for sharing your incredible story. You're the fellow who was struck by lightening, right? Did that have anything to do with how well you played today?"

"You're welcome," replied Kenji with an impish grin.

After that, things happened fast, the paramedics insisted that Kenji ride in the ambulance since he had lost quite a bit of blood. Before they could get to the ambulance, however, Kenji spotted the two vets in the gallery so he crutched his way over to them. "Thank you for your service," he said. "I especially want to thank you for cheering for me today. It gave me the courage to keep on going." The vets both grinned and asked if they could exchange emails with Kenji so they could stay in touch. "Of course," replied Kenji. "It would be my pleasure." He jotted down his telephone number and email address on the proffered programs.

Stu quickly congratulated Kenji on his performance and insisted on accompanying him and Lilly in the ambulance that sped to the emergency room at Queens Hospital. Dr. Joseph was on standby after he had seen on television what was happening with Kenji. In fact all the surgeons who had worked on Kenji sat glued to the TV since the news had hit the airwaves.

效

It felt like a homecoming, coming back to the hospital. Kenji knew so many of the staff and doctors from his past visits.

"What the hell were you thinking Kenji?" asked Dr. Joseph when he got a look at the raw flesh of his stump. "This looks terrible. You know the issue of poor circulation to the outer limbs. You should have had more sense," he scolded.

"I know, Doc. I just got caught up in the moment. We had a chance to win the round. I had an almost perfect game going. You wouldn't have wanted me to bail out on that, would you?" Kenji asked. "Besides, thinking about my dad's ordeal toughened me up a bit."

"It must have toughened you up a lot. Very few people could stand the pain you must have felt walking on this severely injured limb. I'm going to clean it up as best I can and cut away the dead skin. Then we'll load you up with antibiotics. Who knows how many germs you got on it from where it rubbed against the leg socket. The next three days are critical, and I strongly recommend that you hang around town so we can watch it. I want to see you twice a day."

Kenji heard a knock on Dr. Joseph's door and excited voices emanating from the hallway. "Pardon the interruption," a nurse said as she poked her head in, "but we thought you'd both like to know that they just announced it on television. Kenji posted the low amateur score today and set a new tournament record! Obviously his team won!"

"Congratulations, Kenji!" Dr. Joseph said. "You won! Best damned golf tournament I've ever seen!"

"Thank you. Thank you very much," he replied in his best Elvis imitation while grinning from ear to ear.

Dr. Joseph laughed loudly. "You're welcome. See you tomorrow, Kenji."

* * *

Lilly hailed a taxi. As they rode back to the hotel, he looked at her lovingly and said, "Thank you for being here today. I couldn't have done it without you."

Lilly smiled sweetly. "You're welcome, darlin'. For the first time in my life, I'm beginning to understand your obsession with golf. When I heard the huge crowd cheering for you and saw the looks on the faces of those two vets, it all made perfect sense."

Over the next few days, Kenji's leg healed amazingly fast, no doubt because of the number of papayas he consumed daily. "Ah, yes, the magic enzymes are working," he told Lilly with a chuckle.

Epilogue

Although still on crutches, Kenji arranged a celebratory dinner at the restaurant at the Hyatt Regency where they were staying. He invited Vince and Sandy and Lilly of course, because he had a surprise in mind. Stu and his wife and Ernie flew over from Kona for the event. It seemed fitting that the golf foursome should be reunited to mark this special occasion. Kenji had ordered several bottles of Moët Champagne for the toasts he planned to make.

After the waiter poured the Champagne, Kenji, with some effort, stood up, lifted his glass, and said, "Here's to each of you. Thank you for your support. I couldn't have done any of this without you. To good friends and cheeky women!"

They caused quite a ruckus as they all stood up and cheered, other diners curious to know what the hell was going on and looking dismayed because their dinners had been interrupted.

Once they were all seated again, Kenji fished around in the pocket of his sports coat to retrieve the blue velvet box. Then he looked into Lilly's smiling brown eyes and said, "I've been carrying this around for a while — in fact since your birthday — but this moment with our friends here seems to be appropriate. Please forgive me for not getting down on one knee. Lilly, I love and adore you. Will you do me the great honor of becoming my wife?"

Lilly was stunned. All their past misunderstandings suddenly became crystal clear. How could she ever have doubted him? "Yes! Yes! Yes! I love you, too," she responded as Kenji gently slipped the diamond ring on her finger.

Everyone at the table clapped and cheered while extending best wishes and congratulations. Instead of showing consternation, this time the other patrons in the restaurant joined in the chorus, clapping and smiling.

Kenji was still on crutches when the group returned to Kona. There was a welcoming committee at the airport, including dozens of people from the chamber of commerce and the Rotary club. Vince carried the two trophies that Kenji had won. One was for team number fourteen winning, and the other was for Kenji for having shot the lowest round of the amateurs.

Kenji and Lilly were married in February at a small wedding, only their closest friends in attendance. His leg had healed, his prosthesis in place once again as he watched his beautiful bride, resplendent in a stunning, form fitting ivory-colored gown glide down the aisle to become his wife. They exchanged their marriage vows with joy. Kenji had never been happier.

All in attendance cheered the couple after the vows and promises were made, each happy in their own way for Kenji, who had endured so much during his lifetime.

During the reception, Ernie approached Kenji with that mysterious look on his face. "So Kenji, I've been thinking."

"So what else is new?" Kenji said with a grin.

"When you and Lilly get back from your honeymoon, are you ready to get off your ass and come to work? I really need your help, my friend."

Kenji had been pondering Ernie's offer and had discussed it at length with Lilly, who was enthusiastic about the opportunity.

"You can't just lay around the house all day eating bonbons while I'm at work."

He was drawn to the prospect of working with Ernie, who had done so much to help him with his prosthesis and intrigued by the challenges of running a totally different type of business. Without giving it further thought, he quickly said to Ernie, "Sure, what the hell? Why not?"

"Awesome! We'll change the world!"

Two weeks after Kenji and Lilly had returned from their honeymoon to Australia, the golf foursome gathered on the deck at Splashers for breakfast to catch up on everyone's news. Stu shared his plan to open a second practice in Honolulu; Vince happily announced his engagement to Sandy; and Ernie sat quietly thinking, mysterious as ever, a curious smile on his face. A plan was hatched to launch a golf tournament to benefit disabled vets. "How about we call it the Titanium Open?" Kenji suggested.

Vince chimed in, "We should call it the Kenji Watanabe Invitational."

"No, it's not about me," Kenji replied. "I want it to be about the vets. I want to use the proceeds to help provide prostheses and rehabilitation services for veterans on the islands."

So it was decided — the Titanium Open it would be. And that's how it started.

Kenji's new friend Ernie Els thought the tournament was a great idea and promised to participate, writing in an email, "I can probably get a few of my friends to play too, if you schedule it when we're available." Grinning, Els sat at his computer, thinking, *Ah yes, Kenji, I have one more excuse to go to Hawaii. It will be my pleasure.*

Kenji's dream of turning his amazing gift for golf into something worthwhile was going to work out just fine.

Made in the USA
Charleston, SC
13 December 2012